D0423271

The Comfort of Favorite Things

Center Point
Large Print

Also by Alison Kent and available from Center Point Large Print:

The Second Chance Café
Beneath the Patchwork Moon
The Sweetness of Honey
Bliss and the Art of Forever

This Large Print Book carries the Seal of Approval of N.A.V.H.

The Comfort of Favorite Things

Alison Kent

CENTER POINT LARGE PRINT
THORNDIKE, MAINE

This Center Point Large Print edition is published
in the year 2016 by arrangement with
Amazon Publishing, www.apub.com.

This is a work of fiction. Names, characters,
organizations, places, events, and incidents are
either products of the author's imagination
or are used fictitiously.

Originally published in the United States
by Amazon Publishing, 2015.

The text of this Large Print edition is unabridged.
In other aspects, this book may vary
from the original edition.
Printed in the United States of America
on permanent paper.
Set in 16-point Times New Roman type.

ISBN: 978-1-68324-107-2

Library of Congress Cataloging-in-Publication Data

Names: Kent, Alison, author.
Title: The comfort of favorite things / Alison Kent.
Description: Center Point Large Print edition. | Thorndike, Maine :
Center Point Large Print, 2016.
Identifiers: LCCN 2016024599 | ISBN 9781683241072
    (hardcover : alk. paper)
Subjects: LCSH: Large type books. | GSAFD: Love stories.
Classification: LCC PS3561.E5155 C66 2016 | DDC 813/.6—dc23
LC record available at https://lccn.loc.gov/2016024599

I miss holding your big fluffy paws
like best friends do.
I miss rubbing your furry belly,
and snipping off your matted dreads.
I miss feeling you climb onto my chest
and nudge me for pets, purring.
I miss burying my face in your neck and
smelling swamp because you love
sleeping in the flower beds.
I miss seeing you peer through the window
from the top of the fence, and hearing
you announce your arrival.
I miss you walking with me to the mailbox,
and running up the driveway to greet me
when I come home.
I miss you, my hedge kitty, my Bold.
Run wild and run free.

February 5, 2015

❦ Chapter One ❧

Standing in the center of the space she'd leased on Fourth Street for her espresso bar and bakery, Bread and Bean, Thea Clark imagined how her shop would look two months from now when it opened, how it would smell with coffee brewing, and bread and pastries baking.

How it would sound with customers *oohing* and *aahing* over flaky croissants, and delicate baklava, and sweet strudel, the artisanal loaves nestled in their baskets with their unique rustic shapes, their crusts beautifully browned around their airy, flavorful crumb.

Her shop. The words gave Thea such immense pleasure. Even with all the work to be done, she felt like she could float. At the moment, the shop resembled an abandoned storefront, because it was, but even that made her smile. This was her blank canvas, her bolt of fabric, her empty page to fill with words; she couldn't wait to get started.

A year ago she never would've dreamed she'd be weeks away from throwing wide the doors to a business of her own, one that would benefit many and allow her to pay forward as well as pay back. That, more than the challenge of entrepreneurship, was making it a lot easier to get out of bed these days. She had so many people to thank, and so much to be thankful for.

Then again, dreaming was one of the first things she'd dumped from her arsenal of survival tricks. It hadn't made much sense for her to think of anything beyond the day-to-day when Todd, her ex, was always ready to cut her off at the knees for wasting time on pursuits he disapproved of, to pull the rug out from under her for being so bold as to suggest those pursuits were important to her. To send her crashing to the ground. Literally.

But all of that was behind her now, and would stay behind her forever. Her future was in bread. And in beans. Soup beans and coffee beans. The former sold in bulk. The latter ground and brewed into espresso shots downed straight, or used in cappuccinos and lattes.

She smiled at the thought of customers seeing the latte art for the first time, even if she was a complete failure at drawing anything but leaves. Other patterns required a wrist action she'd never mastered; according to Todd, her wrist action hadn't been good for much of anything, ever.

That was why she'd be putting Becca York to work in the espresso bar instead of in the kitchen, where the rest of Bread and Bean's magic happened. Becca had once used dollops of milk foam to draw swimming fish in one cup, and in a second, a three dimensional cat, ready to leap. As much as Thea hated the reason Becca had moved here, she loved having her in the fold.

Flipping on the shop's lights, she crossed from the kitchen door to the long folding table she was using as a desk. There, she dropped her keys into her messenger bag and dug out her phone. Her contractor was due shortly to go over some changes to the build-out specs, and she wanted to look at the plans one last time. Bread and Bean was her baby. She would be the one dotting her *i*'s and crossing every last one of her *t*'s. The women she lived and worked with, Becca and the others, called her a control freak. She laughed at that; she owned the trait gladly.

She'd ordered the shutters for the bottom half of the front windows from Angelo Caffey. He was local and did amazing woodwork. The café curtains that would cover the upper portions were being sewn even now by the very capable Frannie Charles. The fabric Thea—with Ellie Brass's input—had chosen, was a beautiful combination of browns, rusts, and greens. It was earthy and warm, with less a feel of autumn than that of a desert in bloom.

The latte mugs would be arriving soon. Those Thea had commissioned from a pottery near Bandera. One of the women there threw the most gorgeous designs, and the art Thea had requested from her catalog was a perfect complement for the curtains. The hooked rugs to go beneath the shop's small café tables, and in front of the groupings of cushy club chairs, would be longer in coming. They were being made to order and would pull together the color scheme.

Yesterday, the baskets for the bread had shipped from a market in Arizona. The owner sold only handmade items and funneled the proceeds back to the women who couldn't risk putting their name on their work. It was the same with the mugs and the rugs. And while the shutters would bear Angelo Caffey's logo, the label on the curtains above would say Bread and Bean. No one would ever know Frannie Charles had sewn them.

Now, fingers crossed that pulling the trigger and opening the shop in Hope Springs, Texas, instead of Austin—which was overrun with bakeries and coffee shops—or Round Rock—where Thea had grown up but couldn't imagine ever returning to—would end up being one of the few right decisions she'd made. Staying with Todd for so long sure hadn't been, though leaving had probably saved her life, as had buying the house on Dragon Fire Hill.

There never had been a dragon, of course. There had been trash barrels and burning tires and illegal bonfires and campsites. The hill was out of the way, and the house on top, abandoned for a very long time, had been worth little until Thea had saved it. The land had been used—and misused—accordingly by vagrants and drifters and criminal types.

But dragons had teeth. Dragons had scales. Dragons didn't let anyone close. She liked the idea of living where the mythical beasts were known to—metaphorically—tread. Of being able to see anyone approach. Of having heavy doors with heavier locks and ballistic-resistant windows. It had taken a lot of money to outfit the house, but no one uninvited would ever get in, and Todd would never miss the cash.

The renovations made her feel safe, and better able to keep the women who counted on her safe, too. Because that was all that mattered. Seeing that not one of them ever faced another fist or belt, or the base of a blender, or the wrong end of a shotgun, or a knife blade, or even the sting of hurtful words hurled out of hatred or spite. That none of them ever had to visit an emergency room again for any preventable reason: to get stitches, to have bones set, to be questioned and made to feel at fault for suspicious injuries.

Pushing aside the unsettling thoughts, Thea closed her eyes to center herself and listened. The traffic on the street outside was minimal, though she knew from talking to Callum Drake, who owned Bliss, the confectionery next door, and to Peggy Butters, whose Butters Bakery sat on the other side of Callum's shop, that weekends were madhouse crazy.

She liked that a lot. Being too busy with work to think of anything else. Her well-laid plans for Bread and Bean were coming together beautifully. Everything had unfolded exactly as she'd intended. She was where she was supposed to be. Finally.

The only thing left to do, she mused, as she unrolled the shop's blueprint across the floor and dropped to sit in front of it, was hope none of her secrets decided to rear their ugly heads, and pray no one ever found out what had happened to Todd.

There were more things Dakota Keller had forgotten about his teenage years spent in Texas than he would probably ever realize. Self-preservation was like that, and he couldn't regret what he couldn't recall.

But one thing he would never forget was the top of Thea Clark's head. The way at fifteen years old she'd sat on his bedroom floor in a complete split, leaning forward, textbooks spread out in front of her. She would stretch her feet, her toes pointed like a ballerina's, as if the motion helped her think. She'd hold them there like that, scribbling furiously on her homework, then relax them as she lifted her pencil from the page.

The woman sitting similarly on the floor in front of him now was doing the same thing while running a finger over a blueprint. Her brown hair, streaked or highlighted or whatever the process was called that women paid too much for, wasn't quite as dark as it had been in high school; Dakota had looked down at it often enough to know. Sometimes when she was studying, the tousled mess sticking this way and that, a cigarette or a joint tucked behind her ear. Other times when she'd been on her knees in front of him, her lips parted, though it was probably best he not go there, he mused, clearing his throat.

"One sec," she said, thumbing out a note on her phone, then sitting straight, swinging her legs inward, ankles crossed, and scissoring up to stand. It really was something to see, all that flexing, even if the khaki knee shorts she was wearing hid the best parts of her legs, and her toes were covered by black ankle socks and black canvas sneakers.

Her black tank top was just as concealing, not tight or clingy, but almost burlap-sack baggy, and she wore a black sports bra beneath. Thinking of Thea in a bra took his mind back to times and places that were going to make this job hell if he didn't get a grip.

He really needed to get a grip because Thea was looking at him now, and he felt punched in the gut by her eyes. "Hey Clark," he said, adding a shrug for good measure.

"Dakota?"

He watched her throat work as she swallowed.

Watched her blink as if doing so would clear him from her vision. "I imagine you were expecting Tennessee."

"Yeah. I was." Her voice was rough and gravelly, her tone confused as she took him in. Probably wondering how they were going to work together, because that's exactly what he was wondering, too. She tucked her phone in her pocket and asked, "What are you doing here?"

When did you get back? Where have you been? Those were the questions he'd been asked repeatedly since he'd returned to Texas after a dozen plus years away and found himself in Hope Springs. Thea's question was a lot simpler to answer. "I'm here about your build-out."

"No, I mean, what are you doing in Hope Springs? Last I knew, you were, well, not here."

Huh. Seemed he was wrong. He thought everyone in town knew he was back. And why. One of the PIs hired to find him hunting him down. His showing up at the hospital in time to say hello to his new baby niece only hours after Georgia May arrived in his brother Tennessee's life.

"Working with Tennessee," was his answer.

She reached up a hand, rubbed the backs of her fingers under her chin. Beneath her wrist, her pulse beat at the base of her throat. "So Keller Brothers Construction is finally a thing?"

He wasn't ready to go into any of that, even

if he'd been back a year. "It's still Keller Construction. I'm just the hired help."

"Hmm." It was all she said, and he let it lie. At least until she continued to rub at her chin, to look him over . . . Those eyes of hers, and all the things he saw her thinking . . . He needed distance from those eyes, the way she saw too much of the world around her and too much of him.

Seems that was one of the things about her he hadn't remembered, and it was dangerous.

"This is going to be something," he said, walking farther into the space. The layout reminded him a lot of a shop in Idaho where he'd worked as a barista for a year. "Though I still find it hard to believe what people will pay for coffee."

"It's not just coffee," she said from close behind him. He hadn't heard her move, and he inhaled, wondering if she still smelled like warm sugar. "It's the ambiance. The lighting and the music. The smells. The beans being ground. The chocolate and the vanilla and the caramel."

"So I can't get just a plain cup of coffee?" he asked as he turned. She'd moved near enough that he could've reached for her easily. So near he could count the freckles on her nose. But no sugar. A flower, he thought. Maybe lavender. Maybe jasmine.

"Of course you can get just a plain cup of

coffee," she said, crossing her arms, cocking her head. "Though I still find it hard to believe what people will drink when they have so many exotic choices."

"Exotic." It was a loaded word. "Because exotic is better than plain?"

"Isn't it?" she asked, causing him to wonder again what she was doing in Hope Springs. Besides brewing coffee. And making him think about the past he'd spent more than a decade working to forget. He looked over her shoulder to the table set up against the wall, nodding toward the big silver machine sitting there with all its levers and dials.

Pretty penny of an investment. "That thing work?"

She glanced behind her. "The espresso machine? Sure. You want me to make you a drink? Latte? Mocha? Cappuccino?"

But not just a plain cup of coffee. "A latte would be great."

"Oh, good. I can practice my leaf drawing."

Yeah, he should probably tell her he knew a little bit about latte art. "A leaf."

"Yep. Pull the espresso shot, and pour the steamed milk beneath the crema." She used her hands to talk, another thing he remembered, though she was definitely more expressive now than she'd been then. "You have to heat the milk to just the right temperature, without all the foam

16

you want in a cappuccino. Then it's all about the wrist. And the imagination. I have the second, but not the first, so I can draw you a beautiful leaf. Or if you're lucky, a heart."

"Is that what you mean by exotic?"

"Don't poop on my parade, Dakota Keller," she said with a pout. "I'm trying to have fun here."

He could think of better ways to have fun, but her animation intrigued him; she seemed strangely jumpy when she had no reason to be. Or at least not because he was here. "Then by all means. Draw me a leaf. Or a heart. Or a stick-figure pony. Though I'd still be happy with a plain cup—"

"Hey, Thea. You'll never guess—"

That was all Dakota heard before the small black woman who'd stopped speaking rushed the width of the room like a runaway train. She shoved her way between him and Thea with her shoulders, then lifted the arm closest to him and backed him into the wall with her forearm against his throat. She was maybe five four, five five, but she felt like a Mack Truck.

"I don't know who you are, Jack—"

"Down, Becca," Thea said, moving just as swiftly to his side. The other woman held Dakota's gaze with fierce golden brown eyes, eyes as frosty as they were sizzling, and he didn't even think about looking away. "I'm good, sweetie." Thea patted Becca's lead pipe of a forearm. "I'm fine.

This is Dakota Keller. He's here to do the build-out of the shop. And he's an old friend."

Becca didn't appear convinced; her chest rose and fell, up and down, her pulse thudding at her temple beneath the curls of her loose Afro. Finally, she moved away. "Personal space, man. Learn it. Use it."

"Yes, ma'am," he said, because there wasn't any need to argue. He understood damage. A thought that had him wondering what this one was doing with Thea.

"Okay, then," Thea said, brushing at her bangs as if doing so helped further diffuse the situation. "What did you want me to guess?"

But Becca shook her head. "I'll tell you later." Then she turned for the kitchen, the soles of her Converse high-tops squeaking on the concrete floor. She pushed through the swinging doors, and moments later, the back door opened and closed.

Only then did Dakota's breathing return to normal. "You want to explain that?"

Thea sighed. "It's a long story."

"I'm in no hurry." Though his interest wasn't so much in the woman who'd left the room as what she meant to the one beside him.

Thea's reaction was less of a laugh than it was a bitter sounding snort. "You got a lifetime?"

Funny she should ask. "Actually, I do."

Chapter Two

H er name is Becca York," Thea said, still reeling from having Dakota Keller walk into her shop when she'd been expecting Tennessee. She wasn't sure she could adequately explain Becca to him with so much of their shared past on her mind. Oh, the things she knew about the man . . .

Yes, she'd learned them years ago when they were both teens, both too young for such intimacies. But their age at the time, and her memories of it, only heightened her adult curiosity. Her perspective had been through the wringer over the years. It was hard not to want to know this Dakota in context.

"And her hands are registered as deadly weapons?" he asked.

Becca. Right. It took Thea a couple of heartbeats to return to the conversation. She was too caught up in the length of his hair, the scruff on his face. His weary eyes that were too bloodshot for this hour. The size of his shoulders. The scars—and the tats—on his hands. The markings, both the ink and the healed wounds, spoke of a harsh life, and knowing where Dakota had spent his final years as a teen, and his first years as a twentysomething . . .

"Believe it or not, they could be," she said, though she had to stop once to clear her throat. What in the world had he been through to look so broken? So completely fractured? So unbearably worn? Had anyone else noticed? Or was she only seeing the damage because she'd known him so well when he'd been whole?

"She's had training?" He accompanied her to the espresso maker. Not that either of them needed caffeine after the jolt of Becca York. "Military or something?"

"She has," she said with a nod. "Though she picked up a lot of what she knows after her service." Thea frowned at the tamped grounds in the filter. "You'd be amazed at the things you can learn on the Internet."

"Considering some of the things I've used it for . . ."

"Yeah? Such as?" She hit the button, watched the crema rise above the espresso in the mug. She could use a change of subject.

He leaned a shoulder against the wall beside the table and shoved his hands in the pockets of his jeans. "Had to pull a calf one time. I was working on a ranch. Montana."

That made her grin. "You? Worked on a ranch?"

He nodded. "And before moving to Montana, I worked as a barista for a year, so if you want me to show you where you're getting it wrong with your wrist, I can."

"Jerk." It's what she'd always called him when he'd pissed her off, and it rolled off her tongue as if it were the most natural thing in the world. Her heart fluttered. This familiarity couldn't be good. "You let me go on about lattes like you were actually interested."

"I was interested," he said, watching as she cleaned the steaming wand after heating the milk. "I am interested."

"Interested in having the upper hand, you mean."

"It's less having the upper hand, and more the best way to play it." His shrug pulled his T-shirt tight across his shoulders, which she really needed to stop noticing. "Doling out what I know strategically. It's a life hack I learned a long time ago."

"Here, then," she said, holding out the mug and the pitcher, and wondering about a long time ago. If he meant the years he'd lived at home with his mostly absent parents. Or if he was referring to the time he'd spent behind bars. Maybe his life after. "Play your hand. Dole out your own leaf."

His mouth twisted wryly as he took both from her hands. "It's been a while since I've done this. Not sure my own wrist action is up to par."

Oh, the things she could say. And would've said if she'd been an irresponsible teenager and not a mature adult. Flirting, innuendo, risqué repartee . . . Those belonged in the past, when she hadn't known any better. Now she did. Todd had taught her well.

She watched Dakota's focus, his narrowed gaze, the crease in his brow, and followed the motion of his hand as he poured the milk in perfect dollops, lifting up smoothly from one before adding the next, reaching the end of the line then pulling the barest drizzle from the top to the bottom of the row to form the leaf's spine.

"Not too shabby," he said, eyeing his creation as he gave back the pitcher. "You going to tell me about Becca while I drink this?"

"Is that what you want?" she asked, dumping the used grounds and repacking the filter to pull a shot for herself. "To talk about Becca?"

She steamed more milk while Dakota sipped, but when she went to pour it into her mug, he said, "Wait," and set down his drink to reach for hers.

She started to tell him she didn't want the art. She really didn't even want the coffee, but the art was an extravagance. She wasn't a customer. She didn't need to be impressed.

Special touches were wasted on her.

Those words, always in Todd's voice . . . How many times had she heard them? Better question: why was she still listening?

Dakota cupped her mug in one big hand, reached for the pitcher of hot milk with the other. His mouth tugged to the side, a smile that was just short of a smirk, as if he was too pleased with whatever was going on in his head.

She was almost afraid to see what he came up with, but she watched anyway as he poured a stream into the inclined cup, filling it, then rotating the pitcher to keep the milk and froth compact as the design took shape. He shook the pitcher as he reached the cup's lower edge. Another movement or two, and the serpentine twist narrowed to become an elephant's trunk.

"There ya go," he said, handing her the mug after he'd used a stir stick to poke two spots in the foam for eyes.

"Very clever." Smiling, she turned it this way and that. "I think you might just be able to give Becca a run for her money."

"Guess it's a good thing I'm not looking for a job."

"Guess so," she said, lifting the mug to her mouth for a quick sip. "Speaking of jobs, you want to go over the sketches now? Since that's supposedly why you're here?"

He took a long moment to answer, staring into his cup, then using the same stir stick to ruin what was left of the leaf in his mug. "What I really want to know is what you're doing in Hope Springs," he said, his gaze rising to challenge her. "And what it has to do with me."

The look she gave him revealed things he was pretty sure she hadn't meant to before she got those eyes of hers under control. Because as familiar as he found the view of the top of her head, he would never forget her eyes. They were the same coffee brown as her hair, with gold-colored flecks where her hair had similar highlights.

She didn't like what he was implying, or inferring, or insinuating. Pick one. He'd never understood which word to use. Most likely because he hadn't paid a lot of attention in senior English, and then his plans for after graduation, for graduation period, had been cut short. He'd finished high school while in prison, then fast-tracked his bachelor's in under three years, making the best use he could of his time— studying, working out, lather, rinse, repeat.

But where he'd been, language didn't matter. And with his background, he hadn't figured it would matter wherever he ended up. He'd been right. Tennessee didn't care, as long as he could read a blueprint, which his engineering degree guaranteed. It was a degree that hadn't done him much good as a barista. Or when wrangling cattle, fishing for salmon, felling trees.

"Why would you think me being here had anything to do with you?"

They'd known each other in Round Rock growing up, and had fallen out of touch over a decade ago. Yet within a year of each other, they'd both ended up in Hope Springs? A town that was no more than a pinpoint on a map?

He didn't believe in coincidences, and her picking this particular location for her business, out of all the locations in all the towns in all the world, was a big one. But instead of answering her question, he asked another: "Where have *you* been since high school?"

"Here. There." She shrugged. "Everywhere."

"Married?"

Those eyes again. Lying. Or close to it anyway. "A long-term relationship. Very long. Too long."

Interesting. And a lot more than he'd asked for. "You bought the house after it ended?"

She shook her head. Shook loose wisps of hair she then blew away with a puff of breath. "I bought it more recently. I had . . . things to take care of first. After it ended. Get my head on straight." She shrugged again, a really bad effort at nonchalance. "Stuff like that."

As if *stuff like that* was par for the course, or not worth the words to explain. Then again, he didn't know anything about getting over relationships. "Sounds like a tough time."

"Not as tough as prison, I imagine," she said, and lifted the cup she held cradled in both hands.

"Yeah." He looked down into his own cup, frowning at the floating remnants of his foam leaf. "It was."

"I'm sorry," she said, the words coming slowly as if she didn't want to choose the wrong ones. And then she did. "I never came to see you. I should've come to see you. Especially since we spent the last free night you had making sure you could barely walk out of my room."

Uh-uh. He didn't want to think about that night. Not the sex. Not Thea's body naked. Not the way his heart had nearly torn his chest open with fear. The memory punched hard. "Don't—"

But she cut him off, determined. "I mean it. Knowing what you'd done for Indiana—"

"Don't," he repeated, because he wasn't interested in what she knew, or what she thought she should've done. The past could not be reversed. The past couldn't even be forgotten. He knew. He'd tried. For nearly half of his life, he'd tried. "Seriously. Don't."

"Fine." She set down her cup, the coffee sloshing to the rim. "I won't mention again how much I wish I'd come to see you while you were inside because I probably knew you better than anyone else at the time, and I thought the sacrifice you made for your sister was about the most heroic thing ever."

"I'm nobody's hero, Clark," he said, draining his coffee, then placing his cup beside hers and turning to go, her words like an anchor dragging behind him, scraping over the floor to leave a scar.

He didn't care that he was here on business. Keller business. His brother's business. Since he'd come back to Texas a year ago, no one had talked to him so bluntly about prison. He didn't want anyone talking to him about prison at all.

But especially not Thea Clark.

"You're not leaving, are you?"

It was a challenge rather than a question, and he was pretty sure she'd added on the last part to try to fool him otherwise. "I don't know," he said, stopping and shaking his head before looking back. "Are we going to talk business?"

Her arms were crossed, her hip cocked, her jaw tight as if she was ready for battle. As if she needed the armor because standing up to him wasn't the piece of cake she wanted him to believe. "I thought that's why you were here."

He'd thought the same thing. Then he'd thought about looking down at the top of her head. And looking into her eyes. And prison. He glanced at the blueprint that had rolled itself up on the floor.

He could do this. Talk business with the girl who'd been his first, though he wasn't sure she knew that, or why he'd let the thought creep in.

"It is," he finally said.

"Okay."

"But no talking about my past." That was a deal breaker.

"If that's what you want."

"And no talking about yours."

"I can do that. Or not do that, I guess," she said.

He nodded and offered his hand.

She dropped her gaze from his to look at it,

fighting a smile as she did. "A gentleman's agreement?"

"We can put it in writing if you want," he said, still standing there, arm extended, waiting.

"No need," she said, and placed her hand in his. They shook, and she pulled away, rubbing her fingers into her palm while he shoved his fists in his pockets.

They got down to business after that. He knew from going over the plans with Tennessee that nothing about the build-out was complicated. She needed shelves along the walls for doodads and whatnots, a station for the baristas to work their magic and another for the customers to fine-tune their brew. She would also need a front counter to tempt her clientele into buying the breads that were part of the shop's name.

Though that had him thinking . . . "Kinda strange to have two bakeries in the same block, isn't it?"

"It would be if we sold the same things," she said, standing in front of the windows covered at the moment by brown Kraft paper. "Butters Bakery is desserts. Cookies and cakes and pies."

"And Bread and Beans is bread. And beans."

She nodded. "We'll have some breakfast pastries. And biscuits. Those to satisfy the morning coffee crowd. But our specialty, and our focus, will be the artisanal loaves. I've ordered a shelving unit with baskets to go behind the counter. It's on the way."

"And the apothecary cabinet?" he asked, gesturing toward the large piece of furniture with multiple small drawers sitting just inside the front door. "Is that just for show? Or is that where you're keeping your coffee beans?"

"Beans, yes," she said with a self-effacing grin. "Coffee, no."

"Come again?"

"Beans for soup. Navy and pinto and black. Lentils. Adzuki. Anasazi. Kidney and fava and garbanzo, and I'll stop now," she said, laughing. "Because I'm quite sure that's enough about beans for one day."

Actually, he was curious. Especially because of her enthusiasm, which she was using to hide something else. Nervousness, maybe. Though why she'd be nervous about selling beans . . . "Why beans? I mean, I could see if you were selling coffee beans by the pound, this being a coffee shop and all, but soup?"

She rubbed her hands up and down her bare arms, hugging herself tighter. "Soup is filling. *Beans* are filling and fairly inexpensive. And like I said, enough."

Yep. Definitely nerves. And he was pretty damn sure the beans were only tangentially related. "You never did finish telling me about Becca."

"Yeah, well, Becca's story isn't really mine to

tell." She walked back to where he stood, then to the table, picking up their dirty mugs. "Just know she has a good reason for reacting the way she does. Even when she's wrong."

"Sounds like she's more to you than an employee," he said, digging, though he didn't want to think about the why of his interest. Then again, the woman had tried to crush his windpipe.

She looked at him, frowning, her expression conveying a battle of some sort. "And that sounds like you're asking me about my past."

"It was just a question, Clark. No need to get all defensive."

"I don't like it when people are nosy."

"Sorry." He gave her a nod. "I'm not so good at being a gentleman."

"You never were," she said, and turned for the kitchen, pushing through the swinging doors, coffee mugs in hand.

Can't argue with that, he mused, deserving both the dig and the dismissal.

Simple or not, this job was going to go south if he didn't stick to the agreement he'd made with Thea, and the rules he'd set for himself: Get in. Get out. No involvement.

Those rules had served him well for a decade now. For longer. But they hadn't taken Thea Clark into account. He was going to have to rethink the way he'd been living since he'd picked up that baseball bat and nearly ended a life. Because Thea was no longer a distant memory.

She was here.

And in under an hour, with no effort at all, she'd stirred up every bit of the past he'd worked so hard to bury.

Once she heard the front door close behind Dakota, Thea walked through the commercial kitchen and out the back. She found Becca in the alley behind Bread and Bean smoking a cigarette down to the filter.

She was also pacing a trough across the shop's private parking area. Stress shimmered off her shoulders like heat from asphalt, the smoke barely having time to enter her lungs before she was blowing it out on top of a whole lot of not-so-nice words spoken into the air. It was how she coped, the closet ranting.

Thea felt a catch near her heart. Becca had come so far, and seeing her like this sent Thea's joy at the other woman's progress crumbling. But back to the drawing board was how life worked for all of the women living in the house on Dragon Fire Hill, so back they would go.

"I thought you'd quit."

Becca held up what was left of the filter between two shaking fingers. "I just did. Again."

Thea watched the butt hit the ground, watched Becca grind it flat then bend to pick it up. It was a ritual with Becca. Smoking. Quitting. Starting again. Quitting one more time. She rarely had more than a single smoke, maybe two, a month. Things had gotten better since she'd come to live with Thea.

Or so Thea had hoped. "You're going to have to stop doing that, you know. Assuming any man standing close is a threat."

Becca picked at the edge of the charred paper. "It sounded like you were arguing."

"We weren't. But even if we were . . ." She didn't want to lecture. Becca had been lectured enough in therapy. "It's okay to argue. It's even okay to fight as long as it's a fair one and no one gets hurt."

"Someone always gets hurt. You know that as well as I do," Becca said, flipping open the top of the cigarette box she always carried. Sometimes it was empty. Sometimes it held an emergency cig. She dropped the butt inside.

Thea understood the need for the crutch. She'd had plenty of her own over the years. Just nothing that would give her a bad case of vocal fry or emphysema. "I used to sleep with him. Dakota. When we were in high school."

Frowning, Becca asked, "Seriously?"

"We weren't serious"—though she never had been sure if that was the truth—"and I haven't seen him since"—and she was still reeling from that particular surprise—"but yeah. He was hot. I mean, you saw him. Get rid of some of that scruff and the crow's-feet, and his shoulders weren't quite as broad . . ."

Then again, Thea could pretty much take him just like he was, and oh, boy how that could get in the way of their working relationship.

Becca glanced over, her arms crossed, the hand holding the cigarette box tapping it against her elbow. "I didn't really notice anything but how close he was standing to you. And how much bigger he is."

Thea had noticed that, too. Dakota's size. Dakota's being so near. And strangely, she hadn't hated either. Life with Todd had taught her to hate both. To brace against both.

But Dakota wasn't and never had been Todd.

Plus, there was something about the shoulders and crow's-feet and scruff that spoke to a very primitive part of her. And did so separately from her memories of their past.

She was really going to have to be careful about that. "His being bigger didn't stop you."

"I know, but—"

"No buts, Becca," she said, moving closer. "You and I have had enough of the same training that you should know I can take care of myself."

"And you and I swore on day one to have each other's back," Becca retorted, her gaze as sharp as her voice when it met Thea's.

Thea sighed. "And I appreciate you more than

you'll ever know. I just hate the idea of you going through life thinking every man you meet is going to do you harm."

Becca shook her head, returned the cigarette box to her pocket. "I'm pretty much batting a thousand in that regard."

"No," Thea said firmly. "You're not. It may seem like it, but you've had quite a few good men looking out for you. Don't paint them with the same brush as the few who treated you badly."

"Badly?" Becca gave a snort, her eyes growing wide, big circles of white against her dark skin, before filling with tears. She swiped at them with her fingers. "Is that what we're calling rape now? Is that what we're calling being whipped like a cow or a horse or whatever animals cowboys use whips on?"

"Of course not," Thea said, cringing. "And I'm sorry. I was thinking"—*and selfishly so*—"about Dakota and everything he's gone through. I should've chosen my words more carefully."

Becca sniffed, shrugged, scuffed the toe of her shoe against the concrete. "It's no big deal."

"Oh, sweetheart." Thea took a step toward her friend, who was one of the strongest women she knew, then stopped. Becca wasn't a hugger, and Thea had to respect her space. "It *is* a big deal. Hurting you, even inadvertently, is the last thing I ever want to do."

"You didn't. I overreacted. Again. Just now

34

and"—she gave a nod toward the shop—"in there."

The admission was more than Thea had hoped for, and she smiled, relieved. Reaching up to brush her bangs from her eyes, she said, "It's been a while since you have."

"I'm working on it." One shrug. "I'll get there." A second.

"I know you will. And that's because I did. And Ellie has, pretty much. And Frannie will, too. Eventually." Thea thought for a moment about the newest member of their household. "For the most part, anyway."

Becca moved to lean against the rear of her car, an imported hatchback that had seen better days. "You seemed pretty cool with him. Dakota," she added, as if trying out his name. "Even after, you know . . . Todd."

Good to know. Because inside she'd been anything but. "He was always decent to me. We had a lot of fun together." It was all true, though much more complicated, and she left it at that.

"You said he's gone through some stuff?" Becca asked, the question casual, her tone of voice less so.

"I doubt he wants me talking about it." Unlike Becca's story, however, Dakota's *was* public record. And with all Becca had been through, she deserved the truth about who she was working with. "But it's not a secret that he spent three years in prison," she said, adding, when Becca began to bristle, "for nearly beating to death the boy who'd sexually assaulted his sister."

"Wow," Becca said after a long and very still silence. "That's intense."

Thea nodded. "That past also has a whole lot to do with me trusting him, and his dealing with your arm at his throat the way he did."

"Pretty sure I'd have done the same thing even if I'd known. That signal's embedded and too strong to stop. But, yeah," she said quickly when Thea began to frown. "I'm working on it."

Time, Thea mused, for a big fat change of subject. "So what did you want to tell me earlier? When you came into the shop."

And just like that Becca's expression shuttered. "It doesn't matter—"

Another strongly embedded signal: Becca's feeling that she didn't deserve to have anything go right, or anything that she wanted. "It matters. Becca. You were excited. I could tell. What is it?"

"I was excited for about five minutes," Becca said with a huff, digging for the cigarette box before changing her mind. She pushed away from her car, her fingers laced on top of her head and flattening her hair. "Then I woke up."

"Becca York. I swear—"

"Fine," she said, swinging out her arms in an expansive gesture. "Peggy Butters told me she and her husband are retiring and selling the bakery. She asked if I'd be interested in buying it."

"What?" Why in the world would Peggy do such a thing? It wasn't malicious; Thea didn't think the older woman had a mean bone in her body. But needlessly getting up Becca's hopes? Even if just for the seconds it had taken Becca's bubble to pop? Then again, Peggy wouldn't have known that Becca—and Ellie and Frannie and even Thea—basically lived hand to mouth. No one but the women themselves knew that, or the reasons why.

Yes, Thea had money socked away—some she'd saved from her days waitressing at the upscale Austin restaurant where she'd met Todd; the rest was the money she'd taken from his safe and his bank account when she'd split—but it was money earmarked for the business. It had to be.

It was the business that would allow the women she helped to get back on their feet in an environment where they felt safe. And that's what made the idea of another income stream so appealing. "I wonder what Callum would think, having Bread and Bean on both sides of Bliss."

"She didn't ask you," Becca said, miffed. "She asked me."

"Oh, I know." *Me and my big mouth.* "I didn't mean—"

"It doesn't matter. None of it does." Becca headed for the shop's door and jerked it open. "I'll never have anything of my own."

"Becca," Thea said, but it was too little too late. She'd screwed up because she hadn't thought before speaking. It was the one thing she'd always been good at. Or at least according to Todd.

Seemed that hadn't changed at all.

❧ *Chapter Three* ❧

O h, crap," said the redhead who'd slammed into Lena Mining, causing Lena to grab Bliss's sidewalk bistro table to keep from falling. "I'm so sorry. I didn't see you."

The woman had been standing in front of the window of the coffee shop next door as Lena walked by, and had obviously turned as Lena passed, knocking them both off balance. Lena bent to pick up the textbooks she'd dropped.

"Don't worry about it," she said, taking a nerve-settling breath. "You had your hands full."

Pushing the big black frames of her hipster glasses into place, she smiled at Lena and pressed her hand to her chest. "But I should've been paying attention. It's my fault. I'm so sorry."

Lena set the books on the table and waved

the hand still holding her phone, doing her best to be cool. It wasn't easy, and the circumstances sucked, but whatever. She'd been hoping to meet this woman for weeks. Now not to screw it up. "I know better than to text and walk at the same time."

The other woman leaned down to retrieve what looked like fabric swatches hooked in one corner on a ring. But it was the spools of thread rolling all the way to the front door of Bliss that had her groaning. "Crap. Just crap."

She scuttled around, snatching up the little wheel-like runaways, the hems of her jeans too long and tattered because of the wear as they dragged the ground. Her hair, a mass of red waves that looked as if she'd slept in rag rollers, hung to the middle of her back.

"I think you got them all," Lena said.

"I hope so. I'd hate for anybody to slip on one and fall."

Lena, always the cynic, had assumed she was worried because she needed them for a project. "Are you making something?" And what a stupid question that was. Who walked around with spools of thread if they weren't?

"Oh, no, I was double checking the thread against the fabric. How it will look from the shop's interior, and from out here when the sun hits the window. I don't want passersby to be put off by mismatched colors and not come in."

For real? "I kind of doubt anyone will notice the thread."

"I'll notice," she said with a completely beatific smile as a missed spool rolled toward her. She stopped it with the toe of a very tired-looking Birkenstock sandal. "And Frannie will notice. She's the one making the curtains. I'm Ellie, by the way. Ellie Brass."

"Lena Mining," she finally said, still caught by the smile, her heart thudding.

"I know. You work at Bliss." Ellie gestured behind her, her hair flying around her shoulders as she moved. It was nearly copper in the sun, and Lena, an old hand at hair color, knew it was real. It was also stunning. "I work next door. At Bread and Bean. Well, I don't work there yet. When it's open, I'll be in the kitchen. I bake bread."

It was a lot of information delivered in a quick rush of words. Lena wasn't used to talking so much. She was the straight-and-to-the-point type. The less-is-more type. If she had her way, she'd be the completely silent type. She wondered if opposites really did attract. "Cool."

"So . . . apologies again. And I guess I'll be seeing you." A tentative shrug. Nerves, maybe? "I mean, if you like bread. Or coffee."

"Sure thing." Hope Springs was a small town. It was hard not to see the people who worked nearby. "And I dig both."

"I really like your hair, by the way," Ellie said,

waving the hand holding the spools. "I've always wanted to put color in mine. I mean, fun color. Not the color it is. Your pink and purple are great. Oh, and there's blue, too. Really great."

"Thanks," Lena said, pretty sure she'd never had anyone compliment her hair. Comment on it, sure. And Callum joked when she changed it up. But not call it great. Never that. "I'm thinking of going with orange and green next time. Maybe some turquoise."

"Yeah? Those colors will be perfect together. So tropical. And they'll totally suit your complexion. Orange and green are both secondary colors. One is warm. One is cool. For the most part, anyway. It can vary depending on the shade, of course. I mean, emerald green isn't the same as spruce.

"Here," she said, digging through the fabrics draped over her forearm. "This is what we're using for the shop's curtains. It's mostly brown, but the rusts and greens keep it from being overwhelming. Thea—she's the shop's owner—says it reminds her of the desert. I think it looks like a gorgeous fall day."

Lena would've said it looked like an old couch, but she didn't. Also, she was still wondering if the scars on Ellie's forearm were cigarette burns because that was exactly what the puckered circles looked like. She struggled to find her voice. What the fuck was wrong with people?

"I can see that," she finally said. "The fall thing. And the desert thing, too. Perspective, I guess."

"That's why it's going to be perfect." Ellie's grin pulled at the corners of her mouth. "It can be interpreted so many ways."

"Makes sense," Lena said, pocketing her phone and reaching for her books. She hated to go, but she needed to get to work.

"What are you studying? If you don't mind me asking." Ellie rushed through the words as if she was afraid of Lena leaving her alone on the sidewalk. Or as if she hadn't had anyone to talk to in too long and didn't want to lose the connection.

Whatever it was, it made it even harder for Lena to leave. She wanted to keep talking, to have a cup of coffee or something, grab a burger and a beer. Not that Ellie seemed like the burger and beer type. "I'm taking a couple of business courses. Basic accounting stuff. I'm not so good with money. And my mom needs to do a better job keeping a record of her income and expenses. Seemed an easy enough way to help."

Ellie nodded, her green eyes focused and bright above her nose that was as freckled as her bare shoulders. Her skin looked so soft. "What does your mom do? If you don't mind me asking. Again."

Lena came close to telling Ellie to ask her anything. "She's a midwife."

42

"Really? Here in Hope Springs? That is so cool."

"I guess. But not in Hope Springs, no. I mean, we live near Kyle . . . or she lives near Kyle." She was going to blow this if she didn't get a grip. "I just moved not long ago. But she works anywhere and everywhere she's needed."

Another nod, and another question. "You weren't drawn to follow in her footsteps?"

That made Lena want to laugh, though not at Ellie. Just at the thought. "I'm not much for getting that close to people." *Isn't it obvious?* "I do better from behind a counter."

"Or a chair?"

Lena looked down, completely unaware that she'd moved, and in doing so had put one of the bistro table's chairs between herself and the other woman. Idiot. She was so screwed. "Sorry about that."

"It's okay," Ellie said with a laugh. "I don't take very many things personally."

"It wasn't meant personally," Lena said, thinking the remark strange . . . or not, considering first impressions and all that.

Ellie went on, picking up the conversation as if the interlude hadn't happened at all. "I guess you're close to your mother then. If you're taking classes for her instead of for yourself?"

"I figure a business education's not a bad thing to have. It's pretty versatile."

"If you like business, sure." Finally stuffing the spools of thread into her pocket, Ellie shrugged. "Do you?

"I like it more than unemployment." But a whole lot less than setting up the animal shelter she'd been planning for a while now. She'd get around to doing for herself later. After doing for her mom. If the shelter ever saw the light of day, it would be because her mom had kept her alive to make it happen. "Peggy Butters asked me if I'd want to buy her out. Take over the bakery next door. I guess she and her husband are retiring. I figure the classes would help with that."

Ellie's smile, when she spoke, was soft, though it also seemed to be . . . disappointed maybe? As if somehow Lena had let her down? "Are you going to?"

"I haven't really thought about it yet." Desserts weren't really her thing. And the classes would be just as helpful getting the shelter up and running.

"Well, good luck if you do." Ellie backed a step away, raising one hand in a tentative wave. "I'm sorry for keeping you. And for bugging you. And for bumping into you."

"You're not bugging me, and the bump was nothing. But I do need to get to work," she said, turning to go, hating to go.

"It was nice to meet you, Lena Mining."

"And you," Lena said, silently adding *Ellie Brass*.

Becca wasn't sure why she let herself get her hopes up about anything anymore. She, more than anyone, should know better. It was almost as if once she'd left the Fort Worth hospital for the shelter in Austin where she'd met Thea, she'd forgotten every life lesson she'd ever learned.

Do not expect things to go your way. That was the most important one.

Of course, she couldn't say that to Thea. Or to Ellie, really, who was as fragile as she was strong. Thea was a big proponent of not looking back, though Becca wasn't sure the other woman practiced what she preached to any of the women living in the house on Dragon Fire Hill.

Still, Becca had promised to do her best to move on from the abuse she'd gone through. At least her physical scars were on her back, where she couldn't see them. Ellie had to look at hers every day. Yet Becca had to give it to her. Though she chose them occasionally, Ellie had given up always wearing long sleeves.

Becca wasn't sure she would've been that brave. The idea of being faced with that visual reminder every day . . . Oh, who was she kidding? She didn't have to see her scars to remember.

At the sound of the front door opening, she pushed aside the thoughts and looked up from the plans for the barista station, glancing at Ellie as she shut it and collapsed back against it. "What happened to you? You're all flushed."

"I'm all embarrassed, is what I am. Humiliated." Ellie closed her eyes and waved a hand in front of her face like a fan. "Mortified. Absolutely, ridiculously mortified."

Hmm. Ellie Brass's personality defined mood swings, but Becca couldn't remember ever seeing the other woman so fully flustered. All over the place, sure. Up one minute, down the next, yep. But embarrassment was not in Ellie's repertoire. "Ellie. Spill."

"I ran into the woman who works at Bliss," Ellie said, pushing off the door and adjusting her glasses. "Like literally." She crossed to the table set up with the espresso machine and unloaded several spools of thread from her pocket. "Like some movie meet-cute, but it wasn't cute at all. She dropped a big stack of books, though thank God she held on to her phone, and I dropped my swatches and thread. Spools everywhere. Rollin', rollin', rollin'." Ellie frowned as she added the fabric to the pile. "Isn't that a song?"

Becca nodded. "*Rawhide*. A TV western from the early sixties. Clint Eastwood starred as Rowdy Yates."

Ellie stopped what she was doing to consider Becca curiously. "How in the world do you know that?"

46

Becca rolled her eyes and went back to looking at the blueprint Thea had tacked to the wall. "You have to ask?"

"Right. Thea and her retro shows."

Which was probably why they were all living in a house that would've suited the Waltons, another show she only knew about because of Thea's obsession. Not that Becca was complaining. Besides, she had a feeling Thea's choice of entertainment had a lot to do with the past being a lot simpler than the present. "So you ran into the woman next door and . . . what happened exactly? Besides both of you dropping things?"

Ellie leaned against the wall beside the blueprint, her hands at her back, her head rolling to the side on her shoulders. She met Becca's gaze with a fanciful smile. "Do you believe in love at first sight?"

Good grief. Was the woman never going to learn? Becca shoved a hand at her hip and turned to face her friend. "Ellie—"

"I know. I know. It's not love. It's not even infatuation." She pushed away from the wall and crossed to the front windows, peering out through the Kraft paper's loose edge. "Or maybe it is infatuation. I mean, I don't know her. I just met her—"

"Who is her?" Obviously the woman who worked at Bliss, but Becca needed more.

"Her name is Lena Mining. She's taking some

business classes to help her mother who's a midwife. She's got chunks of pink and blue and purple color in her hair, and three rings in one eyebrow, and she was so nice to me, Becca," Ellie said, coming back. "I ran smack into her, and she dropped her books, and she didn't yell or call me stupid or anything."

"Most people don't, you know. Most people are pretty nice."

The words settled between them, and it took a second, but Becca felt the stirrings of a smile, then Ellie chuckled, then both women laughed. The idea of Becca lecturing anyone, but especially Ellie, about the nature of people was absolutely ridiculous. The two of them knew more about what people were capable of than anyone should ever have to.

"It was weird, though," Ellie finally said. "We started talking about her mom, and she moved to stand behind one of the chairs outside on the sidewalk. I don't know if it meant anything. She obviously didn't know she'd done it."

Everybody had their own tell. "But she had."

"I wanted to ask her about it, but she blew it off, and I know better than to push."

They all knew better, Becca mused. Ellie's new crush may not have recognized the move as one of self-preservation, but Ellie had, and Becca would have. Thea, too. "Maybe you'll have a chance to talk to her more later—"

"Goodness," Ellie said, all giddy and syrupy sweet. "I hope so—"

"But Ellie," Becca hurried out with, before the other woman got completely hippie daydreamy in that way that she did, "take it slow. You've been hurt enough for one lifetime."

"And you're a dear friend who worries too much."

"I don't worry too much. I probably don't worry enough." At least not about other people. She worried plenty about herself. "You don't know anything about her or why she thought she needed that chair. It's probably nothing. Could be she was just afraid you'd sew her a curtain," she said, and Ellie snorted. "But it might be more than you need to take on. And now I'll stop lecturing," she said, because Ellie was sticking out her tongue and crossing her eyes, which meant Becca's point had gone as deep as it was going to.

"One thing I do know is that she's thinking about buying Butters Bakery. So there."

At that, Becca's entire body went stiff. "What?"

Ellie nodded. "She said Peggy and her husband are retiring, and Peggy asked her if she'd be interested in buying them out."

So Peggy was trolling for buyers. So what? That's what sellers did. Smart ones didn't offer their property to a nearly penniless abuse and rape victim—No. She was not a victim. She was done with thinking of herself that way. But still. "Dammit."

"Damn what?" Thea asked, walking into the shop proper from the kitchen. "What are you two up to?"

Becca shook her head, so Ellie answered. "I was telling Becca that I just met Lena Mining, who works next door at Bliss."

Thea frowned as she started sorting through the paperwork on her table, pushing aside Ellie's fabric swatches and thread. "That was what the *dammit* was about?"

"No," Becca said, having found her voice and the anger she seemed unable to stop using as fuel. "That was about Peggy Butters having offered her bakery to Lena before offering it to me."

"She offered the bakery to you?" Ellie asked, wide-eyed. "Goodness, that would be so cool. I could bake bread here. You could bake cakes there. I can already imagine the lines out the door once word gets out about your hummingbird cake. Oh, and your pineapple upside-down cake. And your German chocolate with cream cheese."

"It might be cool if I had more to my name than, oh, the nothing I do," Becca said, rubbing at her eyes then looking up to see Thea staring. "What?"

Thea looked from Becca to Ellie and back, a twitch of a grin on her mouth as she crossed her arms. "I think we should bring the subject of Butters Bakery to the table tonight."

To the table. Where the four of them, as a group, discussed issues with an impact on them all.

That meant making Butters Bakery more than just an extension of Bread and Bean. Making it something that would involve all of them, belong to all of them. Be something they could each call their own. A piece of it anyway.

Becca smiled, and for the first time all day, actually felt the emotion behind it.

✨ Chapter Four ✨

Dakota was hunkered on the floor measuring the baseboard when Thea pushed through the kitchen's saloon doors and back into the front of the shop. He'd stepped out front earlier to take a call from Tennessee, and though he'd seen a red-haired woman go into the shop, the place had been empty when he'd gotten back to work.

He hadn't been gone but maybe twenty minutes, but couldn't rid himself of the notion that she'd come back to fire him. Juries who went into deliberations with their minds made up tended not to drag things out.

"Can you take a break?" she asked, looking down at him and swiping at the longest of her bangs. "I want to get your opinion on something."

Because she valued what he thought? With the

way she'd stormed out of here earlier, he couldn't imagine that. But he was curious, so he stood, and though his day had barely gotten started, he said, "Sure."

He jotted down the measurement, then wound up his tape measure and tucked it along with his notebook and pencil in the pocket of his tool belt, where it sat on an overturned box. "Can I leave this here, or do I need to put it in my truck?"

"It's fine." She'd moved to the front door, hardly paying attention to him at all. "We're just going down the block."

That meant the chocolate shop or the bakery, unless they were going to cross the street at the corner and hit the antique store or the pharmacy. He had to admit she had him curious.

"I'm sorry about earlier," she said on their way outside.

Looking over, he was struck again by the clever Opening Soon sign in her window. It was a pencil drawing, an abstract depiction of a hand prying the top off a coffee can. He glanced back at Thea, not sure what she was apologizing for, but he was patient.

"You surprised me," she said, squinting against the sun, tiny laugh lines appearing at the corners of her eyes. "And I hadn't quite found my footing when Becca charged in. I was rude. I'm sorry."

He studied her as they walked, watched her rub her hands up and down her bare arms. He'd never known Thea to easily admit she was wrong. He wondered if doing so made her uncomfortable, or if that was all on him. "I wasn't expecting you either. All I knew was the client's name was Clark."

She stopped in front of Butters Bakery, her gaze searching for something in his. "So we're good then? All the awkwardness out of the way?"

"I don't know about that," he said, as she pulled open the bakery's door. He reached over her head and caught it, following her inside. There he was hit with a blast of a warm sugar scent reminiscent of the perfume she'd worn in high school. "I'm just off a year of reunions. Most have been pretty awkward."

She gave him a quirk of a smile. "I suppose with your past that's not unexpected."

Because no one knew what to say to an ex-con. No one except Thea, who'd always been able to speak her mind. "Yep."

"But since we've agreed not to talk about the past," she said, heading for the long display case, "let's eat cake."

They were here to eat cake? He frowned as he accompanied her. Then he stopped frowning and instead wondered if his eyes were really bigger than his stomach, because he was going to need a whole lot of room for the cake eating he planned to do.

Why had he never come here before?

Best he could tell, he could order just about every flavor under the sun: chocolate, vanilla, coconut, caramel, banana—and dozens of variations of each. There was what he was pretty sure was red velvet. And German chocolate. And cake with cookies. Cake with candy. Cake with nuts. Cakes with strawberries, and with limes, and with frosting roses and ruffles and ribbons.

He listened as Thea ordered several items from the Hispanic woman manning the counter. The two were friendly, though he didn't think they were necessarily friends—a thought that took him back to high school where most of Thea's friends had been kids she wanted something from.

Including his sister.

Including him.

It wasn't at all the vibe he'd sensed between her and Becca. Or sensed now.

"Have I missed anything you want?" Thea asked him.

He breathed deeply again, trying to separate the scent of sugar and the selfishness of the past from the woman in front of him now with slices of most every cake the place sold. "That should do it." ·

"What about something to drink?"

"Coffee would be good. Just black." He sure wasn't going to need it sweet.

"Make it two," she said to the woman filling the

order, digging into her pocket for several folded bills and counting out what she needed.

He offered her a twenty. "Here."

But she waved away his cash. "I've got this. It's my experiment."

Right. She'd said she wanted his opinion on something. He was going to guess it was cake.

They found a small table in the far front corner. Dakota sat with his back to the room, facing the window, holding his to-go cup of coffee while Thea doubled up some of the slices, sliding the empty plates beneath those now overflowing. Then she handed him a fork.

"So what's the experiment?" he asked, his gaze moving from one plate to another. He wasn't sure where to start.

She went with a chocolate cake with creamy fudge icing. "I want to see what the traffic is like on a weekday morning."

"And you had to buy out the place? Why not sit out front?"

"The bistro tables?" she asked, and when he nodded, she said, "Those belong to Bliss."

"Yeah, wouldn't want to get towed," he said, Thea snorting at the joke as he sliced off a big bite of white cake iced with a lemon cream-cheese frosting, though he left the candied lime slice on the plate. "Wow," he said, and sliced off another. "Just wow."

"Good stuff, huh?" She'd moved to the strawberry cake. It had bits and pieces of strawberries in the very pink icing.

"Oh, man." There was the second-best sort of orgasm going on in his mouth.

"You always did have a sweet tooth," she said, licking icing from the fork's tines, and grinning. "I guess that hasn't changed?"

He did his best to ignore the flick of her tongue, but he felt the memory of it and had to look away. "Coming to live with Tennessee and Kaylie, and her baking dozens of brownies every day . . ." He shook his head. "It's a wonder I don't weigh a ton."

"You might before we're done here." She glanced over as the door opened, watching the woman at the counter greet the customer as if they'd known each other for years. Then she looked back, taking him in as she chose a bite of cake with a whipped caramel icing. "And I'll have to join you in that wheelbarrow. This is freakishly good."

"I don't know why I've never been in here."

"I have, but not often enough. For obvious reasons," she said, going for the vanilla.

"Desserts were one of the things I missed most while in prison," he said, taking a bite of what he thought was Italian cream. The cake was nutty and moist and insanely good. "I mean, we'd get a cookie, or bowl of what was supposed to be banana pudding. But everything, even the scrambled eggs, tasted like chemically preserved cardboard. I guess the bread wasn't bad. If you like the white stuff. Tear off the crust. Roll it up into a ball. Those things can hurt if they hit you right."

She was slow to set down her fork, slower still to pick up her coffee cup. She held it with both hands, sipped through the slot in the to-go lid. Her hands were shaking just enough that the lid was a lifesaver. "As much as I missed you after you left," she said, looking down at the cup and not him, "I missed Indiana almost as much."

They'd agreed not to talk about the past. He should probably remind her of that. Problem was, he'd brought it up first. "How so?"

She shrugged. "Indiana?" she asked, and he nodded. "We started hanging with different crowds for some reason, so we didn't see each other as often, or really at all unless we met up somewhere. I would still call her, but after a while, if I didn't catch her at home, she stopped calling me back. She had a really hard time with you being gone."

"Yeah," he said, drawing out the word as he toyed with a maraschino cherry that had come unglued from its cake. He didn't know what else to say.

"I should've been a better friend." She shook her head and blew out a huff. "What am I saying? I should've been a friend, period. I knew she needed one. I guess I figured she had truer ones than I'd ever pretended to be. But I was having a hard enough time of my own without you around, and since selfish was my middle name . . ." The sentence trailed off and she shrugged. "I suck."

That would've made him laugh if his whole gut wasn't knotted up at the thought of what Indiana had gone through after he'd left. Tennessee had been there for her, sure. But Dakota's sentencing had been a quick affair. He'd been guilty, and Robby's parents had pushed hard, wanting Dakota punished to the full extent of the law. Good behavior had gotten him released after three years.

He lifted his gaze to meet hers. "Sometimes I wonder if keeping what had happened to ourselves, you and me, Tennessee and Indiana, wasn't a mistake," he said, the wall he'd built to keep that night locked away crumbling around him.

"You had your reasons," she said, remembering him arriving at her house covered in blood, shaking and angry and afraid.

She thought back to the events of that night, the ones she knew, the ones he'd told her: He'd found Robby in an arcade where he was known to hang out. He hadn't bothered to hide his face. He couldn't let his sister spend the rest of her school years as the girl Robby Hunt had tried to rape. He didn't want her living under that microscope, dealing with the pity or the speculation. It was bad enough she would carry the memory of the attack with her the rest of her life.

It wasn't like Robby was going to brag about what he'd done. It would've been easy to keep it among the four of them, though his siblings had never known Dakota had sought out Thea and shared all. But Dakota hadn't been thinking straight; his sister had just been assaulted. Honestly, though, had any of them? They'd been teenagers, the Keller siblings with absentee parents, Thea with a mother in name only. Dakota had agreed to pay whatever the price might be.

Thea had never told another soul. She'd never even mentioned what she knew to Indiana. "Does Indiana know you came to me that night after . . . Robby? Does Tennessee?"

"They do now," he said, slicing into the banana spice cake with the brown sugar icing. It cracked beneath his fork like a praline, granules of candy scattering over the plate.

She thought he might be eating it because with his mouth full he wouldn't have to talk. She couldn't imagine he really wanted it. Not if his stomach felt anything like hers, all topsy-turvy and seasick.

The door chime rang again, and a woman with two preschoolers came in. The children headed for the pint-sized plastic table with building blocks and giant crayons and coloring books in separate slots.

"That was a stupid thing to do, you know," Thea said. She listened to the woman's order. Two dozen cookies for a school party. A custom cake for a surprise anniversary dinner. When she looked back at Dakota he was waiting, one brow arched, fork full of cake at the ready. She hurried to explain. "Keeping what had happened from your parents. Convincing Indiana not to press charges. Robby should've been the one arrested. He should've been the one to go to prison. Indiana would've survived the gossip. She was strong and smart and knew who she was."

Dakota shoved the cake into his mouth, shaking his head as he chewed. He looked down, sliced off another bite, then said, "Maybe. Maybe not. It's not like she had anyone at home in her corner either way. And at least by not telling them, it never became common knowledge," he said and reached for his coffee. "She was better off with me gone and nobody knowing what had happened than with me being there and everyone pointing fingers and talking behind her back."

Whether or not Thea agreed, and she wasn't sure that she did, she wasn't going to argue about this. It was over with. Done with. What-ifs and might-have-beens didn't do anyone any good. Still . . .

She stared down at the cake crumbs littering the

table. "I should've come to see you. I should've brought her to see you. The few times we connected, that's all she talked about. Making the trip to Huntsville. How hard it was to get there."

He nodded, then kept nodding, as if processing memories to depict what she'd said. "Yeah, well, it was only hard because our parents couldn't be bothered."

And even with all the abuse she'd seen in her life, the indifference of Drew and Tiffany Keller was one thing she would never understand. "That had to have hurt."

"Not seeing them? Not really. Not seeing my brother and sister? That was tougher." He shifted to the side in his chair, bumping one of the legs with his knee, and smiled. "With our folks never around, we'd always had this musketeer thing going on. All for one. One for all. Stupid, I guess."

The three siblings. Not stupid at all. "Does that make me d'Artagnan?"

He chuckled under his breath and sipped at his coffee. "You spent enough time at our house to be a fourth."

It had felt so much more like a home than the house she'd shared with her mother. And that with the Keller parents gone more often than not. They'd provided, in their own weird way. Food and shelter and every material thing their kids could want. Where they'd failed was in the lack of involvement, the dearth of emotional investment in Dakota, Tennessee, and Indiana's lives.

Sad, really. "Indiana did miss you. A lot. And I'm not so sure she wouldn't have been happy to have everyone know the truth if it meant Robby going away and you being home."

He leaned forward, his elbows on his thighs, nearly crushing his cup between his hands. "Didn't we agree not to talk about the past? Besides, I thought you were here to monitor traffic."

"We did," she said, sitting back and leaving her fork on the table. She couldn't eat another bite, but she would get a carry-out container for what remained of the cake and take the slices home. "And I have been. Do *you* know how many people have come in since we've been here?"

"I saw the woman with the kids. And another before that."

He'd obviously been lost in thought when the older couple came in for coffee cake. And the two teen girls who giggled and whispered while choosing cupcakes. "We've been here, what? Thirty minutes? Forty-five? Not counting the children, there were eight customers served, including us."

"Is that good or bad?"

"For Bread and Bean, for Butters Bakery, it's slow but steady."

"But it adds up?"

She nodded. "Plus the phone rang at least five times with people placing orders. The woman working the counter hasn't had a lull yet."

"That doesn't sound like you're scoping out the traffic as much as the competition," he said, adding a raised brow.

Not that she believed in jinxes, but she wasn't ready to talk about her interest in the bakery. She finished off her coffee then got to her feet. "Let me grab a box for the leftovers. Then we can head back."

"I'll be right here taking a sugar nap," he said, waving her on. "Wake me up when you're done."

❦ Chapter Five ❦

"Your meeting at Bread and Bean go okay?" Tennessee asked once Dakota had climbed from the company truck and made his way into the Keller Construction barn.

That was one of the things that had surprised him most upon his arrival. Not that his brother had gone into the business on his own; Dakota had kept a tab or two on his siblings while away and was well aware of the existence of Keller Construction.

But learning that Tennessee had spent the first few months in business single-handedly converting the barn into an office and wood-working shop that he also used as a warehouse and occasionally for client meetings, well, Dakota couldn't help but be impressed.

He wished he'd been around to help with the project. And that had been his first clue that returning to Texas might not have been smart. He couldn't afford to regret what he'd done with his life. He couldn't long for a past that didn't exist. Not surprisingly, he was still having a lot of trouble with the present.

He boosted up onto the second stool beside his brother's drafting table. Tennessee had built an office, but he never used it, preferring the open-air breezeway. His stepmother-in-law, Dolly Pepper, worked for him part time. The office was her domain. "You mean was I shocked to see Thea Clark is the owner?"

"Thea Clark." Tennessee frowned, spinning his stool to face Dakota before his mouth broke into a grin. "Wait. Not Thea Clark from—"

"High school? And my bed? Yeah," Dakota said with a nod, shoving a hand through his hair and raking it from his face. "That Thea Clark."

He hadn't quite come to terms with what he felt about seeing her. He wasn't even sure *what* he felt besides the obvious. He hadn't slept with a woman in a very long time, and he'd never slept with anyone as often as he had with Thea.

They'd been teens, sure, so their encounters

hadn't been the stuff of legend. Or the stuff of two adults who brought more to the table than hormones and curiosity and rebellious natures. At least he guessed Thea had brought some of those things.

He'd been a teenager and horny. He'd only brought one.

It was obvious Tennessee was trying not to laugh. "Dude. I had no idea. Dolly made the appointment after the original contractor bailed halfway through the job."

That wasn't much of an explanation. "And she didn't tell you who the appointment was with?"

Tennessee shook his head, Dakota noticing for the first time a patch of gray at his brother's temple. "I knew we wouldn't be working up the specs, that the client had already paid for those and the outfitting of the kitchen, and that we'd only be dealing with the storefront. And I remember the Clark part of her name. Just not the Thea. Maybe I never knew it to remember."

"Parenthood's making you old before your time," Dakota said, thinking if Tennessee was old, he himself was ancient. Then again his bones told him that when he crawled out of bed every day. "Unless that's just what comes with being married. Like that gut you're growing over there."

Tennessee sucked it in as he looked down at his lap and frowned. "The only thing I'm growing around here is the business."

"Yeah? How so?" Dakota asked, and Tennessee's head came up.

He lost the frown on the way, a smile to rival the one he'd worn at his daughter's birth in its place. "That bid I put in on the art house theater downtown? Looks like the job's ours."

Not ours, Dakota wanted to say. *Yours.* "Nice. Very nice. Congratulations."

"And to you, brother. It's going to be a hell of a game changer. Something that size? With that much prestige?" Tennessee shook his head, the emotion in the words nearly causing him to stumble over them. He brought his fist to his mouth and cleared his throat.

If Dakota had been a better person, a better brother, he would've shared in Tennessee's joy. It wasn't the first time he'd had such a thought since returning, but he hadn't had the thoughts at all until he'd come back. Seems he'd done a better job than he'd realized of shutting down.

It was what he'd had to do. The only way he'd known to survive.

"You ever find out who bought the place?" Dakota asked once his brother had regained his composure.

"Nope. Just dealing with the new owner's people. Which is fine. Sometimes it's even easier," he added, which had Dakota's mind going to Thea. Like their history wasn't going to cause him enough grief as it was.

"I like the plans," Tennessee was saying. "The retro stage. The vintage curtain setup. The seats are probably going to be the biggest headache, but we'll work it out."

"It's a hell of a job." In more ways than one. "You got the crew to take it on?"

Tennessee nodded. Then shrugged. "I'll give Manny a call. Even if he doesn't have anyone to send, he might know of someone looking for work."

Someone meaning an ex-con. Because that's what Manny Balleza did. Sent parolees to work for Keller Construction. It was an arrangement Tennessee had made with the other man while Manny was still Dakota's parole officer, though Manny had pulled the right strings with his people to put Dakota to work away from the scene of his crime. It made things a lot easier, his not having to run into anyone who knew who he was, knew what he'd done.

Tennessee had wanted Dakota to join the business after his release, to turn it into a family gig, to add the word *Brothers* between the *Keller* and *Construction* that adorned the sides of the trucks. It was what they'd talked about doing while still teens. But as soon as he'd been free of the state and able, Dakota had split. Not even Manny had known how to reach him, which was exactly what Dakota had wanted.

Freedom. Anonymity.

Peace.

What he hadn't wanted then, and didn't want now, was Tennessee counting on him. For anything. He didn't want the pressure of living up to any expectations his brother—or his sister—might have. He'd been thinking about that a lot. Thinking what he might have to do about it.

He took a big fat uncomfortable breath. "Good. Because after this job for Thea, I'm thinking about cutting out."

"Cutting out." Tennessee's hands went to his thighs. He stretched out his fingers before drawing them up into fists. His frown deepened between his brows. "You mean leaving? Hope Springs? Texas? What about the business? What about Indiana?"

His brother's questions flew at him like darts toward a board already full of too many holes to count. "Indiana will be fine whether I'm living here or not. So will your business. You can get any of Manny's ex-cons to build barista stations in coffee shops."

"I don't want any of Manny's ex-cons."

"C'mon, Tennessee. It's not like we're working together."

"What's that supposed to mean?" Tennessee asked, scowling.

Dakota crossed his arms. "Think about it. This last year. When have we ever crewed a job together? You go one way. I go another. Or I go out to do the manual labor, and you stay in to push pencils."

Time ticked slowly toward Tennessee's response. "That's what you think I do?"

"I think what you do is what you've always done," Dakota said bluntly. "Been the boss. Taken care of the company you built. Seen to the needs of your wife and your daughter. Indiana."

"You're talking about family."

"Yeah."

"Your family. Not just mine."

"Yeah," Dakota said again, the air around the word crackling.

Tennessee swiveled back to his drafting board then shoved off his stool, pacing several steps away before coming back. He was rubbing at his forehead when he did. "Then there's some kind of disconnect going on here that I don't get."

Dakota didn't expect his brother to get it. Tennessee wasn't the one who'd spent three years behind bars and the rest of his life since aimless. "How about I work the Bread and Bean job, and we revisit this when it's done? I won't go anywhere, or make plans to leave before then."

It had been the wrong thing to say. "Do you want the answer I'd give another employee, or the one I'd give my brother?"

Dakota's spine stiffened. His gut knotted. He leaned his head to one side and cracked his neck. "I think you just gave me both."

"I need the work done right," Tennessee said, his jaw tight as he ground out the words. "I need to know whoever is doing it is not taking shortcuts. That he's not rushing through to get done and get gone."

Because that's what he assumed Dakota would do. Which spoke to the heart of the matter.

Tennessee wasn't thinking about Dakota as his brother, much less his partner. He was thinking about him as an ex-con. "You run into that with a lot of the guys Manny sends you?"

"Not until now."

And . . . stalemate. Tennessee wasn't going to give an inch, but neither was Dakota. That said, Dakota wasn't in the mood to fight, to argue, to explain—none of it. He'd been back a year. He wasn't sure what he'd expected from his homecoming, but knew he needed to figure it out.

He wasn't going to be of any use to anyone until he did.

He stepped down from the stool and took off, leaving the keys to the truck he'd been driving on the hood and setting off on foot for Indiana's cottage.

It had only taken Thea one look at Becca's face to make her decision about Butters Bakery. Well more than one, actually. First there had been the disappointment when Becca had told her about Peggy's offer; with no capital of her own, buying the business was out of Becca's reach. Then had come the defensiveness when Thea had co-opted the idea, turning Becca's *me* into her own.

Becca's dejection upon learning that Peggy had made the same overture to Lena Mining had broken Thea's heart. It was like life had chosen Becca to beat up on for some reason, and there was nothing Thea could do to reverse the bad luck that continually blew Becca's way.

But the look that had made all the difference was the one of hope when Thea had mentioned bringing the idea of buying the bakery to the table. That was how they did things at the house on Dragon Fire Hill. Anything affecting all of them was fodder for discussion over their evening meal.

Yes, it was Thea's money, but unlike the catalyst driving her to open Bread and Bean, this involved more than just Thea's life or Thea's man hours or Thea's recovery from abuse. The bakery would be a group effort from the get-go, meaning an LLC or some such.

And most of the money for the purchase would be Todd's, so spending it for the group was sort of karma. She liked the idea of Todd funding the lives of four women who'd been treated abominably. Especially when she was one of them.

She looked from Becca to Ellie to Frannie Charles to Frannie's two boys, James and Robert.

71

All five of them, six when she included herself in the count, were sitting in the big country kitchen of her house eating supper. Two of the room's walls were taken up with white cabinets. The upper ones were glass-fronted and sparkling, except where they were covered with cardboard. Out of the dozen—six on the north wall, six on the east—she counted three intact. One was shattered completely. Several were simply cracked.

The appliances were serviceable but second-hand, so the stove was an avocado green and the fridge a complementary harvest gold. Very seventies. Save for the one red-brick wall that on its own was quite lovely, but in the retro context was not. Ellie, once an art teacher, had blessed the pairing's color scheme, happy to have a working kitchen, like a sandbox, to play in.

The floor was hardwood. Solid. Scarred. In desperate need of refinishing, but Thea loved hearing footsteps falling against it. The Charles boys' tiny little sneakers slapping. Ellie's Birkenstocks flapping. Becca's high-tops squeaking. Her own Keds doing the same. Supper time brought the noises together, a percussive cacophony beneath the clang of pots and pans, the ring of silver on glass.

Tonight's meal was boxed mac and cheese, green beans from a can, and fish sticks with both tartar sauce and ketchup. There was milk for the boys, and for everyone else a huge pitcher of sun tea that had steeped on the back porch for hours. Frannie had done the cooking, as much cooking as any of the items required, using foodstuffs she'd bought with her monthly benefits from the state.

Frannie had set the big circular table—one Thea had found in a flea market and, with Ellie's help, restored—with her own grandmother's china and silverware, and linens she'd embroidered herself. They were done in an "Eat Me" and "Drink Me" theme, black thread against coral and turquoise. She sold them through the same network Thea had used to outfit Bread and Bean.

The dishes and cutlery were among the few family heirlooms Frannie had saved from the house fire that had left her and her sons homeless—the fire her husband had set after his taking pot shots at her with his shotgun hadn't convinced her to call off the divorce. He was still at large, which was why Frannie, James, and Robert had come to live with Thea.

And why Frannie still flinched at every unexpected sound.

The sounds floating through the kitchen now filled Thea with joy, and Frannie, too, judging by her expression. They were gorgeous sounds. Sounds of living. Every day made succinct in universal ways. Women laughing and little boys giggling and forks clinking against plates and the ketchup bottle blowing out air. The fact that

Thea was able to offer Frannie and the others this ordinary moment, this slice of a simple uncomplicated life, thrilled her beyond belief.

The fact that she was also able to keep them safe, to give them a place to sleep and to eat and to shower, or to just sit and watch a movie or read a book without having to look over their shoulder, or wait for another shoe—or belt, or fist—to drop, or a shotgun blast, was more fulfilling than she could put into words.

She didn't even try.

"Thea?"

"Hmm?" she asked as she set down her iced tea, glancing toward Becca who'd been the one to draw her out of her reverie.

"You had something to bring to the table?"

"Oh, right." She braced her forearms on either side of her plate, and looked from Becca's smile to Ellie's to Frannie who had gone from carefree to worried. Thea reached over to squeeze the other woman's hand. "It's a good something. Don't worry. Becca and Ellie know about it already because they were at the shop today when the subject came up. You've met Peggy Butters, right?"

Frannie moved her utensils out of Robert's reach. "The older woman who owns the bakery on the other side of the chocolate shop?"

Thea nodded. "Peggy and her husband, Pat, have decided to retire, and they have no family to take over the business. Peggy asked Becca if she might be interested in buying the place. She also asked Lena Mining, who works at Bliss. No doubt she's asked others as well."

"And you want to buy it," Frannie said.

"No." Becca rushed to correct her. "*We* want to buy it. As a group."

Thea glanced from Frannie to Becca to Ellie then down at the table and her laced hands. "We'll need a name, you know. For the business. We'll need to form a partnership. Or incorporate. And that's only the beginning. Barely the tip of the iceberg. It'll be huge. And it will not be easy."

And then she looked up, seeing wide eyes and excitement and the thrill of adventure and possibilities and hope. That was the one thing on every woman's face. Hope. Peggy Butters had just given them all something to look forward to. Something more than a life spent hiding here in this house, behind bulletproof glass and doors it would take a bulldozer to down.

"So this would be a real business," Frannie said, gathering her straight black hair from Robert's hands and tucking it down the back of her blouse. "That we owned. All of us."

Thea nodded.

And Frannie went back to frowning, her face pale and marred with exhaustion. "But it would be your money."

"Only to get started. We'd set things up so that

a portion of the profits would go to pay back the initial investment. I don't know how all that works. That's why we'll need an accountant and an attorney."

"Which will cost money."

"The business's money, but yeah. Nothing in this world is free," Thea said, giving Frannie a weak smile.

Frannie offered Robert another bite of fish, then said, "And once you're repaid—"

"Each of us would be a quarter owner." Ellie was the one to answer. "Goodness. Just the idea . . ." She reached for her napkin and blotted her eyes as if the freedom, emotional and financial, that came with a new business was overwhelming.

"What about Bread and Bean?" Frannie spooned up more mac and cheese for James, her own food mostly untouched. "How in the world are you going to run two businesses? If Ellie's baking bread in one place, and Becca's baking cakes in another, who's going to wash the dishes and mop the floors? Who's going to keep track of supplies, or work the front counters? Who's going to be the barista? The three of you were already stretched thin running the one place. I've got my hands full with the boys here and the house, and I'm not going to leave them alone in day care."

"Frannie. It's okay," Thea said. "This is why I

brought this to the table. Trust me. I know how exciting it is to think about owning a business. But you're right. There's no way Becca and Ellie and I could run two shops without hiring additional help. We're going to have trouble running the one. I've already thought about having a high schooler come in afternoons to clean up."

"It would have to be someone who could keep things organized," Becca said, stabbing up a forkful of beans. "And not mix up the rice flour with the tapioca or the almond."

"Exactly," Thea said, glancing at Ellie who was smiling guiltily down at her plate. "Plus, they would need to work independently and be able to make simple decisions. Say we do take on the bakery. Peggy and Pat have been in business for decades. I imagine someone would need to apprentice with them—"

"Hold on a second," Becca said, leaning forward, her head cocked to one side. "Are you saying if we buy Butters Bakery it will have to stay Butters Bakery?"

"Yes and no," Thea said, hating to burst Becca's bubble. "Part of buying a business is taking on the customer base and keeping them happy. So there's that to consider. Bread and Bean is different. We're starting from nothing. We can do things however we want to."

"Peggy doesn't do all the baking herself, does

she?" Ellie asked, reaching for her napkin and blotting her mouth. "I know her husband bakes, too, but don't they have help?"

"We'd need to talk to Peggy and Pat and find out more. For all I know, she bakes using old family recipes she'll be taking with her. In that case, we'd have to come up with a whole new menu. Or maybe the recipes would be considered assets the same as the equipment. Buying an established business is way beyond my experience.

"Could be it's more than we want to take on," she continued, feeling as if she were treading some very deep water. "I don't know. Maybe instead we expand Bread and Bean to include some of Becca's desserts. Things Butters doesn't sell. That said, I do think Peggy's offer is worth looking into further. So that's my vote. We get more details from the Butterses and go from there."

She glanced around the table. "Sound good?"

"Sounds good to me," Ellie said.

"Me, too," Becca added.

Frannie gave a nod, then cupped the back of Robert's head and pulled the sleepy boy close for a kiss. "Okay. As long as my boys are safe with me."

"Always," Thea said, her voice, choked in her throat dropping to a whisper. "Always."

❧ Chapter Six ❧

Ellie had been completely unable to sleep and was up and dressed before dawn. All night long her mind had been caught in a whirlwind of thoughts that would not stop, well, whirling.

First had been the memory of yesterday's encounter with Lena Mining, and the romantic possibilities she did not need to be imagining. But how could she help herself? Lena was adorable, and so incredibly sweet, and chemistry was chemistry, though if it was only one-sided.

Then had come last night's group discussion about buying Butters Bakery. Ellie was probably the least affected by the decision to go forward with the purchase. She had plenty to keep her busy in the kitchen at Bread and Bean, as well as at the house on Dragon Fire Hill.

Still, she mused, pedaling her way into town, an additional business would mean more work for everyone. There would be schedules to adjust, chores to reassign . . . Good thing they were all used to having their status quo fly out the window, and knew not to get too comfortable.

The early summer morning was cool enough that the bike trip left her clammy rather than sweat-drenched. It also had her tightening her shoulders and cringing any time a car approached from behind. She wondered if she'd ever stop being scared, though dealing with the fright was worth it. She enjoyed being the first to arrive and having the place to herself.

The kitchen had been fully functional when Thea had leased the space. Oh, it had needed a few additions to make it workable for Bread and Bean's needs. But for the most part, the appliances had been perfectly acceptable, the wiring to code and stable, the flooring in good shape.

After locking her bike behind the shop, Ellie let herself in. Once the door closed behind her, she stood in the dark and listened to the space around her wake up—the steel of the appliances ringing hello, the baking pans lining up on the work table like soldiers, the yeast blooming, the flour sifting, the butter and milk knocking on the door of the fridge. The sourdough starter yawning awake. The herbs stretching and shedding their scents like confetti.

All of that was in her mind, of course, but she loved the idea of the kitchen coming to life, the dishes all dancing like those in the Disney movie *Beauty and the Beast*. Not that she would ever tell anyone. She'd had enough people thinking her a flighty dingbat. A ninny. An airhead.

She knew how she came across. She also knew who she was. A survivor with advanced degrees in art and art history. And she knew who she wanted to be. For now that was a baker of the most amazing artisan bread to be had anywhere near Hope Springs.

That was one good thing to come of her old existence: After losing her teaching job to budget cuts, she'd found work in a specialty bakery and learned a new trade, which she loved as much as she had her career in art. The only downside at the bakery had been meeting the woman she'd thought was her one true love but who had very nearly killed her.

Now Thea had given her this amazing chance, this amazing new life, on top of the place to live that was more than a house, and roommates who were more than a family.

It was a haven, and Ellie was safe.

Today, as she flipped on the lights, as she turned on the music she liked playing before everyone else arrived, as the kitchen came to life around her, ringing and blooming and knocking on the door of the fridge, she knew she would never be more so.

"I felt so bad about yesterday." Ellie reached across Bliss's front counter and handed Lena the bag with the still-warm sourdough round loaf. She knew she was overreacting. Lena had dropped her books. Ellie had dropped her spools and had to chase them down the sidewalk. No one had been hurt. Nothing had been damaged. Except Ellie's pride. "A peace offering, I guess."

"There aren't any hard feelings, so no peace to be made, but thanks." Lena brought the small brown sack wrapped around the fresh crusty loaf to her nose and breathed in, but her gaze held fast to Ellie's. "This smells good. Really good."

"I'm surprised you can smell it above all the chocolate," Ellie said, looking around. This was the first time she'd been inside Bliss, and wow. These weren't the chocolates she'd expected. They were jewels. Tiny pieces in amazing angles and curves that shimmered and popped with color. "I'd never be able to work in here. I think I've put on five pounds since walking in."

"You get used to it," Lena said with a shrug, peering into the bag. "You made this?"

Ellie nodded, inordinately pleased. As if she had anything to do with the way the butter and flour and yeast and milk and starter came together. As if women hadn't been baking bread since the dawn of time or, well, whenever. She knew better than to take credit where she shouldn't. To take pride at all.

"It's great toasted," she said. "Or broiled with garlic and butter. Or used for grilled cheese."

"I'm a fan of grilled cheese for sure," Lena said, looking up.

"Are you?" she asked, drying her palms on her hips, her heart thumping wildly. "Me, too. Especially with a bowl of tomato soup. I like provolone and Gouda and Havarti and sharp cheddar."

Smiling, Lena sniffed at the loaf again. "All on the same sandwich?"

"Of course! It's so good. And goat cheese works better than cheddar, but that's usually all we have at the house. Cheddar, I mean," she said, rambling. "But at least we have that. Thea says we might not have the most extensive pantry in Hope Springs, but we will always have real cheese."

"Thea."

"Thea Clark." Ellie gestured over her shoulder. "She owns Bread and Bean. The coffee shop next door."

"And you live with her?" Lena asked as she set the bag behind her on the counter.

Ellie nodded. "With her and with Becca. She's our barista, or she will be once we're opened. And with Frannie and her two boys. Frannie hasn't been there long, and I'm not sure when she'll be able to work again . . ." Ellie left the thought alone to trail, realizing she was a little too close to revealing things it wasn't her place to share. "Anyway, it's the house up on Dragon Fire Hill. The big white one that looks like it belongs in *Gone with the Wind*."

"Yeah. I know it."

"Thea likes old movies," Ellie said, reaching up with one hand to twist back her hair.

Goodness, she must look a mess, all sweaty from the kneading and the ovens, flour dusting her sleeves and no doubt her nose. "And old TV. I'd never even heard of Scarlett O'Hara before Thea. Rhett Butler was an ass, but Scarlett. That girl was strong. She knew what she wanted."

"Like Katniss Everdeen," Lena said, her smile indulgent as she picked up one of Bliss's candy boxes.

"I don't know who that is," Ellie said, hating that the admission made her feel dumb when she knew she wasn't. Sheltered. Uninformed. Out of the loop. Yeah. All of those. Though not for long.

"From *The Hunger Games*."

"Is that a movie?"

"It was a book," Lena said with complete patience and without condescension. "A series of books. Now it's a big movie franchise."

"Like Harry Potter?"

"Not quite that big, but yeah. Same book-to-movie concept." She reached into the display case for a chocolate and put it into the box. "I'm going to guess you don't get out much."

Ellie did her best to smile. It wasn't Lena's fault she didn't know the things Ellie had been through. "I'm getting better about it. I've got a lot of catching up to do."

"I can help. I mean, if you're ever looking for something to read. Or to watch." Lena stopped then, and shrugged, as if she weren't sure why she was making the offer.

It didn't matter. Ellie liked that she had. "That would be great."

"Cool. Here." Lena passed her the box with the chocolate. "This is my favorite of Callum's flavors."

"For me?" Ellie asked, hesitant.

"Unless you're allergic to chocolate. Or don't like it or something. It's all good if you don't."

"I love chocolate." Ellie took the tiny brown box, thinking it the most gorgeous thing she'd ever seen, all iridescent and so perfectly shaped. "What flavor is it? Besides the chocolate?"

"Burnt orange and Irish whiskey. Callum calls it Irish Creamsicle. It sounds weird, I know, but when Callum cooks it all up and does his thing, it's truly amazing." Lena stopped, then gestured toward Ellie with one hand. "The filling's almost the same color as your hair."

"Goodness," she said, reaching to toy with a strand, her heart beating with tiny, delicate, tickling wings, fluttering, and she only just stopped herself from asking if that was why Lena had chosen it. "Thank you. I'll save it for dessert after lunch."

"Or you could be a rebel and eat it now," Lena said with a shrug.

Ellie looked from the other woman to the box and frowned. "Is that what rebels do?"

Lena laughed. "I have no idea. I just like the idea."

"Of eating dessert first?"

"Sure. Life's too short not to," Lena said, and Ellie could've sworn the words flipped a switch and changed everything. And so with Lena looking on, Ellie opened the box.

She brought it to her nose and breathed in, much as Lena had done with the sourdough round. She smelled the chocolate and the bite of the orange and a soft hint of vanilla and the barest edge of the whiskey. She wondered if Callum used Jameson, if the oranges were organic, the chocolate fair trade, the vanilla scraped fresh from a bean.

Then she stopped thinking of anything but the expectant way Lena was looking at her and what it did to the big hole in her chest, and bit the candy in half. The chocolate sat on her tongue for several seconds and then began to soften, releasing the rest of the flavors as if in a tide. She closed her eyes and savored the combination that was sweet and bitter and tangy and oh-so-perfect as it swelled.

Tears threatened and she forced them away. She could not appear weak. Not here. Not now. Not with this woman whom she already thought of as a friend, but who she could so easily imagine becoming more.

Tucking the other half of the candy into the box

to enjoy later, she looked up at Lena and said, "I can see why this is your favorite. It's exquisite. Thank you."

Lena's expression softened, as if she'd been worried about Ellie's reaction, and then she said, "And thank you for the bread. I think I'll have grilled cheese for supper."

"Good. Let me know if you enjoy it," Ellie said, turning for the door, hoping that hadn't been too forward but just enough of an opening for Lena to step through.

"Sure thing," Lena said, and Ellie smiled.

Lost in thought, a mug of coffee held between his hands, Dakota didn't look up at his sister's approach until Indiana's boot hit the bottom step of the three leading up to the cottage.

His boots were on the second. His butt was on the edge of the porch. It was as far as he'd made it after forcing himself out of bed, into the shower, then to the kitchen and the coffeemaker. He should've been at work already, but he was beginning to wonder if he'd even make it today.

He was on his second mug and still only half-awake. The hour had been close to five when he'd finally dozed off, and he was getting too old to survive on three of them a night. Not that the blue jay who claimed the branch closest to his window every morning at six gave a crap.

At this rate, he wasn't going to make it to forty. Neither would the bird.

He lifted his drink. "There's half a pot left in the kitchen. Still fresh."

"Tennessee called me last night," was Indiana's answer.

Dakota wasn't surprised. "Yeah? What did he call you?"

She kicked the toe of his boot with the toe of hers. "He didn't call me anything but he had a few choice names for you. And he told me some bullshit story about you leaving Hope Springs. Let me grab a cup and then you can tell me why Tennessee doesn't know what he's talking about."

"Can't wait," he said, leaning to the side to give her room to pass. She took it, but shoved against him anyway. That had him grinning. He was really sorry he'd missed so many years of his sister's life. His brother's, too, but he'd known his brother better. His sister, fourteen when he'd gone to prison, had been a teen girl enigma.

For the first five months after returning to Texas, Dakota had stayed in the three-story Victorian on the corner of Second and Chances with Tennessee's family. He'd hated imposing, because no matter both his brother and Kaylie telling him he wasn't, he knew better.

Yes, the house was spacious. The first floor held Kaylie's successful Two Owls Café, which meant people in and out half the day. Kaylie's father Mitch Pepper, and his wife Dolly, were in and out, too. They did most of the cooking and cleaning while Kaylie took care of Georgia May.

And that was the other thing. Dakota had arrived in Hope Springs the day Kaylie had given birth. Meaning she'd come home from the hospital with a new baby and a brother-in-law she hadn't planned for. It hadn't been hard to stay out of the way; the size of the house saw to that.

But it had been hard to find quiet time. Most of the time he'd done so when late night had become early morning, and he'd walked through the big corner lot with Kaylie's dog, Magoo. The lumbering shepherd-chow mix had taken to spending a lot of his time with Dakota, the baby demanding Kaylie's attention.

With time, things had gotten better, the new family falling into a routine, but when Indiana had married Oliver Gatlin five months later, Dakota had moved to the cottage once his sister had vacated it. Everything in the kitchen was where she'd left it. He figured it wouldn't take her long to get her coffee. She was back in less than two minutes, dropping to sit by his side.

"Now," she said, before he could ask her if she wanted breakfast. He thought he might have an egg or two left. "Somebody hired a PI who put in a whole lot of time to find you for me, and someone paid to see that it happened. Why in the world would you think about leaving again?"

"Oliver finally made you see the light, huh?" Because for so long she'd insisted that her husband had been responsible for locating Dakota.

She nodded as she brought her drink away from her mouth to balance it on her knees covered by the skirt of her sundress. The morning sun sparkled off the rock weighing down her left hand's ring finger. Dakota swore he'd seen smaller bowling balls. "He told me more than once that the man he'd hired was not the one who found you. I wouldn't listen."

And her man hadn't been the one to locate Dakota either. There was a mystery third party involved. "What changed your mind?"

"He took me to meet his PI." She sipped at her coffee. "The man was convincing."

"In ways that your husband wasn't?"

"I thought my husband was trying to keep me from feeling indebted to him for bringing you home." She said it with a shrug. "My PI hadn't had any luck finding you, so it just made sense that Oliver's had. Not once did it occur to me that someone else was looking. Why would it? And you weren't exactly forthcoming with your version of the events."

"Hey," he said, lowering his mug and nearly spitting coffee. "I told you I didn't remember the man's name. I'm sure he told me, but"—he twirled a finger—"in one ear and out the other."

She leaned a shoulder against the railing and gave him a side-eyed glance. "He never told you who he worked for?"

"Nope. No idea if he was local. No idea who hired him. I didn't ask. I didn't think I needed to. All he said was that it wasn't an emergency but my sister needed me home."

"So you came."

"I came," he said with a nod. The timing had actually been perfect. Ironically, he'd been in Indiana, at the end of a job and ready to move on. He'd had ten of them since leaving prison. None of them had lasted much longer than a year. Seemed a year was all the time he could give to any one place. Even the place his sister and brother called home.

Indiana's voice was small and soft when she said, "And now you're thinking of leaving."

He took a deep breath, lifted his cup to have it ready. "I am."

"Okay," she said after a heavy, slow-motion moment, though she was more flippant than before. "But I'm going to need a reason why."

Dakota scraped one boot over a rough patch of porch step and laughed. "Is that so?"

"Yes, it's so. Dakota. Crap," she said, this time leaning toward him and pushing her shoulder into his. "You leave, you gotta know I'm going to come looking for you again."

"Hey, now. I never said I wasn't going to stay in touch."

"So far you haven't said much of anything," she said, smoothing down the fabric of her skirt where it had bunched up over one knee.

"Maybe because someone hasn't given me a chance."

"Then here. Take it. The floor is yours," she said with the wave of one arm. "The whole damn five acres is yours. Just talk to me. Please."

"Fine," he said, though he didn't know what to follow up with. *Now is the hour of our discontent* was a little too dramatic. Plus, it was summertime. And he wasn't really much for Shakespeare. "You brought me back because you were worried about me. You wanted to make sure I was all right. You've had a year to see for yourself that I am. What else is there?"

"What does that even mean?" she asked with another expansive gesture and a break in her voice. "What is there for me? What is there for you? What is there for Tennessee or Keller Construction or the July Fourth barbecue at Two Owls or the rest of your life?" She stopped, took a steadying breath. "I'm not even sure what you're asking me."

Considering everything she'd just said had crossed his mind more than once, yet he was still without an answer . . . "I think that makes two of us."

They sat there for several minutes after that, finishing off their coffee while the sun climbed high enough in the sky to have Dakota reaching for the sunglasses hooked over his T-shirt's neckband. It was June, but it was Texas. Mornings came early, and they came hot.

"Should I put on another pot of coffee?" she asked.

Dakota shook his head. "I don't have time. I'm already running late. I've got to get to the job. Oh. Here's one for you," he said, nudging her with his elbow. "Guess who's opening an espresso bar in the same block as Bliss and Butters Bakery?"

She cocked her head. "It's not just an espresso bar, right? I think I heard they'll also be selling artisan bread."

"Thea Clark," he said, ignoring her addendum and answering his question himself.

"What?" Indiana stared, her mouth hanging open, her eyes wide, the cloud of her dark hair like a frame around her face. "From middle school Thea Clark?"

"It was high school for me, but yeah. That's her."

Shaking her head, Indiana stared off across the front lawn into the unchecked growth that bordered the drive leading past the cottage to the greenhouses. "We lost touch . . . God, I don't even remember the last time I saw her or talked to her. It had to be before I graduated. She was a year ahead of me and already out of school. I guess she left Round Rock after that maybe?"

Dakota remembered exactly when, before yesterday, he'd seen Thea last: the several hours he'd spent with her the night before he'd left for prison. Not that they'd done much in the way of talking. "She lives up on Dragon Fire Hill. The big white house."

"Really? Huh. She bought that place?"

"Seems so."

"Isn't it sort of a wreck?" she asked, frowning as if she couldn't picture Thea living there.

Dakota shrugged. "I haven't been up there to see."

"I haven't either, but I've heard the previous owners had really let it go." She looked down into her coffee, then glanced over. "Is she married?"

He shook his head. "She lives with several other women. I think the same women who work for her."

"That's interesting."

She had no idea. "One of them pretty much clotheslined me with her forearm the other morning."

Indiana gasped at that. "What?"

He nodded, remembering the mix of terror and anger simmering in Becca York's eyes. "Apparently I was standing too close to Thea."

"Well, that's not surprising," she said with a snort.

Dakota only just stopped himself from rolling his eyes. "We were looking at a blueprint. It wasn't like we were having sex against the wall."

Indiana gave a loud huff before finishing off her coffee. "Knowing you two, I wouldn't have been surprised."

"That was a long time ago."

"Time's nothing as long as the chemistry's still there."

He supposed she was digging, but he didn't have anything to give her since he hadn't yet been able to nail down what had passed between him and Thea besides a whole lot of coffee and cake. "I'm not sure there ever was any real chemistry. Just . . . hormones."

"And now?" she asked, a curious arch to her brow.

"Not to burst your bubble, but not long after I got there, she told me I'd never been much of a gentleman and walked off."

She laughed again. "Sounds like the Thea Clark I remember. I'll have to stop by and see her. Interesting that she picked Hope Springs to settle down in. She never seemed the small-town, life-in-the-slow-lane type."

"She's . . . different now," he said, not sure if he could explain how, or put what he meant into more specific words.

"Pretty sure we're all different now."

"Yeah, but she's *different* different." He thought for a moment, then added, "Like she's been through something big and is paying for it."

"I'm going to take a guess and say it takes one to know one."

And with that remark, he was done. Indiana wasn't going to hear about his past anymore than Thea was. He tossed the dregs of his coffee to the ground and stood. "You may be a kept woman, but I've got to get to work."

"Excuse me? Just because my extraordinarily generous husband gave me a rock the size of my head does not make me a kept woman. And just because you derailed me by mentioning Thea, don't think we're done with this conversation. If it would help, we could include Tennessee."

He'd rather not revisit yesterday's conversation with his brother. "Trust me. It wouldn't."

"What about breakfast . . . day after tomorrow?" she asked, canting her head to one side. "Same time? I'll bring food?"

"Do I have a choice?" he asked, already anticipating the answer.

"Well, you're living rent-free in my cottage, so let's just say you owe me."

Dakota knew he didn't, knew Indiana was pulling his leg, but they did need to talk. And so he said, "Breakfast tacos. Eggs, cheese, potatoes, onions, sausage, salsa, and cheese."

"I'll see what I can do," Indiana said, handing him her mug as she got to her feet. "See you at seven."

✤ Chapter Seven ✤

By the time Dakota reached Bread and Bean, he'd put away most of his chat with Indiana to look at later. Yes, he needed to tell her what he'd been thinking. Why, in the long run, his leaving would be the best for all of them. But last night's lack of sleep meant this morning wasn't the best time. He was doing good to put one foot in front of the other. Pulling his thoughts together coherently wasn't going to happen today.

The part he hadn't put away, and was still turning over, had to do with Thea, and that last night they'd spent together before he'd gone away. How it had kept him from losing his mind those first few days behind bars. How he'd continued to think about her while incarcerated, comparing their first time to their last, the changes in both of them—not so much how they'd gone about the whole act with less fumbling and more focus, but how comfortable they'd grown together, the things they'd talked about afterward.

The way that intimacy had become as important as the orgasms, if not more so.

The orgasms had always been the easy part.

Talking still gave him hell.

"I was beginning to wonder if you were coming in."

Having tensed at the sound of the back door opening earlier, Dakota now tensed again at hearing Thea's voice. Funny enough, Tennessee had said pretty much the same thing when Dakota had shown up this morning to fetch his truck. It had been a long trek from the cottage, but he had only himself to blame.

Oh, he could've asked Indiana for a lift, but then he'd have to explain walking out on their brother last night. He'd discovered enough shortcuts over the last year that the hike from Three Wishes Road to Grath Avenue wasn't onerous. Besides, it gave him time for quiet contemplation.

Since prison, it was one thing he hated being without.

He gave Thea the same answer he'd given his brother. "I'll keep doing so as long as you keep writing the checks."

She walked around to the other side of his table saw stand and crossed her arms as she stared at him, her T-shirt and knee shorts baggy, her hair piled on top of her head in a rooster tail of strands going here and there. She looked like she wanted to smile, but was having trouble. Like she wanted to forget yesterday and go forward from here. Her next words, flirty but forced, convinced him he was right.

"And all this time I thought we were more to each other than contractor and contractee."

"I think you're confusing today with once upon a time," he said, pulling a pencil from behind his ear to mark off a measurement for the shop's main shelving unit.

"Now you're just making me sad," she said with a pout that might've been believable on the face of the old Thea but on this one was affected and had his radar pinging.

He arched one brow then looked down to his tape measure and length of pine. "How so?"

"I've been so busy since moving, I haven't had time to meet many new people. It's nice seeing a friendly face." She shoved her hands into her pockets and shrugged. "I like that we've reconnected."

He wondered about the women she lived with, the women she worked with. How long had she known them? How had that motley crew gotten together? Something was going on here with Thea and the two he'd met. New York or Houston or LA, and he wouldn't think twice about multiple roommates sharing living expenses, but Hope Springs?

Which made him curious about her mother,

who'd lived in Round Rock not far from his family, and what had happened to her. "I wouldn't think you'd want to reconnect with someone who wasn't a gentleman."

She laughed at that. "You are more right than you will ever know. But in your case I'll make an exception."

"Because I'm good in bed?" he asked, his brain in the past and the words falling out of his mouth before he could stop them.

It was all Indiana's fault. If she hadn't come by to see him this morning, he wouldn't have had to distract her with the news of Thea moving to town. She wouldn't have teased him about their history. He wouldn't have headed off down memory-sex lane.

Or maybe he should blame Tennessee for calling Indiana so that their sister felt the need to set an intervention in motion.

No. It was his fault for saying anything to his brother in the first place instead of packing up his things and quietly leaving town.

"Well, there is that," Thea finally said. "Or there was that. Can't speak to what may have changed."

He couldn't have asked for a better segue into what he needed to tell her, too, and it was not about how much better he was now at sex. "Enough has changed that I'm not very good with staying in one place much more than a year."

100

She stiffened and frowned. "What does that mean?"

Seemed his meaning had been pretty clear. He positioned his rafter square and drew his cutting line. "That I'm not going to be sticking around Hope Springs a whole lot longer."

She reached up and rubbed at the back of her neck as if the motion helped her think. What it did was show off her triceps and lats, and make him curious what was behind her looking like a bodybuilder when she moved just right. "You're not happy here? With the work? With your family?"

If she had any idea how many jobs he'd had . . . "Things are good with the family."

"Just not good enough for you to give up your vagabond lifestyle."

He'd never really thought of himself that way. Interesting how Thea had already pegged him as such. He tried on the word, shrugged into it, surprised at how well it fit.

Leaving the pencil and the square on the table, he crossed the room to the coffee station and pumped out a cup from the pot there. "I've wondered more than once whether I'd have been able to make a go of the business with Tennessee even if prison hadn't gotten in the way. I'm just not a fan of . . . I don't know—"

"Commitment?"

He huffed and turned back. "Not sure it's that. I don't have a problem finishing a job."

"As long as you can get up and go once it's done," she was quick to add, picking up the pencil he'd left on the table as she did.

"Something like that." Even the idea of leaving was making him itch to do so. He brought the cup to his mouth and sipped, making his way back to where she stood.

"I don't remember you having a short attention span when we were in school. And no," she said, her mouth pulling into a wry grin, "that wasn't a commentary on our sex life."

He huffed. "Is that what we had? A sex life?"

"It wasn't all we had, but I'm not sure what else to call it," she said.

She was staring at him with eyes so clear he thought he might be able to see where she'd been and the things she'd done if he looked into them long enough. Ridiculous, of course. The windows-of-the-soul thing was nothing but metaphor. And he was damn glad it was. He sure as hell didn't want her seeing the life he'd lived, even though he wasn't sure why.

She knew about the worst thing he'd done, and how he'd paid for it. She didn't know what it had been like for him behind bars—no one did, no one ever would—or what it meant to live as a . . . vagabond, he mused, turning over the word, weighing it. He wasn't proud of having abandoned his family, though doing so had seemed the only option at the time.

Later, when he might've returned, too much water had passed under the bridge. He could apologize for being absent and out of touch, sure, no problem. But amends and explanations . . .

He had no obligation to give more than he was comfortable with. It was his life. His business.

"Do you want to know something totally crazy?"

He looked up, surprised to find Thea still staring. More surprised to realize he'd drifted away. "About the sex life we did or did not have?"

"Our sex life, because it was a sex life, was better than any other I've had since."

He wasn't even sure he could process what she'd just said. "Come again?"

"You heard me," she said, moving closer to his table. She braced her hands on the top and leaned forward, the motion showing off the muscles in her shoulders and giving him pause for the second time. "Not one of the handful of relationships I've had since high school was as good as what I had with you. I think you ruined me, Dakota Keller. Absolutely, completely ruined me for anyone else."

Even if she'd given him time to answer, he wouldn't have known what to say; how would any man respond to being told such a thing? But she didn't.

She pushed away and headed for the kitchen,

ignoring his, "Thea, wait," and waving him off. The swinging door bounced closed, leaving him torn between following her and giving her space. He picked up his pencil, tossed it down again, picked up his square, and did the same.

Then the front door opened, making his decision for him. He stayed where he was and watched Becca York walk in. Once she'd shut the door behind her and caught sight of him, she reached up to pull her buds from her ears, then she wrapped the cords around her phone and pocketed them.

"Mornin'," he said, nodding while keeping his hands where they were and his voice soft and level.

"Mornin'," she said, returning his nod, her Afro, a brown that was tinted almost red, bouncing. She pushed away from the entrance to pace back and forth in front of his table, rolling her next words around on her tongue. "Look. About the other day . . ."

He started to cut her off, to tell her not to worry about it, but he was curious enough to let her have her say, so he lifted his mug to drink and waited.

"I'm sorry. I overreacted." She stopped walking to dig a crushed cigarette box from her other pocket. "I do a lot of that. Leaping before I look. Or at least leaping before I know what exactly it is I'm seeing."

"No harm, no foul." As sins went, it was pretty minor.

"So you're okay?" she asked, flipping the box open, flipping it closed. "Your throat?"

"I'm fine," he said, and found himself swallowing as if test-driving the equipment. "Not even the hint of a bruise."

"Then we're good? Because both of us being here, both of us working for Thea . . ." She stopped in front of him, much where Thea had been standing earlier. "I don't want her in the middle of some stupid shit storm."

"We're good," he said. "No reason for a shit storm."

"Okay," she said, her eyes wide and worried, her dark skin—shoulders, arms, chest—clammy from the heat, and her muscles just as buff as her boss's. "It's hard for me . . . I don't do well . . ." She stopped and rubbed at her forehead. "I'm shit with meeting new people. Complete and utter shit."

"That's okay." Her floundering caused him to smile. "I'm not much of a people person myself."

She shook her head, gave a short huff, then stuffed the cigarette box back into her pocket. "Bet you've never tried to crush someone's windpipe before you even knew their name."

No, but he'd done a pretty good job crushing the jaw of a kid he'd thought was a friend. And he'd done it with a baseball bat. At least Becca had used her arm. "I've got a few regrets of my own."

"I never said I regretted it."

Her words took a second to register, and then he laughed out loud, reaching up to scratch at his neck as he did. "I'll keep that in mind for the future."

"No need," she said, grinning, too. "I'm pretty sure we're on the same page."

He nodded. He liked this one, her sense of humor, her twisted sense of self. "How did you and Thea hook up? And, yeah. I know her story's not yours to tell," he added, repeating Thea's words since they did the job as good as any.

"But you're asking me anyway," she said, walking closer, leaning against the wall beside his table where he'd tacked up his blueprint, her hands behind her, deadly weapons out of sight.

He tried for casual. "I'm just asking you about your side of things. Tell me that instead."

"Why should I?"

"Might make our working together easier if we understand each other a bit." Though he wasn't sure how much of his own story he wanted her to know.

She seemed to consider his answer longer than it required. "We're not exactly working *together*."

True enough. "We're working in the same place. And for the same woman."

She thought about that for a while, too, then

shifted her weight from one hip to the other. "Thea said you'd been in prison."

So that's how it was. Thea could talk about him, but not vice versa. "Yep."

"Because you stood up for your sister."

"That's not exactly how it went down, but"— he shrugged—"close enough."

"Thank you," she said.

He nodded again, then added, "You're welcome."

It seemed a strange exchange to have with someone who hadn't been there in the past to know what he'd done and why.

She dropped her gaze to the floor, shifting again, frowning as out of nowhere she said, "I was raped. More than once. While in the navy."

"Becca. Oh, man." He stopped, his heart thudding, his pulse a drumbeat at his temples. "I'm so sorry. I had no idea."

"That's because Thea's really good at keeping secrets," she said, her mouth twisted wryly.

He filed away the comment, thinking he might need it later. But at the moment all he had room for was the hell of what she'd endured. "That kind of shit should never happen. To any woman." He was babbling. He had no way to make things better, and everything out of his mouth sounded lame. "But not to be safe when defending your country? That's just obscene."

"Yeah, well," she said, scuffing the sole of one shoe against the floor. "There's still a lot of good ol' boys club members out there who don't agree."

"Becca—"

"Don't make me sorry I told you," she was quick to say, one eyebrow lifting archly.

Yeah, he mused as he nodded. They were going to be okay. He raised his mug, casually asking, "Is that how you know Thea?"

Becca cocked her head. "Really? You're prying into her side of things now?"

"Just making conversation," he said, hiding his grin as he drank.

"If you want to know, ask her sometime," she said as she shoved away from the wall and headed for the kitchen door. "You two have enough of a past—"

Crap on a cracker. "She really has been talking to you about me, hasn't she?"

"It's no big thing. That day I tried to choke you she told me you two were old friends."

"Right. Friends."

"Most people who sleep together regularly are friends, aren't they?" she asked, then pushed her way into the kitchen, leaving a cauldron of laughter behind.

Hearing both Dakota and Becca's voices in the shop, Thea left the kitchen through the back door and made her way around the block to the front. It took her several minutes to get there, which

108

gave her just enough time to stomp off her frustration—With herself? With him? With their past?—and she wondered if this was going to be her thing now, walking out on him because it was easier and so much less painful than staying to face the music like the adult she was.

Or maybe it was just ingrained. Inherited even. Part of her DNA. She couldn't speak to her father; she'd never met him, she didn't even know if his walking out had been his choice. She did know her mother, and walking out had been one of the things Muriel Clark did best. But Thea was not her mother. And Dakota deserved better treatment than what she'd shown him. He was her contractor, but even more than that, he was a human being. And he was her friend. Or he had been anyway.

Her reasons for moving to Hope Springs were several. It had been time to get on with life on her own. She'd spent a year in the shelter she'd moved to after leaving the safe house that had originally taken her in. During that year there had been no word from Todd, and while she understood the practicality of losing herself in a city like Austin or Dallas, her state of mind required something serene. She couldn't deal with looking behind her at every new noise and seeing crowds.

It was when she'd seen Indiana's engagement announcement in the paper that she'd first considered settling in Hope Springs. She hadn't kept in touch with Indiana after graduation. She'd been busy trying to make it on her own, and Indiana had her thinking too much of Dakota. She was sure it was why they'd fallen out of contact in the first place. Dakota was what had brought them together. He'd been the foundation of their friendship. The original glue. Then he was gone.

But the main reason, the true reason she'd chosen Hope Springs was the possibility of seeing him again. She'd known it was a long shot. His brother had set up his business here, she'd learned. His sister had moved here and married. Surely, Thea had rationalized, there was a chance Dakota might show up one day, to visit maybe. Except she'd been so wrapped up in the red tape and paperwork of buying the house and setting up the shelter that she hadn't kept up with the Keller siblings.

Dakota had returned to Texas and she hadn't even known.

She'd gotten exactly what she wanted, and now she didn't know what to do with it. Had she thought they could start fresh? Get to know each other as adults without the ball-and-chain of the past dragging behind them and weighing them down? One thing was certain: She would not keep running out on him. She was done being afraid of all the scary places he might take her. The conversations she didn't want to have with him. The memories she'd locked away sure to bubble to the surface.

She pulled open the door to the shop, walking in just as he was walking out. "Where are you going?"

He arched a brow, as if she was one to be asking questions when she'd left him hanging not so long ago. "I need to run to Kern's Hardware."

"Can I hitch a ride?"

"To where?"

"Just a ride." She didn't have anywhere to go. She just needed to apologize.

"Truck's right there," he said, nodding to the space in front of her shop.

It was an older model, and still had a bench seat. A lot like the truck he'd driven in high school. Buckets were comfortable, but there'd been something about cuddling in the front of his truck, his arm around her shoulder, their thighs pressed tight, the windows down and her hair whipping into her face . . .

Not that any of that was going to happen now, she mused, slamming the passenger door and buckling up. Still, the recollection was a nice one, even if it had her revisiting the rest of the things they'd done in his truck's front seat. Taking a deep breath to dispel the thoughts had her swimming in his scent.

She was so screwed.

"You're going to have to tell me where to let

you out, or it's the hardware store for you."

Staring out her window as he drove, she smiled. "Kern's is fine. I can walk to String Theory from there."

She'd pulled the name of the fabric shop out of her hat. It was across the street and two doors down from Kern's. Still, while she was in the neighborhood . . . "I need to get a couple of patches for the chairs in the kitchen at home. They've seen better days. Though that's pretty typical for hand-me-downs."

"You got that right. Take it from someone who's used a lot of spit and baling wire on other people's garbage."

He'd left home at eighteen. He'd spent the next three years in prison. He'd been on the road for over a decade since, save for the last year when he'd lived first in his brother's home, then in the cottage that belonged to his sister. Thea supposed he was just as familiar as she with secondhand things, though maybe she'd started first, her crib coming from a garage sale and all.

And then she blurted out, "I'm sorry," because she didn't know how else to get there.

"For what?" he asked, and snorted. "Me having nothing to my name?"

"No. I mean, well, yes." Could she be any clumsier? "I am sorry about that, but the apology was for walking out on you earlier."

"What about yesterday? Do I get one for then, too?" he asked, giving her a side-eyed glance. "Or maybe I need to be apologizing to you. I ruined you for other men. I've never been a gentleman. Hell, with that résumé, it's a wonder you trust me to drive you to buy . . . What was it? Patches?"

"Fine. I don't really need the patches. I mean, I do"—Frannie's youngest had found holes in the fabric of two of the kitchen's chairs and gone to town—"but the chairs aren't going anywhere, and you were."

"And you figured if you were in a moving vehicle it would be harder to walk out if things got tough."

Something like that. No. *Exactly* like that. "What are we doing here, Dakota? And I don't mean going shopping."

"You mean how did two crazy kids from Round Rock end up together in Hope Springs?"

She knew her story. She just wasn't ready to tell him that he was a big part of her being here. And she knew his, so . . . "Are you going to be able to do this job, or am I in your way?"

He slowed at the corner stop sign, glanced over as he put the truck into motion again. "That's a hell of a loaded question, Clark."

Was there anything about their relationship that wasn't? "It's all I need to know today. Just the one thing."

"I guess it depends. If we stick to our agreement not to talk about the past, to keep to business and the present"—he checked his rearview and both side mirrors, though his truck was the only vehicle on the road—"we should be okay. If not, I can have Tennessee put someone else on the job."

"And then you'll leave?"

He shrugged his answer. He'd already told her he was thinking about hitting the road, but the idea of his going even sooner because she couldn't keep her mouth shut . . . He was here. She was here. She had to be satisfied with that. She had to stop looking for answers to questions put to bed long ago.

What good would it do now to find them? she mused, staring out the window as they passed the insurance office and the art house theater. "I heard the theater was going to be renovated."

"Yeah. Tennessee got the job."

"That's great. Wow. You've got to be excited."

"He's excited. I won't be here."

"You're going to leave before it's done?" she asked and glanced over, watching his pulse tic in the vein at his temple.

"I'm just the hired help, remember?" he finally said in response.

And as stupid as it was, she pushed. "Is that all you want to be?"

"What's that supposed to mean?"

"I remember high school. You and Tennessee talking about doing construction together."

"We were kids."

"So were we," she said, not sure if she was reminding him or herself of how young they'd been when they'd shared their bodies as well as pieces of their souls.

He pulled into an angled parking spot in front of Kern's Hardware, then shut off the truck, but made no move to get out. Instead, he stared at the steering wheel, twisting his hands around it. "You just can't help yourself, can you? You just can't let it go. You have to keep bringing it up. You have to keep digging. What is wrong with you, Clark?"

She stared at her hands where she'd wound her fingers together in her lap, her vision blurry, though she refused to cry. He was right about it all, but she still couldn't answer his question. All she could do was push out of the truck and head for String Theory, hoping she hadn't just screwed up the single best friendship she'd ever known.

Becca spent the rest of the day in the kitchen organizing the supply shelves. Ellie was a genius when it came to baking bread but a complete disaster grouping and classifying her flours and herbs and spices. Who put cinnamon next to sage? That didn't even make sense. Essential savory herbs were not shelved next to spices.

115

Especially when the cinnamon alone required an entire rack. There was Chinese, Vietnamese, Ceylon, and Indonesian. There were powders and oils and sticks and bark.

But every time Becca walked into the kitchen to help Ellie wash the mixing bowls and baking pans, or to mop the floor free of spilled flour—which she did, like, five times a day—she found the spelt flour next to the turbinado sugar and that next to the coconut oil. Honestly. The mess of bottles and bags and jars and cans and tubes and droppers had her wanting to pull out her hair. And Ellie's hair. Which would take forever.

Then again, Ellie didn't think of the supplies as simply as Becca did. She was into the medicinal properties of everything as well as the culinary. Sage for respiratory health. Cinnamon for digestive upset. Becca didn't know how the other woman knew the things she did, or why she came across as such an airhead when she was degreed and anything but. Becca wanted to punch people who made fun of her. Ellie just laughed it off.

Becca wished she had more of Ellie's Zen, she mused, alphabetizing the red peppercorns and the black peppercorns and the white and the green and the pink. And more of Ellie's smarts. Ellie and Thea both were so much better about thinking first. Becca just barged in and reacted. If Thea hadn't been there to stop her when she'd slammed her arm into Dakota Keller's throat . . .

She didn't want to think about it. She couldn't think about it. She had to get her temper and her impulses under control or she was going to hurt someone, and she knew too much about hurt to ever want to subject another person to anything like what she'd gone through.

Moving to the new rack with the specialized bins for dry goods, Becca flipped through the legal pad of notes she and Ellie had made for the labeling of the flours. Closer to the door into the shop now, she frowned, hearing Dakota talking to another man. Probably related to the build-out. It was well underway, even if it seemed to her Keller Construction was moving at a snail's pace.

Then again, what did she know about what it took to turn an empty storefront into an espresso bar? As long as she had a nice counter to work behind, one tall enough and wide enough to keep the public on their side and out of her space, she was fine with whatever Thea decided on.

Except Thea hadn't been the only one involved in the decisions. Like with everything that came from living in the house on Dragon Fire Hill, the workings of Bread and Bean had been brought to the table, though Becca thought Thea, as owner, was taking the democratic process of their shared living arrangements too far. Or maybe it wasn't democratic. Maybe it was socialist.

Becca didn't know squat about government,

even after spending four years in service. She hadn't had time to learn. She'd been too busy fighting off unwanted advances—without much success—to do more than see to the shine of her shoes and her made bed.

She also thought Thea was spending more money on parts of Bread and Bean than was necessary. Take the flour bins, for example. Ellie would be just as well served with Rubbermaid totes. They were water- and bug-proof, right? That had been the draw of the custom storage unit. Keeping the flours from losing their nutritional value, or some such spiel.

Sounded like a bunch of bunk to her, Becca mused, then frowned as the voices in the shop grew louder and more distinct.

"You can make the manpower happen? If Tennessee needs it?"

That had been Dakota, obviously back at the coffee machine since she also heard the squeak of the table and the *whoosh* of the pot being pumped.

"Not a problem. Though it might be if you don't let the owner in on it."

That man, she didn't know, though he seemed familiar enough with Dakota and rather bossy. Curious, Becca crept closer to the swinging doors.

"Yeah. That thought already crossed my mind," Dakota said.

"Had to mention it," said the second man. "It's what I do."

What? Becca rolled her eyes. *Tell other people their business?*

"I know, and I will. Depending on what I decide." Dakota's phone rang then. "I'll take this out front. It's Tennessee. Be right back."

The front door opened and closed as Dakota walked out. Becca stayed where she was, realizing too late the lack of noise coming from her side of the door, when she'd been making all sorts of racket before, was going to give her away. That and her breathing. And it didn't take long for it to happen.

"You make it a habit to eavesdrop on private conversations?"

Crap. She hung her head, shook it, then turned and pushed open the door and walked into the shop where the bossy man stood in brown deck shoes, his hands in the pockets of his khaki pants. He wore a navy sport coat, the sides flared out behind his elbows. His shirt was white, his tie loosely knotted and patterned in blue and tan.

"I wasn't eavesdropping." Though, of course, she had been. "I work here. I have every right to be here."

"Never said you didn't."

It was then that she realized he was Hispanic. His voice hadn't given him away, but his black hair and complexion and the set of his intensely dark eyes did. He was also too gorgeous for words, his lashes long, his dimples deep, his crow's-feet made by very big birds. They extended from his temples to his cheekbones, and gave him the look of someone intent on having fun.

But he was still bossy. And he wasn't very tall. "You're a friend of the construction guy? Dakota?"

He pulled his hands from his pockets and crossed his arms, gave a nod that didn't seem very convincing. "You could say that. I'm a better friend of Tennessee."

"Okay." She didn't care. She didn't even know why she was still standing here. She had a to-do list that was easily a mile long.

Yet she didn't move because he didn't move. He didn't come closer. He didn't gesture or reach out or say anything inappropriate. He didn't say anything else at all.

She wasn't used to extricating herself from a situation so completely dull. She was used to fireworks. "I guess I'll get back to work," she said, gesturing toward the kitchen.

"You a baker?" When she frowned at the question he added, "The bread?"

"No. I mean, I help. I clean up. I make sure Ellie has everything she needs. But she does the baking. Of course we're not selling anything yet, but sometimes she uses the kitchen here to bake what we need at the house." And why in the world was she talking so much?

"Sounds like a fair division of labor."

"We all do our part. It's how we make it work." Again with the blabbering. At this rate, he'd know her social security number and what had brought her to live in the house on Dragon Fire Hill.

"You all live together, then? Like roommates?"

She scowled. "What makes you ask that?"

"You said your friend bakes the bread you need at the house," he said with a shrug, ambling a couple of steps toward the long table they were using as a coffee station. Now that he was closer, she could see the strands of gray in his hair and noticed he could use a shave, his beard graying, too.

"Oh. Right." See? She was giving away way too much information. Which was why she needed to keep her mouth shut. She watched him move, like he was taking his time, but making sure he wasn't doing anything wrong. "Yeah. We're . . . roommates. I guess you could say."

He nodded, looking around. "When's the place set to open?"

A safer subject. "We should've been open already, but the first guy doing the build-out bailed."

"That's when Keller took over?"

She stayed where she was, the door at her back

121

and convenient. "I thought it would go a lot faster, but Thea said we're on track."

"Thea's the boss?"

"The owner. Boss. Same thing. She owns the house, too. On Dragon Fire Hill." And that's when she decided to bite off her tongue. What in the world was wrong with her? She did not spill her guts. She did not give up advantage.

"That's where you live?"

She didn't know this man. Who he was. His connection to Dakota, whom she barely knew. What he was doing here. Yet she was telling him things that were none of his business. Things she would never in the past have said to a complete stranger. Because that's what he was.

A complete stranger.

"I need to get back to work."

"I'm sorry." He held up both hands. "Where you live is none of my business. I know better than to ask."

"Okay." It was the only word she had. Guys, in her experience, didn't apologize. Unless it was the only way they could get what they wanted. The thought had her frowning. "What do you want?"

"Nothing." He lifted both brows and shrugged. "I just stopped to talk to Dakota. He stepped out for a minute. I'm just waiting for him, but I can wait outside if it would help you breathe easier."

"I'm not having any trouble breathing."

"Coffee's good for that, too. Caffeine."

"I'm not having any trouble—" But then she stopped because she was. Her heart was slamming around in her chest and doing something weird to her lungs, and all she wanted to do was run—not out of fear, but something else. Something she didn't understand.

The front door opened then and Dakota came in, pocketing his phone, his hair hanging in his face, his T-shirt powdered with sawdust. He lifted his chin when he saw her, and said, "Hey, Becca. This is—"

But she was already pushing through the swinging door into the kitchen, singing, "La, la, la, la, la," in her head. She didn't want to know the other man's name, or more than the last ten minutes had told her about him. It was bad enough that he'd read her like a book, and that she was bent over struggling to inhale because of how easily he'd been able to do so.

❧ *Chapter Eight* ❧

Thea spent most of the night staring at the paint peeling from the tongue-and-groove ceiling in her second-floor corner bedroom. Staring and trying to figure out why she'd said what she had to Dakota, about his ruining her for other men. She didn't even know if it was true.

The words had just rushed out. They weren't words she'd practiced or considered or previously established as truth.

Yes, she'd thought of him often over the years. She'd wondered where he'd gone after prison and what he'd done with his life since. And, yes. For some unfathomable reason, she'd compared her time with her adult lovers to the years in high school she'd spent sleeping with him.

She'd missed him. He'd been a boy, she'd been a girl, and she'd missed him.

But the idea that he'd ruined her for any other man? Seriously? Was that what her subconscious had decided while she'd been getting on with her life after Todd? Rearing its head once Dakota was back in her life to remind her of how good they'd been together?

Then again, thinking back on her two short years with Dakota made her realize the concept wasn't that far out there. Not when they'd bared as much of their souls as they had of their bodies. She just didn't want to believe it.

Believing it would give credence to the idea that she and Dakota were . . . soul mates, or whatever. Destined to be together. Meant for each other. Spiritually or metaphysically bound. And that just wouldn't do. For one thing, she had a brand-new business to run and she couldn't afford the dizzying distraction of being caught up in whatever lingered of Dakota's damage.

That damage . . . It didn't frighten her as much as it bothered her, and worried her, and she had so much on her plate already, with Frannie and Ellie and Becca, not to mention herself.

Had he told her he was thinking of leaving so she'd try and convince him to stay?

The question remained with her all morning as she straightened her cheerful and comforting but very Spartan room. She'd kept nothing of Todd's but his money when she'd closed the door of his condo behind her. On her way to the safe house where she'd slept the first night, she'd stopped by the storage unit where most of her belongings had been sitting in boxes since high school. It was a crappy warehouse, but it was cheap. That had been the main draw since she couldn't afford a big monthly payment anymore than she could afford to leave what she valued in her mother's house.

Todd had asked that she not bring her old things into his new home. She'd been young and dumb and incapable of discerning between being loved by a man and being under his thumb. He'd paid attention to her, and at the time she'd needed to feel like she mattered to someone. To anyone. Her mother didn't care. She didn't know her father. Dakota was gone . . . Like she'd said. Dumb.

From her stored things that day, she'd grabbed the same comforter she was using now. It was worn, stuffing poking through tears in the cotton, but it was soft and warm, colored in a palette of water blues with dolphins romping across it. She'd had a lot of dolphins back then.

Her bed was a full, and unlike some the others slept on, had a headboard, a footboard, and a frame. Frannie preferred her mattress on the floor so she didn't have to worry about Robert rolling off. James was older and less of a concern, but with the bed at that level, the only thing she had to think about when turning in for the night was locking the door so the boys wouldn't wander.

The room the family of three shared was on the first floor, and it would take a bulldozer to get into the house after dark. Or, for that matter, during the day. A large chunk of Todd's money had gone to secure the premises from men like him, and women, too, and others who were worse.

Thea had moved in before anyone else. Her bed had come from a junk store that claimed to sell antiques. The mattress was new, but it was the only thing that was. She'd painted the bed and the side table white, and had made curtains out of navy sheets identical to the set she slept in. Her ceiling fan was cheap white cane, but did the job perfectly, and she'd installed it herself.

One of these days she'd get around to painting everything else because the room was an absolute mess. The ceiling was high, and needed sanding, and the idea of so much physical labor with everything crowding her to-do list . . . she couldn't do it. Not now. And the walls were no better, plaster peeling, studs and pink insulation and wads of old newspaper showing through in more than one place. The outlet closest to the door didn't work. Neither did the closet light fixture.

Maybe she could get Dakota . . .

No. She wasn't going there. She couldn't afford to hire him, and she would *not* ask him the favor. The manpower, the paint, and the other supplies were not in the household budget. And bringing a painting crew into the house, well, flying pigs and frozen underworlds would become the norm before any of the women she lived with would open the door to a man.

Look what had happened in the shop when Becca had first seen Dakota. And Becca had *known* about the contractor's visit. Thea had survived this long in less than ideal living conditions, and she would continue to survive them as long as her finances and the women she lived with required she do so.

And as far as Dakota Keller went . . .

Neither his staying in Hope Springs nor his leaving Hope Springs was any of her concern. She had absolutely no intention of trying to convince him to do one or the other.

Not a bit of intention at all.

• • •

"I've been thinking about something."

It was the first thing Thea said to Dakota after arriving at Bread and Bean. Initially, she'd thought she was early, then she'd realized Ellie must've slept in. There wasn't a single loaf of bread or a biscuit in the kitchen. Thea usually arrived to the smell and warmth of both. There *was* a fresh pot of coffee in the shop. That was due to Dakota having been the one to get the worm.

He looked at her over the rim of his mug as he sipped. "And that's supposed to be a surprise?"

"Back in high school—"

"Uh-huh. No talking about the past," he reminded her, sipping again, steam from his drink drifting up like smoke signals, softening the hardness in his gaze and warning her away.

She would not be warned. "We never agreed not to talk about high school," she said, hoping she remembered things correctly as she pumped coffee into her own mug.

"I think *the past* covers high school."

Good. She had. "Only if you're going by the letter of the law instead of the spirit."

He didn't respond right off, giving her time to look him over while they both pretended the coffee was the most important thing in the room. His eyes were bloodshot, as if he hadn't slept, the dark circles beneath confirmation. Neither had he bothered to shave, though that didn't make

128

him look tired as much as it did unkempt. And even that turned her on way more than it turned her off.

There was something about this undone Dakota Keller—

"So," he said, interrupting a train of thought that had the wheels of her heart turning and picking up speed. Dammit, but she did *not* need him complicating her life. She did not need to care. "The spirit of the law is why you felt it okay to tell Becca about me?"

Thanks a lot, Becca. She shrugged. "We were talking—"

"Talking a lot from what I hear," he said, his voice teasing and gruff and making her shiver. "About me. Me and prison. Me and you."

"Ah," she said, holding up one finger. "That was *before* our agreement."

"Was it?" he asked, lifting his mug again, snagging her gaze again, taking her back again to a time when they'd made sense. Except they had never made sense. They'd been too young, and they'd slept together for reasons that were even less about hormones than about being cool.

But she would never get over the way he'd looked at her then because it was the way he was looking at her now, and she was having way too much trouble separating the two.

Seemed the perfect time to hit him with the question that had been giving her hell all day.

"Why did you tell me you want to leave Hope Springs?"

"So you would know," he said with a lazy shrug, the motion drawing her gaze to the roll of his shoulders beneath his T-shirt.

She took a deep breath, then exhaled, blowing away the distraction. At least she tried.

And she might even have been successful if he hadn't emptied his mug then, the motion of his arm as he drained it pulling the shirt up and exposing a strip of skin on his torso. Skin showing off a puckered scar, the wound having been stitched without a single thought for cosmetics.

She looked away, and did her best not to wince as she picked up the conversation. "But if you don't leave until you're done with the job, why would it matter? Why would I care?"

"I didn't say that you would," he responded, his brows drawn into a frown.

"There has to be more to it than that." Unless she was just wishing there was.

"Not really," he said, returning his mug to the table, then reaching for the safety goggles he'd left on his table saw stand. "I told Tennessee. I told Indiana. Manny knows. Figured you should, too."

His brother and his sister. His parole officer. The three people she assumed to be most important in his life. And her. Which brought her back to her original question. "Is it because of that night before you went to prison? Because you left me without saying good-bye?"

How was he supposed to give Thea an answer when he hadn't been able to give one to Indiana, or Tennessee, or Manny, or even himself? He didn't know why this urge to leave was pushing him harder and harder away from the most important people in his life.

Or why Thea was in that number. Only that it was, and that she was—which at least explained why he'd felt compelled to tell her.

And that's what she was asking. Not why he was leaving, like the other three had demanded to know, but why he had given her the news, too. Because she was right.

His putting Hope Springs behind him would have no impact on her, as long as she signed off on the Bread and Bean job before then.

Then he frowned because what she'd said finally registered. "Did I really leave that last night without telling you good-bye?"

She nodded, her topknot flopping from one side of her head to the other. "I was out of it, having cried myself to sleep. But I heard you get up and get dressed, and you may have been talking to yourself, but you never said anything to me."

"Huh." He remembered the sex. He remembered her crying. He'd cried, too, but he was pretty sure she'd been asleep by then and missed the show. At least he hoped she had. If she'd said anything to him then, he wasn't sure he'd have been able to leave. He'd been that torn up, that frightened and desperate to find a way out. "I must not have wanted to wake you."

"For something like that?" she asked, her eyes wide, her voice raised. "You going to prison? Me not seeing you for three years? Three that turned into so many more?"

He shrugged. It was all he had.

"And would you stop doing that," she said, waving her hand. "That shrugging thing."

"Sorry," he said, toying with the strap on his goggles. "I thought that was universal body language for 'I got nothing.'"

"It's not that," she said, rubbing at her forehead with one hand. "Never mind. I'm just . . . frustrated."

With him? With the job? Sexually?

He tossed the goggles back to the table. "My mind was all over the place that night, Clark. I was ready for it to be tomorrow. To get all of that over with. To be *in* prison. Not to be waiting to go. The waiting was the worst. The not knowing what it would look like. What it would smell like. What the men inside would say to me. What they would do to me. What they would want."

He reached up and scrubbed both hands down his face. Why was he telling her this? Why was he talking about prison at all? And even as he asked himself the question, he went on. "I thought I was going to die of a heart attack that day. Or an aneurysm. My head and my chest. My gut. I don't know why I bothered eating. I lost my breakfast before we were out of the driveway."

"Oh, Dakota," she said, tears brimming in her eyes and threatening to spill, then the sound of the back door opening and closing keeping either of them from taking the subject further. "That's probably Ellie. I knew she'd be in since the bread at the house got finished off with breakfast."

He didn't mind the intrusion. Hell, he welcomed it. Anything to keep him from going on about something he'd deemed off limits. Besides, he'd been wondering about something anyway so the timing was perfect. "Are you paying her and Becca? For the hours they're here?"

"Since Bread and Bean's not open yet, you mean?" When he nodded, she returned to the table and pumped herself a refill, taking the time to come up with an answer. "Yes and no."

Yeah. He could see why she'd needed time to come up with that. "Thanks. Things are so much clearer now."

She rolled her eyes in response. "I'm not paying them yet, but I will. They keep track of the hours they put in here that aren't personal. Becca organizing the kitchen is business. Ellie baking bread for the house is not."

Seemed fair. "And when Becca has to clean up after Ellie?"

Thea laughed, her mug cradled in both hands. "You've noticed that, have you?"

He nodded. One of the first things he'd done in prison was grow eyes in the back of his head. "Becca was doing a lot of work in the kitchen yesterday morning, and mumbling to herself more than once when I walked through."

Thea frowned down into her mug. "Ellie's not the most organized person in the world. Brilliant, yes. Like an absent-minded genius. But I've yet to find anyone whose bread holds a candle to hers. You think Becca's forearm was something, be glad you didn't run into Ellie's, all that mixing and kneading and hefting those huge bags of flour."

That was another thing he'd noticed. About all of them. Their shoulders and killer guns. "She's been doing it awhile then."

A sip of coffee, a careless shrug. "She was an art teacher before budget cuts had her looking for a new line of work. She decided bread made for a safe bet."

"And luck sent her your way."

"I wouldn't exactly call it luck," she said, picking up a pencil from his table saw stand and bouncing the eraser end on the surface. "But I am very fortunate that we crossed paths."

Another thought went through his mind. "So

with Ellie baking, and Becca pulling shots, who's going to clean the kitchen once you're open?"

"Funny you should mention that," she said, putting the pencil back in its place. "We actually talked about it at dinner last night."

"You going to hire additional help?"

"Yes, once we're closer to opening."

That didn't make a lot of sense. "Why not line up someone now? Someone to wash all your coffee cups and mop the floors, at least. Sounds like the perfect job for a kid wanting to earn a few bucks. Have Ellie teach him or her to bake. Becca could do the same with the latte art. You'll end up with a jack of all trades who can fill in anywhere you need him."

She looked at him as if he'd just made an argument she couldn't refute. "You've put a lot more thought into this than I have."

For a pretty simple reason. "I've been a jack of all trades. More than once."

"Sounds to me like you should be the one running the place."

And it sounded to him like Thea Clark was in over her head. Why would she put off something as easy as advertising for a dishwasher? Then it hit him how many of their conversations had gone off the rails, and how many of his questions she'd never really answered.

Thea Clark was hiding something big. As well as he'd known her in high school, he was surprised it had taken him three days to recognize the signs now. He pushed a bit further. "If you've got a reason to wait, then wait."

She reached up with one hand to smooth the hair at her nape. Another tell. "Let's just say it's complicated and leave it at that."

Complicated. Another word for "none of your business." It was her life. Not his. Her money. Not his.

But curiosity *was* his, and a normal human condition. His suspicion, however, came from three years in the state pen and a decade of being the vagabond she'd labeled him. Something was rotten in the state of Denmark—or at least in Hope Springs. "So you're footing the bill for everyone. The rent. The utilities. The food. Everything."

"Well, not everything." She drained her coffee and returned the mug to the table. "But again. It's complicated. We all chip in, whether that's manpower or cash. In some cases, in most cases, it's both. Once the shop is open, we'll get everything sorted out. Including the extra help."

And that was that. He wasn't going to get anything more out of her. In fact, getting anything out of her at all might take a lighter touch than he was capable of.

"Listen. I'm having breakfast with Indiana in the morning. At her cottage. You should come. The two of you could catch up." *And keep me from having to let down my sister for a few more days.*

Her eyes grew wide, animated, all traces of the barrier she'd erected to ward off his questions gone. "Oh, I'd love to see her. But I wouldn't want to be a third wheel."

"If you were going to be in the way, I wouldn't have invited you." It was only a tiny lie.

"Okay, then. Should I bring something?"

"She's bringing breakfast tacos, but I only ordered for me."

"I'll grab something then. Kolaches, maybe."

Man, when was the last time he'd had a good kolache? "With cream cheese? Or peaches?"

"You have a microwave to heat them?"

He nodded. "I do. And I have coffee."

"Like that's a surprise," she said with a snort, pushing through the kitchen door and leaving him alone to wonder if Indiana would be too happy at seeing Thea to be mad at him.

And to wonder what in the world was going on with the women who lived in the house on Dragon Fire Hill.

❧ Chapter Nine ❧

Lena had no idea what she was doing. Well, that wasn't true. She was taking cheese to Ellie Brass. The why of the cheese was escaping her, though it had seemed like a good idea at the time.

She'd been standing in the grocery store's expansive deli department, looking for something fresh for dinner because she was so effing tired of frozen when she'd wandered into the cheese aisle. Or the cheese section really. Wedges stacked on barrels, wheels nestled into refrigerated cases, tubs bearing brands she'd never heard of, bricks in flavors she'd never seen.

There was just something about the cold and the smell and the bakery just beyond with the loaves of fresh bread she couldn't resist. She'd picked up a wedge of hard Parmesan and remembered Ellie talking about sharp cheddar. She'd grabbed a slab of extra sharp aged, then her gaze had fallen on a container of local chèvre, and she'd added it into her cart.

She knew Ellie had bread; the house on Dragon Fire Hill would always have bread with Ellie living there, but the rest of the pantry . . . Minutes later, Lena's basket held Gouda, Havarti, provolone, too. And fresh soup, which she'd found in the same section as the made-in-store hummus. A good grilled cheese with a bowl of tomato basil soup and an olive hummus appetizer. Lena wasn't sure when she'd last had such a simple meal, and her stomach had started rumbling.

None of that explained what she was doing here, however, climbing the steps to the porch of Ellie's residence unannounced, unexpected, having driven straight from the grocery store to the big *Gone with the Wind* plantation house. She was pretty sure the women who lived here weren't big fans of visitors. She didn't know their stories, but Ellie wasn't exactly hard to read.

Lena knew about causality and figured whatever Ellie had faced in her past was a big part of the need she now had to overshare. As if a big strip of duct tape had been ripped off her mouth. Or she'd been let out of a room where she'd lived alone with no one to talk to for years. What Lena feared was that Ellie had suffered a combination of both, even if metaphorically, and that sucked.

She lifted her hand to knock, really hoping neither of those was the case, though if they were, they weren't her business. She was only here for soup. Soup and hummus and a grilled cheese sandwich. And if she was the only one hungry, well, that was fine. She had no trouble taking the groceries home and cooking for herself. She was used to it. It was how she spent most nights.

Ellie, not one of the others, answered the door, but only after a lot of noisy tumbling of locks. She seemed pleased, more than baffled, though she'd had no idea Lena was coming, leaving Lena to wonder if her arrival had been captured by a camera, and her image fed to a monitor inside.

"Lena. Hello." Ellie's smile was welcoming, warm and soft and genuine as she adjusted her glasses on her nose. Lena's stomach fluttered happily. "What are you doing here?"

She lifted the plastic grocery bags. "I brought cheese. And deli soup. Tomato basil. There's also some hummus and naan. I thought if you had bread—"

"Goodness. Tomato soup and grilled cheese for dinner? And I can't even remember the last time I had hummus." Ellie's face lit up as if Lena had brought her a rib eye and a stuffed baked potato. With apple pie for dessert. Then again, that was Lena's favorite meal. For all she knew, Ellie was vegetarian. "Do you know how good that sounds?"

"Actually, yeah. I do." Lena exhaled deeply and smiled. "That's why I'm here."

Ellie took the bags from her hand and peered inside. A lock of her wavy hair fell forward, and she flipped it back over her shoulder, the motion —and the porch light—showing off another bunch of small circular scars above her collarbone. "And there's plenty for everyone. Oh, Lena. You're so sweet. Do you mind? If the others share?"

"Of course not." She just hoped she'd brought enough. And that whatever had happened to Ellie had been over with quickly and healed without a lot of pain. "I had to guess at how much everyone would eat."

"Oh, this is more than plenty. So much more," she said, as if the idea of not having to go hungry was foreign.

The flutters in her stomach having tightened into knots, Lena cleared her throat. "And you don't mind if I stay? I don't want to make anyone uncomfortable, showing up like this."

Ellie lifted her gaze and gave Lena a look. A longing sort of look, not lusty, but unfulfilled, as if she hadn't had a true friend in a very long time. As if she'd been left emotionally empty and lost. Those were the words that came to mind. They were ones Lena wasn't sure what to do with. Having Ellie as a friend was wonderful. But having her as more . . .

"I absolutely insist you stay." Ellie backed into the room and reached for Lena's wrist, pulling her inside. "No. I demand it," she added, laughing and shutting the door. She bolted it, then turned another lock and another, finally setting some sort of electronic alarm on the tablet mounted beside the door.

The one showing the image from the camera outside on the porch.

Still holding Lena by the wrist, Ellie guided her through the house's big front room. Lena wasn't able to see much of it. There was the basic furniture: a couch, a loveseat, a couple of tables and chairs, a lamp or two, though neither was on, and a big fireplace.

The floor was hardwood. The walls, plain. She had no idea if there was a color scheme since everything was in shadow. It was a big house. Made sense they wouldn't light rooms they weren't using. But something left her thinking there wasn't anything chic about the sense of shabby.

"Watch the flashing on the floor here," Ellie said as they crossed out of the big front room into a kitchen and eating area equally huge. "It's loose and I've tripped too many times to count."

Lena stepped carefully then looked up. It was obvious the room used to be at least two, like a separate cooking area and dining room, and maybe even three. Near the back door, both the ceiling- and floorboards ran perpendicular to those in the rest of the space. An old washroom? Or a mudroom? "Were y'all the ones who gutted the rooms, or was it like this when you moved in?"

Ellie carried the bags to the counter. She unloaded the four one-quart containers of soup, then read the labels on each chunk of butcher-papered cheese. "You're seeing it in all its pre-renovated glory. Thea has all kinds of plans, but for now it's a roof over our heads, and that's all that matters."

A roof with some serious windows and doors, Lena mused, catching sight of a monitor similar to the one at the front door beside the back. The kitchen itself, well, it was as homey as something in its condition could be, she guessed. The sink and cabinets and all the appliances sat to the right of the door she'd come through, which pretty much bisected one wall.

To the left, toward whatever the other room had once been, a big round table sat in one corner. In the other were three cushy but mismatched club chairs, and two small side tables piled with books and craft projects. She wondered if the women living here didn't use the front room at all.

"It's really not as bad as it looks," Ellie said. "Though your expression is saying otherwise."

"No, no," Lena hurried to say, feeling like crap for being so judgmental, even if she'd been doing all the judging—and speculating—in her head. "It's fine. I wasn't really expecting Tara."

"Tara?" Ellie frowned for a moment before her eyes went wide. "Oh. *Gone with the Wind* Tara. No. It's nothing like that. We don't even have drapes for our windows, much less to make into dresses. But we do have blinds, even if they're not in the best shape."

"Hey, whatever keeps the Toms from peeping

in," Lena said, the words hanging there until punctuated by Ellie dropping the tub of chèvre she'd been holding.

They bent at the same time, Lena's hand closing on top of Ellie's over the lid that had—thankfully—only loosened and not come off. Ellie's fingers were cold, her grip deadly. Lena had to use both hands to pry the cheese away.

"I am so sorry." She wanted to shoot herself. What in the world was wrong with her? She'd seen the security system and the size of the front door and Ellie's scars. "I didn't even think. I'm bad about that. Spouting off when I shouldn't."

"You have nothing to apologize for," Ellie said, shaking her head, her eyes watery, her smile weak. "They're just words. I shouldn't let them get to me. I've never even had a peeping Tom."

But she'd obviously had something go wrong. And someone she didn't want looking into the house where she lived, seeing her making soup and sandwiches. Lena wasn't going to push. If it was important for her to know later, she'd push then. She certainly understood what it meant for one human being to wound another to the point of words turning unexpectedly into weapons.

Just then a toddler boy and another of preschool age came running through the kitchen, the older one jumping into one of the chairs, the younger leaning over the seat and giggling. Lena stood. Ellie followed. She was working at removing the top to the chèvre when a woman Lena assumed was the boys' mother appeared.

She stopped just over the threshold, looking from Lena to the far corner of the room where the boys had pulled out a box of giant Duplo toys from behind one of the chairs and were dumping them on the braided rug. "I didn't know we had company."

Ellie left the cheese on the counter and stepped forward quickly. "Lena, this is Frannie Charles, and those are her sons, Robert and James. Frannie, this is Lena Mining. She works at the chocolate shop next to Bread and Bean. Look what she brought us for supper."

"How nice," Frannie said hesitantly, glancing toward her boys. "What's the occasion?"

The woman was gorgeous, though terribly gaunt, her dark hair lank, her skin olive and flawless, save for the circles beneath her big eyes. The vibes she was giving off told Lena to tread carefully. "I was hungry, and Ellie brought me a sourdough round yesterday morning, and waxed poetic about the joys of grilled cheese."

"I did not," Ellie said, giggling. "I don't have a poetic bone in my body."

"Mommy! Mommy!" The older boy caught sight of his mother and came running, slamming into her legs and wrapping his arms around her. He peeked at Lena with one eye. "Why is that lady's hair purple?"

Embarrassment stained Frannie's cheeks. "Well, I suppose she likes the color. But let's not talk about what other people look like, all right?"

"It's cool," Lena said, quickly adding, "that he's curious, I mean. I don't mind him asking about it."

"Did you hear that, James?" Ellie said, leaning down and ruffling his hair. "If you want to ask Ms. Lena about her hair, go ahead. As long as it's okay with your mom."

Frannie nodded, so Lena dropped to the boy's level and held out her hand. "Hi, James. I'm Lena."

He was tentative at first, then reached to shake. "Is purple your favorite color?"

"I do like purple," she said, canting her head forward so he could see all of it. "Do you know what color this is?" she asked, lifting a scissored chunk that hung above her ear.

"That's blue!"

"You're exactly right," she said, pointing to another stripe at her temple. "And this?"

"Pink!" he said, clapping his hands. "You have pretty hair."

"Thank you, James," she said, smiling and too aware that his clothes had probably been handed down a dozen times. His jean shorts were washed nearly white, and his T-shirt, once blue with a big red dog in the center, was just about as faded.

"Why do you have earrings in your eye?"

"James!" Frannie gasped, mortified.

Lena waved off his mother's objection. "They're eyebrow rings. Though I guess they do look like earrings."

"Do they come out?"

"They do. Would you like to see?"

James nodded excitedly, his mother saying, "You don't have to do that."

"It's fine. I offered." She crossed her ankles and sat on the floor. James came close, holding on to his mother's hand as he watched Lena pull open the hoops and slide them from their holes. She'd worry about getting them back in when she got home.

Setting each in the center of her palm, she opened her hand to show him, then pointed to her eyebrow with her other hand. "They go through these tiny little holes. Just like earrings go through tiny little holes in ears."

James let go of his mother and moved closer, hunkering down to look at Lena's eye. "Does it hurt? When you poke them in?"

"Not anymore," she said. "It hurt some when I first had them done."

"Did it bleed?" he asked, his little lips turned down, his eyes sad. "Did you get a butterfly?"

A butterfly? Oh, a bandage, right. Lena shook her head. "It didn't bleed much, so I didn't need a Band-Aid."

James let that sink in, frowning when he said, "Mommy needed a butterfly one time for her eye when Daddy hit her."

"James!" Frannie reached out and lifted the boy away, carrying him toward the chairs where Robert was still busy with the blocks, leaving Lena to stare at the hoops and try to remember how to breathe. Wow, she mused, and shuddered with the hurt. Just wow.

"C'mon," Ellie said, urging her to her feet. "There's a big mirror in the bathroom off the front room's hallway. It'll make it easier to put them back in. Just watch the hole in the floor right outside. It's got a pillow covering it, but sometimes Robert likes to drag it away."

Lena followed her out of the kitchen and through the big dark room at the front of the house to a hallway she hadn't noticed before. It led to the rest of the first-floor rooms, and the staircase to the upper stories. The bathroom was the second door they passed.

"You were so perfect with James," Ellie said, pushing the bathroom door open and flipping on the light. It sputtered several times before it finally caught. "He's such a good boy, but I know being here all the time with just us and his mother is hard."

"He doesn't go to preschool or have play-dates?" Lena asked, walking into the room with the huge claw-foot tub, the porcelain chipped away from its gilded feet, which appeared to be rusted to the floor's worn black-and-white tiles.

Ellie shook her head, her frown causing her glasses to slip. "Frannie rarely lets him out of her sight," she said as she pushed them back up her nose.

"She didn't seem overprotective," Lena said, leaning close to the mirror and smoothing her eyebrow before pushing the post of the first ring into place. "Just wanting him to have good manners. And, well, not talk about what went on at home."

"Unfortunately, talking about it is the only way he seems to be able to deal," Ellie said with a shrug, her hand on the doorjamb at face level. "He talks about it all the time."

"About the abuse?" Lena asked, finishing with the second ring and catching Ellie's reflection in the mirror, her heart catching, too.

Ellie blinked, then looked down as she said, "And his dad setting fire to their house."

Her stomach bunched in knots, Lena's hands stilled as she turned and met Ellie's gaze. "Are you serious?"

"I wish I wasn't."

"But they're okay?" What a stupid question. How could anyone be okay after that?

Ellie nodded. "Physically. And they're staying here to make sure they remain so."

"The dad doesn't know where they are?"

"No." Ellie pushed off the doorjamb. "Though I imagine he's trying his best to find out."

Lena couldn't keep it in any longer. "This is a shelter or something, isn't it? For abused women. I mean, don't worry. I'm not going to say anything. I saw the scars on your arms—"

"We're all just staying here, living here, for now," Ellie said with a shrug, pulling down on one sleeve then the other as she did. "We're all fine. Just . . . careful."

"It's good to be careful," Lena said. *God, why did she have to keep saying the wrong things?* "And I'm sorry. I seem to be stepping over a lot of lines I shouldn't tonight."

"You, Lena Mining, are so sweet to worry," Ellie said almost sadly, placing her hands on Lena's cheeks then leaning close and kissing her.

It was a soft kiss. Quick and gentle. Just Ellie's lips touching Lena's and pulling away. Nothing more. Nothing insistent. But so unexpected Lena didn't have time to react before Ellie took a step back, gesturing over her shoulder. "I'm going to run and get started on supper. You know where the kitchen is. Come find me when you're done."

Then she was gone, leaving Lena with the last of her rings to deal with, and the invitation she'd been waiting for. Now to figure out how to answer it without making a mess of things.

❧ Chapter Ten ❧

Dakota was standing on the cottage's tiny square of a front porch when Indiana arrived the next morning, guiding her low-slung Camaro to a stop next to his truck. He had his first cup of coffee in hand. He'd hoped to be on his third by now. Dealing with his sister and her questions and Thea on top was going to require a lot of caffeine.

His brain wasn't there yet. Sleep would've helped, but it was getting harder and harder to come by. Something about suppressed thoughts bubbling to the surface when he closed his eyes. His degree might be in engineering, but he'd taken enough psychology classes and seen enough shrinks while in prison to figure that out for himself.

So he wasn't exactly sorry to see Thea pull in behind his sister as Indiana got out of her car. Good, he mused, watching Indiana turn to see who else had arrived so early. The two could catch up and maybe this whole intervention could be put off for another day. Though in a perfect world everyone would just leave him alone now and get together after he was gone.

Bringing his mug to his mouth, he saw recognition dawn in his sister's expression. She

151

left the sack of what he assumed were his breakfast tacos on top of her car and ran to Thea.

Thea had just slammed her door, and left the bag of what he assumed were his kolaches on top of hers, meeting Indiana between the Subaru's front end and the Camaro's back.

Their hug was huge. They rocked back and forth. They pulled away to get a closer look. They screamed and they cried and they gestured wildly and held hands and jumped for joy.

Great. His breakfast was going to get cold and stale and soggy while they revisited a decade plus of life. He whistled once, waving for both women to grab the food and get their asses in gear.

Indiana waved back as if telling him to hold his horses. Thea just ignored him. He waffled between heading inside for more coffee, or heading down the steps to the food. The word *waffle* did him in. As much as he wanted to wait them out, his pride tasted like cardboard.

He set his mug on the porch and took two long steps to the ground before crossing the yard to the cars. He reached across the Camaro's roof for the first bag, across the Subaru's for the second. Then he growled out the words, "I'm hungry," and returned to the cottage.

In the kitchen, he dug two tacos from the bag to heat and shoved half of a kolache in his mouth while he waited. He was still chewing when the door squeaked open and laughter filled the front room. It nearly choked him when he tried to swallow. It was the laughter of his teen years, the same two voices he'd listened to through the wall adjoining his bedroom to Indiana's.

He reached first for his empty mug, then for the coffee pot, pouring while he tried to hide his cough but spitting crumbs everywhere. The women walked into the kitchen to find him with his hands full as he spewed the remnants of his kolache into the air.

"Good grief. Are you all right?" His sister came toward him, brushing his shirtfront clean and taking the carafe from his hand, then patting his back as if that actually helped. "You're making a mess."

"Trust me," he said, barking another cough before sipping at the hot coffee to clear the rest of the kolache from his throat. "Not what I intended."

"Why didn't you tell me Thea was coming?" she asked, fetching two mugs from the cabinet. "I would've brought more food."

"I brought plenty of kolaches." Thea stood at the kitchen's entrance, one brow arched as she added, "Or there were plenty last time I looked in the bag."

"I had one," Dakota said, holding up a finger to defend himself. "One. And half of it ended up in my windpipe."

"I don't remember you being one for wasting food," Thea said.

And then his sister responded, "No, but he was always one for making a mess."

He came so close to mentioning the mess that had sent him to prison, but managed not to be stupid. Just annoyed at being ganged up on, though it served him right for bringing both women here. "I'll clean up the mess. And the rest of the kolaches are yours." He nodded toward the microwave. "I'll just take my tacos and coffee to the porch while you two have a nice long visit."

Indiana grabbed his sleeve before he took a step. "Not so fast, big brother. I see what you did there."

Of course she would have. "I don't know what you're talking about."

She glanced at Thea, then arms crossed, glanced back. "You mean it's completely coincidental that you invited an old friend to join us for the breakfast where you and I were supposed to continue yesterday morning's conversation?"

He shrugged off his guilt. "I thought you two might like to catch up."

"I asked you about this when you suggested I join you," Thea said, waving a hand she then shoved to her hip. "You told me I wouldn't be in the way."

"You're not in the way," he said with an expansive gesture, nearly sloshing what was left of his coffee from his cup. "Plenty of room. And once I get out of here, there'll be even more. You can get on with your girl talk, and I'll get to work."

"As lovely as it was of you to surprise me, I didn't come here for girl talk," Indiana said. "Thea and I can do that later. When we have more time and I don't need answers from you."

"I don't have any answers to give you, Indiana. I don't have any answers to give Clark here. Hell, I don't have any to give myself."

She looked down for a moment, frowning, her lips pressed tight, then said, "Fine. Deny it all you want, but there's got to be a reason behind your wanting to leave. You told Tennessee you were going. You told Thea—"

Well that hadn't taken long, he mused, looking at Thea. "Thanks."

She shrugged. "I didn't know it was a secret."

"It's not. It's just—" He looked from Thea to Indiana, then hung his head. Screw it. Might as well get this crap over with so he could get back to his life—what there was of it—and to work. "Look. I don't want to disappoint Tennessee more than I already have. Okay? Happy now? Moving on is just a simple way to exit a bad situation."

"Why do you think you've disappointed him? And how in the world is moving on going to make anything better? And what bad situation are you talking about? Because honestly . . ." Indiana stopped, gathered her cloud of dark hair and held it at the back of her head, then let it go. "I think you're overreacting to something. I just can't figure out what."

His sister. Poking holes in everything as always. And probably more right than he wanted to admit. "You know he and I talked about making a go of the construction gig as partners. Keller Brothers. We discussed it for years. Well, turns out I'm not much a fan of construction."

"Have you told him you don't like it?" Indiana asked, as if doing so was the most logical thing in the world. "It's not like he's making you work for him."

No, but guilt was, an admission that sounded as dumb as it probably was. "I'm not going to say anything. And neither are you. I'm not going to let him down. At least not like that. He's been talking about our finally being in business together since the day I got home."

"Give him some credit," she said imploringly, rubbing at her forehead as if her head was hurting as badly as his. "He's not going to buy this bad situation bullshit anymore than I am."

"Uh, guys," Thea said, interrupting. "I'm going to head outside—"

"No." Dakota said the word without even thinking, his gaze on his sister when he did.

156

Indiana leaned both hands against the counter in front of the sink and stared out the window above.

That was when he let his gaze drift to Thea. Her arms were crossed and she was staring at the floor, the rooster tail on top of her head flopped to one side. He could see a few strands of gray at her temple where the morning sun through the window lit the side of her face.

Stress? Worry? Secrets she was having trouble keeping?

He was still looking at her when he said, "I'm not happy here, Indiana. Can't we just leave it at that?"

"No. We can't. Not without you giving me a reason why." She faced him again, stomping one boot and nearly wailing the words. "I don't understand. Are we not enough for you? Me and Tennessee? What's out there"—she waved one arm, nearly slamming it into Thea—"that you don't have here?"

"Don't even say that. That you're not enough. It's not that." But it was, wasn't it? He needed something more. He needed answers: Why had he been duped by the boy who'd assaulted his sister? Why hadn't he been able to see the truth beneath the surface of Robby Hunt? Why had he thought that beating half to death someone he'd considered a friend would make what had happened to Indiana any better?

Why had he chosen a path that made things worse?

And then. To walk out on his brother and sister when he was almost twenty-two years old. Indiana had still been in high school, Tennessee in college. He could've gone home with them the day he'd left prison, but he'd had to live for three years with the truth of what he'd done.

How he'd ruined their lives as completely as he'd ruined his own.

Now he was living with the consequences. "And I don't know."

"Neither one of those is an answer," Indiana said with a sigh. "And neither one of them explain why you have to leave town."

He spun on her then. "What exactly am I going to do if I stay in Hope Springs?"

"Whatever you want to." She was waving her arms again. This time Thea backed out of the way. "Go into business for yourself."

"Doing what? Using what money? What credit? I got nothing, Indiana. Nothing." And admitting that in front of both of these women was one of the lowest moments of his life. "Don't you get that? Is that so hard to understand?"

Tears welled in her eyes. Her mouth trembled. "Tennessee and I can help you. What do you want to do? You've got a degree. Do something with it."

"That degree on my résumé . . ." Was he the

only one who got the joke? "Isn't there some saying about lipstick and pigs?"

"It's not that hard to turn a bad situation into a good one, you know," Thea said.

Yeah right. He looked at her, all covered up and inaccessible, hiding, really. That's what it was. "Is that what you've done? You and all the women you're supporting?"

Her eyes flared. Her nostrils, too. He expected any second to see smoke coming out of her ears. "We're doing just fine, thank you. Not that it's any of your concern. And not that my circumstances have anything to do with yours."

"You sure about that, Clark?" he asked, goading her and unable to stop. What a joke, pretending they could avoid the past. It was alive in this very room, clawing at them both, angry and hurtful and refusing to let go.

Thea was barely civil when she said, "I'm going to pretend you didn't just go there."

"Go where?" Indiana asked, looking from one to the other. "What am I missing?"

"Listen—"

"No," Thea said, raising a hand to cut him off. "You and your sister finish this up. I'm in the way." She gave Indiana a hug. "It's good to see you. We'll do lunch soon and catch up properly?"

"Absolutely."

"I'll see you at the shop," Dakota said because he couldn't deal with leaving things this way.

"Can't wait," she said, the roll of her eyes adding another tangle to the knot of Dakota's gut.

Once she was gone, he leaned against the counter across from the sink where his sister still stood, and dragged his hands down his face. He was too tired to think. Too fed up with being tired to even know what he was doing. Something had to give. Something had to change.

He looked at his sister and saw the girl she'd been in high school. Her dark hair. Her freckles. Her innocence that he'd very nearly let get ruined. "I'm sorry I wasn't in touch. I'm sorry you had to send a PI to find me."

"I missed you. I needed to know you were okay. I needed you in my life." She stepped forward and laid her palm on his cheek. "I love you."

Then she turned and left the kitchen, left the cottage, and moments later, left the property on Thea's heels.

Dakota grabbed his keys, his lukewarm tacos and cold kolaches, made sure the coffee pot was off, and headed out the door. He slammed that one so hard the front room window rattled. Then he slammed the one in the truck so hard he set off the alarm. "Shit."

Why in the world had he told anyone he was thinking of hitting the road? He'd never told anyone previously. He'd finished a job and vanished, given his notice and gone. Sure, this was different; he was working for his brother. Turning in his resignation wouldn't be as simple as it had been in the past.

Tennessee would've asked the same questions. He'd have gone to Indiana. That part Dakota could understand. He owed his siblings more than he'd given them the last time he'd split. But Thea was different. She was a job. He was a contractor. He didn't owe her a thing. Except he did. He owed her all.

She was why he was still in one piece and for the most part sane. And he was going to tell her that when she said he'd ruined her? Not likely. Though, he mused with a self-deprecating snort, she was very possibly the reason he was alone. Meaning she may have ruined him, too. That was when his snort became a laugh, because what a waste. Of years. Of trying not to think of her when he was with other women.

The idea of being meant for one single person didn't work for him. He didn't buy into all that woo-woo crap. Besides, he and Thea weren't involved beyond their working relationship. The years they'd spent together, he realized as he pulled to park behind Bread and Bean, had been one of those moments out of time. It had mattered then. It wasn't meant to be repeated. That's just how things worked. Just how it was.

It couldn't be any other way.

Checking to see that he hadn't missed anything

in the cab, he slammed the truck's door and headed for the bed and his toolbox.

"Hey, dude."

Dude? He glanced toward the chocolate shop next door. The woman who worked there, the one with the chunks of colored hair, was walking toward him. "By 'dude' I guess you mean me?"

"Yeah, sorry. I don't know your name."

"Ditto."

"Right. I'm Lena Mining. I work at Bliss," she said, gesturing that direction with her thumb.

"Dakota Keller." He held out his hand. "I work wherever my brother sends me."

She frowned, as if parsing out his words, but she did shake his hand. "Your brother. So he's the boss? The one I'd want to talk to about a job?"

"You can talk to me."

She thought about that for a moment, then asked, "Do you only do commercial work? Like the stuff here for Bread and Bean?"

"Nope," he said, unlocking his truck box and setting his tape measure inside before retrieving the case for his saw. "We do it all," he added, hearing the snap of a smartphone camera and turning. "Can I help you with something?"

She turned her phone toward him and showed him the photo of the sign on his door. "Just grabbing your contact info."

"I think I've got a card somewhere if you want it. Probably on the visor. Or the glove box."

"This I won't lose, but thanks," she said, turning away with a frown, then turning back with a quick, "Nice to meet you."

"You, too," he said, thinking this job had put him in the path of some of the most interesting women he'd ever run across in his life.

Needing a break from the drama of Dakota Keller, as much as she needed something new to read, Thea had parked in front of Bread and Bean once she'd arrived in town. Instead of going inside, however, she'd started walking. She was hungry and wished Butters Bakery sold more than sweets, but it was either a cookie or a chocolate bonbon from Bliss. She opted for the cookies, one oatmeal raisin and one peanut butter, figuring at least she'd get some fiber and protein with her sugar and fat.

The cookies kept her busy for the several blocks walk to Cat Tales. The new-and-used bookstore was one of her favorite discoveries after moving to Hope Springs. She could understand why the resident tabby found the place the perfect home. Browsing the shelves gave her time to think about the morning's failed breakfast with Dakota and his sister, and to remember how, during their early teen years, she'd shamelessly used her friend to get to her brother.

She'd loved being around Indiana because she was so . . . normal. Even with weird hippie parents as examples growing up, Indiana had never been brainwashed by their propaganda. She'd always thought for herself, known what she wanted, and gone after it. Thea had envied that. She'd been absolutely without goals— except Dakota.

At first, it had been a conquest thing; every girl she'd known had had a crush on Dakota Keller. Later, she'd wanted him for a grippingly honest reason: never in her life had she had a better friend. She'd been able to talk to him about things she wouldn't have felt comfortable saying to his sister. She'd told him the truth about her problems at home, her problems at school—all of which she'd hidden behind her bad-girl façade. Not once had she worried he'd use her confessions against her, or throw her admissions into her face.

Then again, he'd been just as forthcoming talking to her.

That had been then.

Now just being in the same room with him was enough to make her want to crawl out of her skin. Or to be less dramatic . . . the comfort was gone. Completely. He made her nervous. He made her sweaty and itchy and jumpy. If he'd been anyone else, she would've left him to his work and written a check when it was done.

But Dakota Keller had always been one of her favorite things. And she hadn't realized how much she'd missed having access to his ear and his shoulder until she'd looked up from her blueprint that first morning and found a grown-up version of the boy she'd known looking down.

Why did things have to change? Why did his choice to go after his sister's attacker have to screw up everything they'd had? Except she'd been equally at fault, hadn't she?

She hadn't gone to see him in prison.

She hadn't tried to find him after his release.

She hadn't trusted her instincts when they'd screamed that Todd would never be Dakota, even though they'd shared the same body type, the same coloring, the same dry sense of humor . . . even if the temperament she'd *thought* similar, well . . . Could she possibly have been more wrong?

Yes, Dakota had it in him to be violent. But not like Todd. Never like Todd.

Enough.

The day was paint-by-numbers gorgeous, and the sun tempting, so she veered off the sidewalk and through the entrance to the small city park she'd walked by earlier. She had a new-to-her Megan Chance novel to read, and indulging in a few pages now before having to see Dakota again was just what the doctor ordered.

So what if she was self-medicating?

Heading for the closest bench as she flipped through the book, she looked up just in time to avoid a collision with a woman pushing a stroller. The little girl waving her arms in excitement was probably a year old, though Thea was really bad with ages. The woman—

Thea found herself smiling. "I know you."

Frowning, the little girl's mother looked over. "You do?"

"I'm sorry. That was so rude. I'm Thea Clark," she said, her book closing on one hand as she offered the other. "I'm opening Bread and Bean on Fourth Street."

"The coffee shop, right?" The woman shook Thea's hand warmly. "My husband's firm is doing work for you I think."

"Right. You're Kaylie Keller."

"Yes. Good grief." Kaylie pressed her fingers to her forehead. "I'm usually much better at introductions. Motherhood has made mush of my brain. I'm so sorry."

"I started us off on the wrong foot," Thea said, following Kaylie to the bench where they both sat. "My fault."

Nodding toward Thea's book, Kaylie said, "I guess you've been to Cat Tales."

Thea waved it casually. "I needed something to take my mind off the construction."

Kaylie frowned. "It's not going well?"

"Oh, no. Everything's fine." *Way to go. Stepping without looking again.* The woman's husband was doing the work, for goodness sake. "I'm just hearing hammering and sawing in my sleep."

Kaylie laughed, reaching into her daughter's diaper bag for her chirping phone. "Having gone through a Keller Construction project myself, I can totally relate."

Tennessee had remodeled Kaylie's three-story Victorian, turning the bottom floor into Two Owls Café. That was how the couple had met. That was when they'd fallen in love. Thea knew all this from gossip, but there was absolutely no correlation to Dakota building out Thea's espresso bar.

None at all. "I need to get back, but can I ask you something? Before I go?"

"Sure." Kaylie scanned the text message, then blanked her phone's screen and tucked it away. "What is it?"

How best to put this . . . "Do you know why Dakota's thinking of leaving Hope Springs?"

"What?" Kaylie's gaze narrowed. "Leaving? Dakota?"

And once more with the big mouth. "I thought you probably knew. He mentioned having told Tennessee. I just assumed . . . Sorry. I shouldn't have said anything."

"I'm glad you did," Kaylie said, bending at her daughter's shout to retrieve a toy dangling against the stroller. "Tennessee doesn't usually keep secrets from me."

"I'm sure he has a good reason," Thea said,

though she wasn't sure of anything of the sort.

"Oh, I'm sure he does. Like wanting to deal with it on his own because he doesn't like to rely on anyone." Kaylie rubbed at her forehead again. "That seems to be a family trait with the siblings."

Because they'd had no one else to rely on growing up. "Have you met their parents?"

"Actually, no. They've been overseas since Tennessee and I married. I've heard plenty of stories, though."

"Then you probably understand why said siblings tend to think they have to figure things out on their own."

Kaylie shrugged. "Tennessee and I almost never disagree, you know? We get along so perfectly it's frightening. But when we do, ninety percent of the time it's because he doesn't want to talk about his brother when I ask what's going on with him or how he's doing."

Thea frowned. "You mean with the work?"

"With anything. With everything." Kaylie glanced over. "It was Indiana who hired a PI to find him. Not Tennessee. Did you know that?"

Thea shook her head absently, brushing at her bangs the wind had teased into her eyes. "Does Tennessee feel bad about that? Like he should've been the one to do it or something?"

"I don't know. He won't say." Kaylie pressed her legs together, her hands laced tightly in her lap. "I imagine on some level he does, though once Indiana told him, he was onboard. He insisted on paying half the expenses."

"That's got to be good."

"It is. And I know he loves him. There's just something between them that seems to need settling," she said with a sigh, then shaking her head. "For some reason they can't get there. I can't figure out why."

Thea had a feeling . . . "Is it Indiana's assault?"

"It's the only thing that makes sense."

"I imagine that's hard for them to deal with. Having been there at the time it happened. Not knowing and unable to stop it." Her chest tight, Thea glanced toward the playground as a boy James's age flew giggling off the end of the slide. "And it's got to be even worse for Indiana, seeing her brothers butting heads over something that happened to her."

"I think about that all the time," Kaylie said, shuddering, on the verge of tears. "It keeps me awake nights, when Tennessee and I have argued. I just don't know how they can do this to their sister. This rift . . . These men . . . They've got to repair it before it ruins the rest of their lives."

Chapter Eleven

Dakota stared at the chalk outline of the barista station he'd drawn on Bread and Bean's floor, his thoughts split into two columns. One a list of things he needed to say to his sister. The other, twice as long, the explanations he owed Thea. Across the top of the mental page he'd scrawled the question of the day: *What in the hell is wrong with you?*

He wasn't ready to say that inviting Thea to breakfast had been a mistake. He was glad she and his sister were once again on each other's radar. If nothing else came of this morning, there was that. What he hated was Thea being caught in the middle of his issues with Indiana. She'd been his sister's friend, if not as close as some, and yeah, because of him, they'd fallen out of touch.

One more thing to add to the list of wrongs he needed to make up for. It was going to take the rest of his life.

At the sound of the front door opening, he glanced over his shoulder to see Manny walking in. Dakota didn't even give the door a chance to close or Manny a chance to speak before he jumped. "Please tell me you've lined up more help for Tennessee." Knowing he could leave after this job was probably the only way he'd get through it.

"I've got a couple of guys I'll be able to send him to talk to. If you're sure about this."

Dakota stayed where he was, arms crossed, as Manny made his way to the makeshift coffee station, stepping through the chalked lines of Dakota's visual aid, and helped himself to a cup. "I am," he said, though even he noticed the hesitation and doubt that had Manny staring at him over the edge of his cup as steam from the coffee rose like a fog between them.

"Not quite sure I heard that right," Manny said, then blew over the surface and sipped. "Did you say you're still thinking about it?"

Funny man. "What I'm thinking about is the placement of the barista station you're standing in the middle of," he said, nodding toward the sketch he'd made on the floor.

"Didn't you hash all this out with the owner?" Manny asked, frowning as he glanced from the station's shell sitting across the room to the chalk dust his feet had stirred up.

"We're working from the original contractor's specs, but I'm wondering if Becca might want more room." He stepped to the other side of the drawing and faced the door. "We could give her another foot without impeding the flow of traffic."

Manny sipped again, then shrugged. "Works for me, but then I'm just the manpower guy. You want me to have Tennessee talk to these guys now, or are you not ready to hit him with the fact that you're leaving?"

"He knows," Dakota said. "Might as well set up the interviews." Then through the front door's glass, he caught a glimpse of Thea on the sidewalk. Nothing else mattered after that. "Give me a minute, will ya? There's a bag with a couple of kolaches in the kitchen if you need something to go with your coffee."

"Thanks," Manny said, turning that way as Dakota headed for the door, his heart hammering, his throat tight.

Thea had parked in one of the shop's angled spaces and was standing in front of her car, her hands in her pockets, her shoulders hunched. She was staring across the street, at what he didn't know, and though she would've heard him come out, she had yet to acknowledge him. He didn't think that was a very good sign.

"Can we talk about this morning?" he asked as he stopped beside her. Might as well get it out of the way.

"I don't think so," she said, doing nothing to hide her sarcasm. "I mean, this morning's in the past, right? And we don't talk about that."

Yeah, okay. He deserved that. "Give me a break, Clark. I'm no better at this getting reacquainted business than you are. And I'm sorry."

She turned then, her head cocked as she looked

at him. "What if we just call off the agreement? If the past comes up in conversation, so be it. Will that make you happy?"

Happy enough to stay? Was that what she was asking? He wasn't thrilled with her suggestion, but . . . "I don't want to argue with you. Or fight with you. If the trade-off is the occasional trip down memory lane, I can deal with that."

"For as long as you're here, you mean."

"I'm offering an olive branch. A white flag. Whatever you need it to be."

He watched her purse her lips, then fight against a grin, though almost as quickly she grew pensive. "You know what our problem is, don't you?"

He didn't, though he was sure she was going to enlighten him.

"Unfinished business."

"How so?" he asked, frowning.

"We never broke up."

O . . . kay. "Come again?"

She moved to lean against the front of her car, her hands on the hood at her hips. "We had a crazy night of sex. Or a night of crazy sex. Then you left. I never saw you again, or heard from you again, until a few days ago when I looked up and there you were. We've spent more than a decade and many many miles apart without closure. And that after being together constantly for two years. We need that. Closure."

He stared at her, waiting for more but that seemed to be it. He couldn't think of anything to ask but the obvious. "So you want to break up now?"

She nodded. "I think we should."

He was struggling really hard not to laugh as he played along. "You know we weren't ever officially going out. I didn't ask you to be my old lady or anything."

"Doesn't matter," she said. "I told everyone that you had."

"That so?" he asked, unable to keep a straight face. "No wonder Debbie Hollis wouldn't have anything to do with me."

"Debbie Hollis?" she asked, scrunching up her nose. "Seriously?"

He shrugged. "Cheerleaders have always been one of my favorite things."

"Somehow I don't quite believe you."

"When have I ever lied to you?" he asked, then immediately wanted to grab back the words.

Thea looked at him with those eyes that saw everything, that gave no quarter. "You told me you'd write me from prison. You never did."

Well, hell. He hadn't expected that to come back and bite him. "I was busy. I couldn't think of anything to say."

"That's just dumb."

"Which part?" Because the second was the absolute truth. "I studied. I worked out. I ate and I slept and got really good at making the right friends."

"You could've told me about that. How you went about it. What you looked for." She stopped, then she snorted at whatever thought she'd just had. "I could've used the help."

She was talking about her ex. He was certain. But that didn't change anything about what he'd had to do to survive. "It was another world in there, Clark. Nothing else existed. I couldn't let it. I had to shut out everything I'd known to get through. It was hard even to see Tennessee and Indiana when they would come, and my parents the few times they did. I needed to be the brother they knew. But I'd left him at the door when I went inside."

Unexpectedly, she reached for his hand, rubbing her thumb over his knuckles and the remnants of the tattoos there. "What was here? What did it say?"

The tats had been crude, the ink not as deep as it would've been if professionally done. He'd had the letters removed with a laser, though had kept the dot beneath each one as a reminder. "It said 'wait.' "

"Like waiting for something?"

He nodded because that was true, too. Waiting to get out. Waiting to see her again. At least until he'd changed his mind and hit the road. "More like not being stupid and rushing into something without thinking about it."

"Would waiting have made a difference? With Robby and what happened?"

A question with no answer, so he shrugged. "I'm a lot more patient now than I was then. I guess it worked."

She squeezed his fingers once then let go, pushing off the car with a shudder as if she needed to get away from the time he'd served and all that it meant.

"You okay?" he asked.

She nodded. "I think I'm still hungry."

He couldn't help himself. "I hear Malina's makes a mean egg taco."

"Gee, thanks. I wouldn't know."

And he'd downed enough for both of them. "You should've told me you hadn't eaten. I just sent Manny into the kitchen for the rest of the kolaches."

She looked at him, one brow arched. "There were some left?"

"I ate mine and Indiana's. I saved your three for you."

"Aw," she said, punching lightly at his shoulder. "That's so sweet."

"Then all is forgiven?" He hoped.

But she shook her head. "Not a chance."

At the sound of the kitchen door opening, Becca looked up expecting Thea, since she was late. Or even Dakota, since he went through more coffee than anyone she'd ever known.

What she got instead was the man who'd told her caffeine would help her breathe. The man responsible for her being unable to. The man who'd asked her questions she'd fallen into answering as if she'd opened a vein.

That wasn't going to happen today.

He stopped near the kitchen's front stainless-steel work counter, and hands at his hips, looked around. Usually by this time bread for the house would be rising there, but Ellie hadn't made it in yet, so Becca had taken advantage of the quiet kitchen to bake.

"Dakota said there might be some leftover kolaches back here," the man finally said.

"There might be. There might not." Because two and a half of the three that had been in the sack Dakota had left on said counter were now in her stomach. She finished centering the third cake layer on the other two she'd already iced together before looking up. "Sack's there at your elbow."

He frowned into the bag that held the remaining kolache half. Then he shrugged and reached inside. "Beggars can't be choosers."

"You're just full of all sorts of wisdom, aren't you?" she asked, bending to eyeball the cake. It was as level as it was going to get, so she reached for the bowl of icing, scooping out what she'd need to cover the top before moving on to the sides.

The man with the devil in his eye and the smile that chewed away at her resolve came closer, coffee in one hand, the last remaining bite of the kolache in the other. He ate it while she worked, watching her closely. She didn't like being watched. Not by anyone.

But she refused to let his attention get to her. She knew what she was doing. She was as comfortable frosting a cake as Ellie was kneading a loaf of bread, as Frannie was caring for her boys, as Thea was running the show.

She spun the cake on its stand and started in frosting the sides.

"That smells really good."

"I know," she said, the cinnamon, sugar, and vanilla aromas hard to ignore.

"It looks really good, too," he said, stepping back to set his empty coffee cup in the sink and toss the ball of the paper sack in the trash.

"I know."

"Is it for a special occasion?"

"Eating," she said, getting a perverse pleasure out of the tit for tat, and waiting for him to come right out and ask for a slice.

But he took a different tack instead. "You train professionally? Through some classes or something? Decorating and baking?"

She shook her head and spun the cake another turn, her spatula smoothing the icing layer. "I learned from my father. He started working in a bakery as a dishwasher and by the time I was in high school, he was decorating cakes."

"From the ground up then. For both of you."

"You could say that, I guess."

"So what's the occasion? Somebody's birthday or something?"

Besides having a few extra bucks to buy the hummingbird cake's ingredients? And struck with the urge to splurge after pawning the belt buckle she'd stolen from her cowboy ex?

She didn't know why she'd held on to it for so long. Maybe it was just enjoying the knowledge that he'd loved it, he'd bragged about it, he'd shown it off everywhere they'd gone, and now he didn't have it anymore.

Neither did she know what had had her digging it from the bottom of her dresser drawer. But something had finally pushed her to ditch it. Something she couldn't put a finger on, though that something was in no way related to thoughts she'd had for days now about the man standing in front of her.

She wasn't that oxygen-deprived. "No occasion. Just in the mood to bake."

"You going to cut it soon? I mean, if you're not taking it to a potluck or saving it for any particular reason and it's just for eating," he said, and she swore she heard his stomach grumble.

She reached for the bag of shredded coconut and sprinkled a handful over the cake's top. The recipe called for macadamia nuts, but she couldn't justify the cost when coconut alone would do. "I thought it would be a nice surprise for after dinner."

"I think it would make a nice breakfast."

"It would, wouldn't it?" She bit down on a grin. "I'll definitely have a slice tomorrow."

"I wouldn't mind having a slice today." Another, louder growl. "If you need a taste tester—"

"I don't—"

"Or you just want to feed a hungry man who's only had half a stale kolache all day. One who can't remember the last time he had a piece of cake fresh from the oven."

Now he was just playing on her sympathies. Except she'd lost most of those long before she'd pawned the belt buckle. Which didn't explain why she was looking at the finished cake and trying to decide the best place to start cutting.

It was something she'd picked up from her father. She couldn't even count the number of times she'd sat on a stack of phone books in a kitchen chair while knife in hand, he'd looked a cake up one side and down the other before slicing into it.

She'd held her breath, her gaze moving from her father's studied expression to the cake's perfect surface—sometimes smooth, sometimes mounded with whipped-cream dollops, sometimes decorated with a lattice of icing ribbons—until he'd made his decision. Then he'd taken the twelve-inch serrated blade he used only on cakes, and sliced.

She'd bought herself an identical knife to use for the same purpose. Then Dez had used it on the last cake she'd baked him to hack it into pieces, as much ending up on the ceiling as the floor and the clothes she'd been wearing. He'd made her climb onto the counter to clean the mess. And he'd snapped his whip behind her, the threat a real one.

No matter how she hurried, she hadn't been fast enough.

"You okay? I mean, if you don't want to cut the cake, that's fine," her visitor said. "I didn't mean to make you cry."

"I'm not crying." *Dammit.* She swiped the back of her wrist over her eyes. "Just having a hard time with the things some people can do."

"Like balance peanuts on their nose?"

The man really was a piece of work. "Like how they can hurt those they say they love."

"That's a song, you know. You only hurt who you love. Or something like that."

"I'm pretty sure that's not the way love's supposed to work. But whatever." She found her knife in the drawer where she'd left it and slid it into the cake. Before she made the second cut, she looked up. "How big of a piece do you want?"

His eyes went wide, his smile, too, all sorts of dimples and laugh lines lighting up his face. She expected him to ask for half of it, but he said, "Just a normal size piece is fine. Thanks. I really am starving."

"Tell that to the bottom button of your shirt there," she said, counting off eight pieces before cutting his wedge. "Is that enough?"

But he was busy looking down at the fit of his shirt. "I'm going to have to blame this on the fast food."

"Just don't blame it on me," she said, finding one of the saucers they used for breakfast and a fork. "There's bananas and pineapple in the cake so you can call it a serving of fruit. There's pecans, too, so whatever nuts are. Protein I guess. But, yeah. It's still cake."

He glanced at the plate he held in one hand, then down to where he'd used the other to flatten the fabric to his stomach. "Maybe I shouldn't."

"Fine," she said, "I'll eat it," and reached to take it back. It wasn't like he had more than a five-pound spare tire. More like the shirt had seen better days. "No one's forcing you to do anything you don't want to."

But he kept the cake, and kept his gaze on hers as he took up the fork and dug in. He didn't say anything, but for some reason she heard him asking about what she'd been forced to do. Even unspoken, the question fell softly between them, and it was all she could do not to tell him about Dez.

Luckily, he finished the bite and spoke before taking another, saving her from being foolish when she swore she was done with that. He gestured toward the cake with the fork. "This is probably the best not-chocolate cake I've ever eaten. No, not probably. It is."

"This coming from the man who ate half a stale kolache."

"I was hungry."

"That, or you have no taste."

"I don't have to. It's all in this cake. You going to sell this here, too? Because I was already planning to be a regular for coffee."

"You can get coffee on the highway when you stop for your greasy egg muffin."

"But the coffee here comes with more personality."

"And you can get cake two doors down," she said, ignoring the flutter in her belly at the idea of seeing him even after the shop was opened and Dakota gone.

"Not this cake," he said, his head shaking as he ate more. "Not *your* cake."

He might be able to. If the Butters Bakery deal happened. But she couldn't say anything about that, so she cut herself a slice and joined him.

❦ Chapter Twelve ❦

Tennessee was at the Keller Construction barn when Dakota arrived from Bread and Bean. Thea had split midafternoon, not long after they'd talked out front. Pretty much like she'd split from the cottage this morning, though this time she hadn't told him. He'd found out when he'd stepped into the kitchen to ask her if she'd mind him making another pot of coffee.

Ellie had been there. And Becca. Working together quietly in the corner on labels for some bins. Neither knew where she'd gone. Neither knew when she'd be back. Judging by their moods, which he had to say were pretty upbeat these days, it seemed Thea hadn't said anything to them about breakfast at the cottage, or the mess he'd made of things with her later.

He supposed he should be thankful for that. It was bad enough having Thea know who he was. Working around the other two was already like navigating a minefield. He couldn't imagine how bad it would get if they learned what a shit he was to his siblings. It was hard enough getting through the day without the truth of his actions seizing up in his chest like gears gone bad.

He hooked his tool belt on the pegboard just

inside the door as a reminder to fix the buckle before going to work tomorrow. "I had breakfast with Indiana this morning," he said to his brother. Seemed best to get it out in the open.

Tennessee tapped his pencil against the ledger on his drafting table. "The way I heard, there wasn't much breakfast involved."

Dakota shrugged. "I had plenty. In the truck on the way in. Most of it cold."

That had the other man laughing. "If I weren't your brother, I'd say it served you right."

"It did serve me right," Dakota admitted, shoving a drafting stool between his legs and straddling it. "You being my brother shouldn't keep you from telling the truth."

Tennessee was silent for a long moment, his pencil still, his jaw working. "The truth is, it's my fault for calling Indiana. I should've let you be the one to tell her. It wasn't my place."

An apology. Wow. "It doesn't matter who told her. She needed to know. Now she does."

"And Thea Clark was there."

Dakota nodded. "She hadn't seen Indiana yet. I figured it would be a good time to get them together."

"And keep you from having to talk to Indiana," Tennessee said because he was a Keller, too.

Another nod, and Dakota crossed his arms. "We talked. Not sure we said anything. But we talked."

"Listen, Dakota." Tennessee set down his pencil and spun his stool to the side. "I need to explain about the other morning."

"No. You don't." It was the same response he'd given his brother each time Tennessee had broached the subject. "You own the business. You need to look after the business."

"You're my brother. I need to look—"

"No. You don't." He felt like a broken record. And his siblings both seemed unable to accept that he was no longer eighteen. "I can look after myself. I've been doing it for a lot of years. The last truly bad decision I made was the night I left the house with that bat."

Tennessee crossed his arms, his body language a mirror of Dakota's, a level playing field as they hashed out what had been over and done with long ago. "So you *do* think it was a bad decision."

Dakota tried not to bristle. "Obviously you do."

"I meant that as a question," Tennessee clarified. "I know you didn't at the time. Neither one of us did. But, yeah. I've wondered if you'd changed your mind about going after Robby being the right thing to do."

"Have you?"

Tennessee sighed heavily, moving his hands to his thighs. "Maybe. I don't know. I should've gone with you. I do know that much."

A gust of wind blew through the barn's open

doors. Dakota cleared his hair from his face. "And have Indiana feel responsible for both of us paying for that?"

"Who knows?" Tennessee said with a shrug. "Things might've turned out differently if I'd been there."

Right. "Because I'm a hothead and you're the one who thinks clearly?"

"Not anymore, I hate to say." He laughed, dragging both hands down his face. "Getting a full night's sleep would help, but I can't imagine that will ever happen again."

"Kids," Dakota said, then rubbed it in. "Feedings and diapers then playground bullies then driving and dating and sex—"

"Whoa, now." Tennessee raised both hands. "I think you skipped a few steps there. A few big ones."

He could do this with his brother all day. "Like the years when Georgia May believes the world revolves around her dear old dad? The same years where she keeps him wrapped around her little finger?"

Tennessee sighed. "No one told me it would be like this. All day long . . . Every decision I make . . ." He stopped, scratching at his jaw. "It's like I can't do anything without considering the impact on her."

Dakota enjoyed seeing this side of his brother, uncertain and uneven. It made him more human somehow. Made him more . . . relatable. "Pretty sure that's called being a parent."

"Are you really?" Tennessee's eyes darkened. "Because I can't remember our parents ever taking us into consideration with any decision they made."

"Yeah, well." Dakota shrugged. "There are parents, and then there are parents."

"And then there's whatever ours were."

"*Are,* brother. They're still alive. At least as far as we know."

Tennessee glanced over, his mouth twisted. "You know when I quit caring?"

"Not a clue." Though it was interesting to hear that he had.

"You remember that calendar that hung next to the phone in the kitchen?"

Dakota pictured it clearly. The precisely penciled numbers and letters. "The one with all our schedules? Baseball and volleyball and SAT dates?"

"That's the one. Even after you were gone, Indiana kept it up, and on the weekends when we didn't have a conflict, she put down your name. She knew if she didn't, they'd never remember to leave time for our trips to Huntsville."

Dakota slapped his palms against his thighs and hopped down from the stool. "That worked out really well, didn't it?"

"Most of the times when Indiana and I came

alone? After I had my license? They didn't even know. We would sneak out before they got up. Or we'd leave after they'd gone to save whatever part of the planet was in danger that day." Tennessee stopped, snorted.

"What?"

"The only time they did notice, the only time we got in trouble . . ." He waved one hand absently as he pushed off his stool. "They had a big conference of some sort to get to. I had no idea Dad's car was out of commission. Alternator or something. We always took Mom's. No different that day."

"Bet that went over like a lead balloon," Dakota said, picturing his siblings making that long drive, both teenagers, both still in high school, at least during his first two years locked up. He tried to swallow, but his throat was swollen, and he had trouble clearing it.

"They'd called a cab. So they hadn't missed anything. But, yeah. We got a lecture about responsibility within a family, respect for all family members." Tennessee rolled his head on his shoulders as if the weight of the memory had him stiff. "That was about the time I got up and walked out. I was afraid of what I'd say if I stayed. But Indiana didn't hold back."

Interesting. "Oh yeah?"

"Yeah. I sat at the top of the stairs and listened to her rant about how they had time for every cause that came their way except the three they owed the most. The three they'd created. She asked them over and over why they wouldn't drive us to see you. Why *they* wouldn't come see you more often than they did. It was like she'd been saving up for a year and couldn't deal anymore. She laid into them, just flayed them. And they took it. They didn't say a word. Even when she finally wore herself out . . . nothing. She was all out of tears, and they told her to go to bed. She walked right past me and I got up to go after her but she just slammed her door. She was crying, so I knocked. She told me to leave. Later I heard her on the phone with Thea—"

"Thea? I didn't think they'd stayed in touch."

"I don't know how long they did, but I do know they talked a lot the first year you were gone."

Dakota blew out a big puff of breath. "I spent the night before going to Huntsville with Thea. At her place. Her mother wasn't home. Her mother was never home. She told me once she liked being at our house when we were all there because it felt normal. Like what a family should be."

"If she only knew the truth, eh?"

"She knew. Hell, everyone knew. She never said anything, but we wouldn't have gotten away with half of what we did if our folks had been around."

"And when they were . . ." Brow arched, Tennessee let the sentence trail.

Dakota shoved his hands to his hips. "What a joke, huh? They had no idea who half the kids coming into our house even were, but boy did they ever know how to put on a show."

"Especially for Robby Hunt."

That had him wondering . . . "You think that's why they've been scarce all these years?"

"What? Like they actually woke up and realized their part in Robby being able to get close to Indiana? C'mon. That would mean they'd paid attention. They didn't then. They don't now. Georgia May's a year old. Mitch and Dolly are the only grandparents she knows. And Dolly's only related because of marrying Mitch."

"Not a bad set to have."

"The best. She's got an honorary aunt and uncle in Luna and Angelo. And then she's got her Uncle Oliver and her blood kin. Indiana and you. And that's why you can't just up and leave."

"Tennessee—"

"No. Let me finish. It's not just about my girl. It's about our sister. And it's about me. I want you here. I need you here. We spent the first half of our lives in side-by-side bedrooms, fighting and pulling pranks and lying to our parents to cover for one another. We spent the second half apart. The three years you were on the inside, I saw you a few dozen times, and always with a partition between us. Then you were gone. For all those years. I didn't talk to you. I had no idea

191

if you were alive or dead. And it took our hard-headed sister—"

A shudder had Tennessee rolling his shoulders and walking away, rubbing at the back of his neck as he did. Dakota crossed his arms and looked down at his wide spread feet. Then he closed his eyes because it was easier to pretend he was anywhere else but here. That he wasn't putting his brother through this. That he hadn't ruined his siblings' lives by staying away. Hell, he'd ruined his own life just as completely.

That's what he was having the most trouble coming to grips with. Not what he'd done to Robby Hunt, but what he'd done to Tennessee, to Indiana, to himself. And there was no going back.

It was done. It couldn't be fixed. Meaning he had no reason to stay. He stayed, they'd all be pretending that life was beautiful all the time. It could be, he supposed, for some people. Other people. He couldn't risk things getting worse because he didn't listen to his gut that was screaming for the open road, the next job, enough cash in his pocket for one more day, then one more night. It was an easy life. A good life.

Except it wasn't anything more than existing. It wasn't living at all.

"I should've looked for you sooner." Tennessee had turned and come back. His hair was disheveled, having been raked with his hands repeatedly, and his eyes were bloodshot and bleary, but dry. "I shouldn't have waited for Indiana to do it. I want to kick my own ass into next week for being too . . . I don't know . . . whatever, to do it."

Dakota found enough of his voice to ask gruffly, "Why didn't you?"

Tennessee stopped, his hands laced on top of his head keeping him in place, as if letting go would have him spiraling into the ground, round and round until he was planted, unmoving. "Because I was afraid of the truth. Afraid I would search and never find you. Afraid I'd find you dead. Afraid you'd be alive and kicking and want nothing to do with me."

"Why would you think that?"

"Why *wouldn't* I think that? Any of it. You weren't in touch. *You weren't in touch.* You couldn't have called? Or dropped a postcard in the mail once a year at Christmas? You couldn't have let us know you were alive? You let us think the worst. You let us believe you'd written us off. That you didn't care. That we didn't matter. Indiana—"

Tennessee cut himself off, his voice raw and strained and finally choked by emotions that had him turning away again, had him walking the length of the barn and standing in the far entrance, as far away as he could get without leaving the premises.

It was a distance all too familiar, one that continued to expand the closer they got, or at least the closer they tried. Dakota wasn't sure what to do, what to say. His brother was right. He hadn't been in touch. He'd left his siblings hanging, while at the same time he'd kept tabs on their lives. Not exactly a fair exchange of information, and they didn't even know.

So, yeah. Tennessee had a point. He and Indiana had deserved more consideration. And Dakota had one more thing to atone for. He was going to need to live a hell of a long life to cover even half the list, he mused, turning at the sound of an approaching car and thankful for the interruption.

Checking the directions on her Mini Cooper's dashboard GPS, Lena made the turn onto Grath Avenue and headed for the barn at the end of the road. Since it was the only building around, she assumed it housed Keller Construction. The company website hadn't said anything about the hours they were open. She didn't even know if they had a regular office; Grath Avenue was pretty much out in the sticks.

Probably stupid to come all this way when she could've talked to the dude working at Bread and Bean. She just didn't want anyone there to hear what she had to say. Since Bliss hadn't been busy this afternoon, Callum hadn't minded her cutting out an hour early. Especially since she'd finished her end-of-the-day cleanup before the day had come to an end. He'd do the mopping once the doors were locked. He always did.

She was probably making a fool of herself, but there was something about seeing how Ellie and the others lived in that house on Dragon Fire Hill that Lena couldn't get over. It was a big house. There was plenty of room. The women weren't tripping over each other to get around. But they were tripping over the flooring, and the flashing, and dodging potholes on the way to pee. And they were locking themselves inside that disaster because it was where they were safe.

Ellie covered her scars with her sleeves and her hair. Becca covered hers with bravado. Frannie hadn't yet found anything to hide behind but her boys, and that wasn't going to work. She needed to find her own strength or she'd be putting them in danger. Lena could tell her. Lena knew.

Thea was a different story. And harder to figure out. She was the pro at camouflaging her emotions. Maybe she'd been out of her personal hell longer than the others. One dinner and a couple of hellos outside their respective shops wasn't enough time for Lena to get a read, though it was obvious there was something between her and Dakota Keller.

It wasn't right that they were living in such crap conditions when Lena could so easily do something about it. So they'd hit bad patches in their lives. Lena and her mother could compare stories until the cows came home. Honestly, it was a wonder the two of them were still alive. She thanked her lucky stars every day that her father wasn't. Cruel? Not a bit. Heartless? Not in her world. Did she miss him? That question was tougher, because it had more than one answer.

Yes, she missed the man who'd sat with her on her bedroom floor and taught her how to play chess, who'd decided she was plenty old enough to choose her own bedtime stories, and had read her Stephen King's *The Stand* at a time when she'd been too young to understand much of the plot. But that was okay. He'd read to her. She'd heard the words in his voice. She'd cuddled close to his side. She'd loved him.

No, she did not miss the man he'd become after whatever it was had ruined his mind: drugs, depression, drink. A combination of all three. The genetic predisposition to madness. Because that's the only word her young self had been able to attach to his actions. The violence that came out of nowhere. The zombielike numbness that followed. The flashes of clarity in his eyes that were lost to his inner anarchy.

So . . . yeah. She knew about lives that started out most excellent and crashed in a way that meant there was no going back. She didn't want to go back, but at least she'd been left a really hefty insurance payment when he finally croaked. Like big time major hefty. Enough that she could go through the rest of her life without working, if that's what she wanted to do. She didn't. She wanted to be normal—colored hair or no—not the poor little rich girl with the crazy old man.

She parked her car, snagged her key fob from the ignition, her phone from the passenger seat, and got out. The barn door was open; now that she was closer, she could see it wasn't the home for cows she'd feared. Dakota was standing inside talking to the dude she assumed was his brother. They looked like family, both tall, both built, both pretty hot in that scruffy, golden-eyed and caramel-brown hair sort of way. She wouldn't kick either one of them out of bed if she liked men. Oh, wait. The brother was wearing a wedding ring.

She looked from one man to the other, thinking she must've walked in on something heavy because there was some major tension going on between them. Dakota was the first one to speak.

"Lena, right?" he asked, pointing at her.

Since they'd exchanged names earlier in the day, big points to him for remembering. "Yep. Lena Mining," she said, introducing herself to the man she didn't know.

"Tennessee Keller," he said, shaking her hand.

"I figured." When his brows drew together in a deep frown, she added, "It's Keller Construction. And I know Dakota. You were the only one left."

"Okay," he said, as if he couldn't wait to split. "I'll leave you two to whatever brings you here."

"What brings me here is a job," she said, before he'd gone more than a step.

"A job?" Dakota was the one to ask the question as his brother took that same step back.

"What kind of a job?" Tennessee asked.

"Construction." Duh. "But it's a little tricky."

Tennessee didn't seem concerned. "I imagine we've run across whatever you can throw at us."

"It's a house. It needs a lot of work. But it's not mine." Here came the tricky part. "I want to pay for the renovations, but I don't want the owner to know where the money came from."

"I don't understand," Tennessee said.

Lena shrugged. "You will when you see the house."

"No, I mean . . ." He waved a hand as if stirring up words. "I don't get the anonymous thing."

Oh. That. "That's my business."

"So where is it?" Dakota asked.

"Here," she said. "In Hope Springs. It's the house on Dragon Fire Hill."

"That's Thea Clark's place," Dakota said, frowning and suddenly hooked.

Finally, Lena mused, and nodded. "But she's not the only one who lives there."

"Right. I've met a couple of the others." Dakota shoved his hands in his pockets and looked from her to his brother and back. "I get the feeling it's some sort of shelter."

Good to know she wasn't the only one whose

thoughts had headed in that direction. "I doubt she'll tell you if it is."

"Makes sense she'd be keeping it off the grid."

"Hold up a sec," Tennessee said, raising one hand, his other at his hip. "You two have me at a disadvantage. I know we're working Thea's coffee shop—"

Lena corrected him. "Espresso bar—"

He waved off the details. "Whatever. What's this about a shelter?"

"I don't know that it is a shelter," she said. "There are three women living there with Thea. The same three women working with her at Bread and Bean. Or two of them anyway. I'm not sure about the third. She's got two little boys."

"They're not Thea's family?" Tennessee asked, looking from Lena to Dakota and back.

She'd about had it with the questions. "I'm not even sure they've known each other all that long, but that's not the point. The point is the house needs work."

"How much work?" Dakota asked, frowning in that way people did when concentrating. "Is it a complete pit?"

Lena shrugged. "Define pit. Holes in the walls. Holes in the floors. It's probably no worse than a frat house."

"But those aren't nineteen-year-old college boys living up there," Dakota said.

"That's the thing," she said. "They pool what

money they have to make ends meet. But they can't afford cheese to go with their bread. They have blankets and sheets and mattresses, but in a couple of rooms, the ones I saw downstairs, those are on the floor."

Dakota spit out some pretty foul words. "And that's where Thea lives."

Lena nodded. She'd been right about him and Thea having a thing. "It's weird, though," she found herself admitting. "The doors aren't going anywhere. Neither are the windows. The house may fall down around them, but no one is getting in."

"I don't want to put a damper on things," Tennessee said after letting that sink in, "but do you know what a construction project like what you're describing will cost?"

Lena didn't care. She wouldn't touch the inheritance she'd received from her grand-parents. That she was saving for the animal shelter. But she kinda liked the irony of using the insurance money she'd received from her old man to help abused women. It was just sitting there. Had been for over ten years. Spending it on herself would be too much like forgiving him.

Not even when hell froze over. "Will a million dollars cover it?"

The two men looked at each other, then back at her. Dakota was the one to finally speak. "You're willing to spend that much on a house that doesn't belong to you?"

"Is it going to cost that much?"

"God, I hope not."

"Then no big deal. I have a friend who lives there."

"She lives there now," Dakota said. "That doesn't mean she'll be living there in five months."

She'd thought about that. Then she'd thought about two little boys whose father had burned down their home while they looked on, and who had holes in the walls of their bedroom. Even if Ellie did leave, Lena couldn't imagine Frannie Charles doing so for a while.

And there would always be another Frannie Charles. And another Robert and James. Yeah. This would be a great legacy for her old man to leave behind. Darryl Mining paying for the sins of abusive bastards everywhere. "I imagine Thea will be. She owns it."

"You know her well, then?" Dakota asked.

Was he prying? Had she read him wrong? "I work next door to her shop, which you know. We've talked. I've eaten supper at the house. Is that well enough for you?"

"But she's not the friend you're doing this for."

"Does it matter who? Or why? Because I don't have a bit of trouble offering my cool mil to someone else. The house needs the work. The women living there deserve better than they've got. I've got the money to make it happen. I mean, it's not burning a hole in my pocket, but yeah. It's a good cause and it feels right. And it will make me a lot happier to spend it on someone I know than donating to a charity who'll waste ninety percent on administrative costs and maybe put a new roof on a house I'll never see."

She waited for Dakota to say something. Then waited for Tennessee. Neither did, so it looked like it was still her turn. "What's it going to be?"

Dakota looked at his brother, watched Tennessee scrub a hand down his face. "We in?"

"It's a big job. Supplies. Man hours. Money."

"Check with Manny? See if he has anyone else he can send you?"

"He sends me everyone he can."

"An ad in the paper then?"

"Manny's guys will be better vetted," Tennessee said. "That could be a big deal considering the client."

Lena had no idea who Manny was, but she wanted an answer. "I didn't come here for a Ping-Pong match, but it sounds like we're on the same page. As long as you can figure out a way to get into the house and see what needs doing and let me know. Not sure how easy that'll be."

"I've got a way in," Dakota said with a nod. "I just need to talk to her first."

❦ Chapter Thirteen ❧

Later that night found Dakota back at Bread and Bean waiting for Thea. His mind was full of his brother and his sister and what Lena Mining had told him and Tennessee about Thea's living conditions.

What he needed was a beer. Or a long drive with his truck windows down and Axl Rose wailing "Sweet Child o' Mine." He wondered what had happened to all of his old cassette tapes. Then he wondered if he was as out of touch with the rest of the world as he felt.

He hadn't been inside but three years, and he'd been almost twenty-two when released, but he hadn't played college baseball with his peers, or attended classes with students his own age. He hadn't gone to clubs hoping to hook up, or concerts to get wasted, or hiking or white-water rafting or parasailing or just goddamn bowling.

Those three years had made a difference. Once he was free, he hadn't known where to start to catch up with anything . . . music, movies, TV, sports. And he hadn't much cared. He'd been too busy breathing, eating. Learning what it felt like to walk a full mile without a fence to stop him, or a guard to yell at him that he'd gone too far.

He'd paid attention later, sure, falling into the

zeitgeist over the years. It was pretty hard not to. Social media shoved it down his throat. He'd binge-watched *Breaking Bad* and *The Walking Dead* like most of America. Taylor Swift wasn't his type, but he would've been hard-pressed not to follow along as she took over the world.

But most of the time he felt . . . unsettled. As if he didn't belong. His own fault. He'd walked out of prison and turned his back on everything he'd known. He had no one to belong to. No place. No history. Robby and the bat and the trial meant he couldn't go back to Round Rock. That had meant leaving Indiana. And Tennessee.

Because as much as he'd tried to convince himself otherwise, they were as big a part of that night as he was. And as long as he continued to see them on a regular basis, he'd never be able to forget.

He wanted more than anything to forget.

A jangle of keys at the front door caught his attention. He stilled and waited, listening as the door opened, as Thea—because he recognized the sound of the key ring as hers—shut the door behind her and pocketed the keys.

"Hey, Clark."

"Good grief. Dakota. You scared me. What are you still doing here?"

For one thing, he was working, but since he was on his back inside the shell of the barista station, that was pretty obvious. For another, he was avoiding both Indiana and Tennessee, and this was the best place to do that since neither could get in.

Mostly, though, he was waiting for Thea. He knew she stopped by on the nights she wasn't the one to lock up at the end of the day. He hadn't seen her since this morning, and Becca had been the last to leave . . . "If you're going to ask me that every time we run into each other, it's going to get old. Especially since you're paying my brother for me to be here."

"I just mean that it's late," she said, standing over him; he could see her from her ankles to her thighs when he glanced at his feet, her baggy knee shorts, her black socks and black shoes, a uniform he hadn't yet worked out, unless Old Navy gave her a bulk discount or something. "I know *what* you're doing here."

He crawled out from beneath the cabinet and rolled up to sit, draping his wrists over his knees, a screwdriver in one hand, a flashlight in the other. "I wasn't in the mood to go home. I had a burger at the Back Alley Pub. Nothing on TV. I already reached the end of the Internet," he said, and she snorted. "Thought I might as well work." He looked her up and down.

She backed into the wall behind her, giving him room. "And why do I have a hard time believing you keep up with what's on TV?"

"Because I don't," he said. "Unless it's football

season. Or that Victoria's Secret runway show thing with all the big shoes and big wings and big—"

"Yeah, yeah. I get the picture." She gave him a look, all judgmental and haughty. "I figured you'd be home making travel plans."

Home. Was that what the cottage on Three Wishes Road was? Because that was not what it felt like. Neither did Hope Springs. Even after a year. "I'm about to ditch them just to keep Indiana and Tennessee off my case."

"They love you," she said, frowning, as if his siblings' emotions were the yardstick he was supposed to use to plan the rest of his life.

"And I love them," he said, handing her the flashlight. "But if Indiana wanted to up and move to, well, Indiana, I'd throw her a party."

She flicked the flashlight on, flicked it off. "If Indiana were to move, she'd have a reason that made sense."

He tossed the screwdriver at his toolbox and missed. "Because being unhappy here doesn't?"

"Actually, no," she said, holding his gaze as he got to his feet, back to flicking the flashlight on and off, on and off. He grabbed it away from her. "Unhappy is a state of mind. Moving's not going to help it."

And now it was amateur shrink hour. "You know that because you're a licensed psychologist?"

206

"It hasn't helped you yet, has it?" she asked, her question serving as an answer. "All the moving?"

"I never said I was unhappy living elsewhere." He squatted in front of the toolbox, stowing away the screwdriver and flashlight both, thinking he hadn't been particularly happy anywhere for a very long time.

"Were you?" she asked because she was Thea and couldn't let it go.

"I don't know." He let the toolbox lid slam shut. Then he shrugged and stood. "I never really thought about it."

She was still leaning against the wall. And he was almost right in front of her. And it seemed way too close for them to be standing when the idea of kissing her to put a stop to this conversation was rattling around in his mind. Also the idea of kissing her just because that's what he wanted to do. They never should've broken up . . .

She responded with a huff. "So you were just struck with the urge to move."

Struck was pretty damn accurate. Like a fist to the gut. Or a bolt of lightning. He'd given notice and then he'd gone. Just like that. Every time. He bent for his toolbox, hefted it up like a blockade between them. "New place. New people. New food. Sure. Why not?"

She pushed off the wall and moved to the table where she picked up a loose receipt and slipped it into a folder. "Did you tell me where you worked as a barista?"

"Idaho," he said, setting the toolbox next to the kitchen door.

"Why did you leave?"

"It was too cold."

"Where did you go?"

"Montana," he said, laughing at the irony before she could, though he did catch her smiling.

"Was that the ranch?"

He shoved his hands in his pockets, leaned a shoulder against the jamb. "Yep. Wrangled cattle."

"Outdoors," she said, finally looking up from the folder. "In Montana," she added, tapping the edge against the table. "Because being a barista in Idaho was too cold."

He shrugged, wishing this didn't feel so natural, this back and forth, this sense of things being right and comfortable and normal. "I never said it made sense."

She dropped the folder into her messenger bag then sat in the table's folding chair to shut down her laptop. "Did you tell me where you were when the PI found you?"

"Indiana." He watched her stretch to unplug the cord from the wall, bend to slide the machine into its sleeve in the bag, reach for the pencils she'd left scattered about, the highlighter, the Post-it flags.

"Doing what?"

Another minute and she'd be packed. She'd have no reason to stay. Their conversation would be over. He wasn't ready for that to happen. Besides, he needed to talk to her about the house. "Some of what I'm doing now. Construction."

She set her bag in her lap and looked at him. "Did you have friends in all those places?"

"I knew people."

"Did you date?" she asked, her expression tightening in a way that surprised him.

It made him almost hesitant to answer, but he did. "I saw women."

"You slept with women."

He shrugged, shifted his weight to his other hip, ready for a change of subject. "I made them happy. They made me happy."

"Aha." She narrowed her eyes, a sort of I told you so, and pointed. "So you haven't always been unhappy."

"I've never been unhappy when I'm having sex," he said, but because he didn't want this to devolve into a never-ending game of twenty questions, or a discourse on his sex life, he moved them back to the original topic. "I don't know that I'm unhappy really. I'm just not . . . happy. It's been coming on stronger for a while. And it's gotten a lot worse since I've been in Hope Springs. But it's been like this for the past decade of my life. Longer, really."

Neither one of them said anything for a long,

tense moment, Dakota wondering what in the hell was wrong with his mouth that all this crap kept pouring out. Knowing it was because of the woman looking at him as if the agreement they'd made to not discuss their pasts had been a ridiculous endeavor from the get-go and they'd been right to give it up.

They *were* each other's past.

Yes, they'd been teenagers, and prone to exaggerated emotions, but that didn't mean those feelings had been baseless or false. It just meant they'd been less capable of dealing with them.

Then again, they weren't doing such a great job now.

"So it's not my fault," she said, her tone of voice soft, pensive. "This need you have to leave."

Where was that coming from? "Why would it be your fault?"

"What I said to you the other day. About you ruining me for other men." She frowned down at her bag, plucked at a loose bit of stitching on the flap. "I shouldn't have ever said that."

Best he recalled, she'd said it after he'd told her he was cutting out, but in light of his current musings, he was curious. He pushed off the doorjamb, moved to stand at the end of the long table, keeping the six feet of office and coffee supplies between them. "Is it true?"

"Not those words. Not . . . ruin."

Well, that wasn't much help. "But the senti-ment?"

She took a deep breath, slouched over her bag as she blew it out, and sat like that, hunched in on herself but looking at him, vulnerable. "I haven't been with anyone that I haven't compared to you in one way or another. Is that what you want to hear?"

He dropped his gaze from hers, crossing his arms and frowning down at the table's wood-grain surface. "You do remember that I was only seventeen, eighteen back then. A kid."

She nodded, laughed softly. "Age is just a number."

The throaty humor in her laugh twisted him up. "Are *you* happy? I mean, from what I've seen, your life's not exactly . . . conventional."

"I think you have that market cornered." She got to her feet, setting her bag on the table and checking the closures. "I haven't been to prison. Nor have I lived in a dozen different places and held down just as many jobs in that many years."

"Then we're both unconventional. Just in our own ways."

"Not sure that makes me feel any better," she said.

Because it would mean they were meant to be? A perfect match? Two crazy kids who'd survived some rough spots only to find each other again?

Man, he did not need his thoughts to go wandering in that direction. "Actually, I'm glad I caught you. I wanted to run something by you."

"Something more than switching out coffee vendors?"

He'd made the suggestion recently after a particularly bitter pot, but he'd been thinking less about her market research than his own preferences, so he ignored the dig. "The house you're living in. The one up on Dragon Fire Hill." As if there were another.

Her head came up slowly. "What about it?"

Here's the wind-up . . . "I know from the rumor mill that it had been empty awhile," he said, choosing his words carefully.

"It had," she said, going about her business.

The pitch . . . "I also heard that vagrants had taken advantage. And that it wasn't in the best of shape."

"It wasn't," she said, then added, "It's not. It's up to code, and it passed inspection, though even I have trouble believing that sometimes."

And swing! "Then you wouldn't mind if Keller Construction came in and fixed it up."

She huffed at that, hooking her bag's strap over her shoulder. "I don't have money to have it fixed up."

"You don't need to. We have it covered."

"I'm not going to let you work on my house without getting paid," she said dismissively, heading for the door behind him. "Charity's not my thing."

He turned and leaned against the table. "We will be getting paid. Just not by you."

That stopped her. "What are you talking about?"

He wasn't exactly sure what to say, or how to say it. He couldn't imagine being called a guardian angel would sit well with Lena Mining, but he couldn't think of a better description. "The costs are being covered by an anonymous benefactor."

"Uh-uh. No way." She was shaking her head, loose strands of her topknot flipping back and forth. Her laugh was bitter. Her hand white-knuckle tight around the strap of her bag. "Besides, that's still charity, and I'm not going to make it that easy for someone to get their clutches into us."

Us? "You mean someone like an ex."

"Exactly like an ex," she said, waving her free hand expansively "Ellie's, in fact, could easily afford to do this, and is exactly the sort of person who would do it, then hold it over Ellie's head. And Ellie's *so* easily swayed by random acts of kindness and so *so* susceptible to guilt."

Ellie wasn't the one he was interested in. "And your ex?"

She hesitated a moment, as if needing to weigh her words carefully and find a truth that worked. "At one point, yes. Now, I couldn't say."

"You don't need to worry," he said after that had settled. Sort of. "It's not anyone's ex."

She was back to choking her bag's strap again, this time with both hands. "If you know who it is, then tell me, because I can't think of anyone who'd be that invested in my house."

It wasn't about the house as much as its inhabitants, though he couldn't explain that either. He shook his head. "I can't. That's the only string that's attached."

"Thanks, but no thanks," she said. Then she turned to go.

Crap. He needed a convincing argument, a line of reasoning she couldn't refute. "You know it's going to cost a small fortune to cool that place this summer without proper insulation. And leaky pipes mean wasted water and wasted cash."

She stood facing away from him, her head falling back on her shoulders as she huffed and shook it and muttered beneath her breath. "We'll make it work. It's what we do."

"But that's the thing. You don't have to." He raked his hands through his hair, then settled them at his hips. "C'mon, Clark. You and Becca and Ellie are going to be working your asses off here with the coffee and the bread and the cleaning and ordering and organizing, not to mention dealing with all the locals who'll be hanging out, bending your ear all day."

"So?" she asked, turning toward him again, her brows arched, her exasperation clear.

He felt like he was reaching now when he knew the hard sell wasn't going to work with her. She had always needed to make her own way. "Do you really want to go home and flip a coin to see who gets to use the hot water to shower? Or eat cold cuts for dinner because the microwave keeps throwing the breaker? Or wear the same clothes the next day because the dryer's on the fritz?"

"You're talking appliances." She said it as if he was wasting her time. "I can replace appliances. Eventually. And Frannie cooks and does the laundry, so we're covered there, and what's wrong with cold cuts?" Then she asked, "Anything else?" and waited.

Maybe softball was a better way to go, he mused, frowning down while he gathered his thoughts. "You don't have to be a martyr, Thea. Sometimes it's okay to let people do nice things for you. Not all gifts have strings attached. Not everybody wants something."

When he looked up again, he found her shaking her head, her eyes watering, her shoulders slumped as if she were about to collapse beneath some unbearable weight. He stayed where he was, wanting more than anything to go to her, to pull her close, to wrap her up in his arms and carry the burden for her. But he knew she would never let him. And so he stayed.

"This is going to cause all kinds of problems."

Not exactly the reaction he'd expected, but considering his suspicions that the house was more that it appeared to be . . . "You're not paying for anything. You're not arranging for anything. What problems besides inconvenience could you possibly have?"

She twisted up her mouth as if the words wouldn't behave. "I can't have strange men in and out of the house. Not with the women there."

"Strange as in men you haven't yet met? Or strange as in weirdos? Because I can guarantee they're not going to be any weirder than me."

"It's just . . ." She took a deep breath, shuddered it out. "Frannie, especially, isn't comfortable around men she doesn't know."

"We'll make sure everybody meets everybody before things get started. Trust me, Clark. The men Tennessee hires are good guys," he said. "If there's anything in any of their pasts that looks otherwise, it will have a legit reason for being there."

"Like you and the baseball bat and Indiana?" she asked.

"Yeah. Like that," he said, grinding down on the words, his jaw aching.

"I don't know. God." She reached up to rub at the back of her neck. "The whole anonymity thing. It makes me twitchy. And the money. You haven't even seen the house. No one has seen the house save for Lena who works at Bliss next door. How could anyone know what they're getting into? We're talking a small fortune here. A large fortune, if you get right down to it."

"I know," Dakota said, though the work wouldn't require but a fraction of what Lena had offered. Hell, with that kind of money they could raze the place and rebuild from the ground up. But he and his brother had talked after she'd left and agreed to pinch every penny. They wouldn't take advantage of her generosity. And the business would absorb the cost of the labor. "Just like you know you'd be a fool to turn this down."

She nodded. "Let me talk to everyone first. See what they have to say."

Now he was the one feeling twitchy. "It's your house, isn't it?"

"It is," she said, backing into the kitchen's swinging door. "But it's not just my life."

❦ *Chapter Fourteen* ❧

Bringing the subject of the home repairs to the table wasn't as easy as that of Butters Bakery. Buying the bakery would benefit everyone living at the house on Dragon Fire Hill. So would having Keller Construction do the renovations to the structure that wasn't quite falling apart around them but was close.

The problem was the bakery wouldn't require a bunch of strangers to tramp around the house. The renovations couldn't be done any other way. Dakota trusted Tennessee's judgment and Tennessee trusted his employees. That didn't make Thea feel a whole lot better. And she wasn't feeling good at all about the anonymous benefactor thing.

It was going to come back and bite her in the butt. She just knew it. Yet how could she turn down the chance to give the women living with her now, and others who might come later, a place worth calling home for as long as they were there? Yes, a home could be as simple as four walls and a roof overhead, but did that roof have to leak, as theirs had been doing since a storm in February sent an icy tree branch crashing down?

The hardwood floors were serviceable but they were scuffed and pitted, and mopping did nothing but dull them more. She would kill for a new kitchen sink, stainless steel to replace the chipped porcelain, and a new faucet with a spray head that worked. And though the appliances were perfectly fine, even if the fridge motor was a bit loud, they weren't the least bit energy efficient. Same with the central air and heat.

She'd spent the biggest chunk of her initial budget on safety concerns, the doors, the windows, the equipment for the security monitoring. Though she hadn't been a homeowner before, she was savvy enough to research maintenance and repair costs. She'd known what she was facing buying the place as is. Then she'd had to prioritize. Cosmetics could wait. Saving money couldn't . . . and that had driven her decision.

She would bring the subject of the home repairs to the table, but she'd already called Tennessee on her drive home to accept the Keller Construction —and her guardian angel's—offer. Whatever the price she had to pay down the road, she'd deal with it then. In the meantime, the women in her care would be comfortable.

Because of her hour at the shop with Dakota, she'd been later than usual getting home, and Becca and Ellie had a big pot of spaghetti ready to eat. James was helping Frannie set the table. Robert was asleep on one of the chairs in the corner of the big room. Thea nodded toward him. "Is he feeling okay?"

Frannie glanced over, a concerned frown on her face. "I think so. He's not feverish, so I don't think he's coming down with anything. He woke up way too early this morning, and it threw off his day. He exhausted himself playing. He needs to eat, but I'm not sure I want to wake him."

Thea knew zero about being a mother, but it sounded like Frannie had things under control. She ruffled James's hair as she headed to the counter for the pitcher of sun tea, then returned to the freezer to fill glasses with ice. Becca carried the spaghetti to the table. Ellie followed with a loaf of fresh, crusty Italian bread.

It was one of Thea's favorite meals. Becca's one-pot spaghetti recipe was so simple and absolutely stellar. Scooped up with Ellie's bread . . . *mmm-mmm-mmm*. Usually, Thea had seconds. Tonight, she was having a hard time getting through the first bowl she'd dished up, and an equal amount of trouble paying attention to the conversation.

Ellie was the one who noticed. "Goodness, Ms. Clark. What's going on with you? I've never seen you not eat spaghetti the way you're not eating it tonight. The crust on the bread's not quite the right texture, and I'm sorry for that, but it still tastes good."

"Yeah," Becca said, tearing a chunk from the loaf and mopping the sauce from the bottom of her bowl with exaggerated savagery. "I'm going to get a complex over here. Me and Ellie both. Not to mention the sun. You haven't even touched your tea."

Thea grinned. She loved these girls. Adored them. It wasn't fair for her to keep secrets. She smiled at both, smiled at Frannie, picked up her tea and drank. Then she wound her fork through her spaghetti, her eyes on her food as she said, "We're going to have some people in and out of the house the next few days. A couple of weeks at the outside, and probably not that."

Frannie pulled in a sharp breath, looking from James, as he shoveled spaghetti from his bowl to his mouth, to Robert where he slept, his cheeks red, his blond curls damp against his head. She got up and crossed the room. "What people? Why?"

Becca snorted. "Great. People. We all know how much I love people."

Ellie just frowned and studied the hunk of bread she held in both hands.

"I don't want any of you to panic," Thea said, though judging by the reception of her audience, it was probably too late. "You don't have anything to worry about, or to fear. There's just some work that needs to be done on the house, and a local contractor is going to take care of it."

"Last I heard, we were going to have to live with the work needing to be done because we didn't have the money to take care of it," Becca said, tossing the last bite of her bread into her bowl, then changing her mind, frowning, and grabbing it up.

"We don't," Thea said. "But it seems we have a guardian angel who wants to make sure we have toilets that flush, and sinks that drain, and a roof that doesn't sprout a new leak with every storm, and flooring that doesn't curl up at the corners."

"Goodness," Ellie said, her voice shaky. "That's some guardian angel."

Thea couldn't argue with that.

"You don't know who it is?" Becca asked. "Who's footing the bill?"

Thea shook her head. "Not a clue."

"What about strings?"

The question came from Frannie, catching Thea by surprise. Frannie's concerns usually pertained to her boys. To see her taking an interest in the house was encouraging. "There are none."

"Not now, maybe," Frannie said, hefting a sleeping Robert onto her shoulder and returning to her seat. "But what about later?"

"I'm not exactly comfortable with this secret-squirrel thing either," Becca said. "But if the contractor is getting paid, I'm having a hard time seeing a downside. It's not like he's going to come take out the new toilets and bring back the old. I'm assuming it's Keller Construction?"

Thea gave Becca a nod, then turned to Frannie. "What do you think might happen?"

"I don't know," Frannie said, reaching over to brush James's hair from his forehead. He was more intent on his food than the conversation. Robert, whom she held on her lap, had yet to wake fully, his feathery lashes drifting down over his sleepy eyes. "It just makes me uncomfortable. It's like the thing with the bakery—"

"Do you think it might be Bobby?" Ellie asked out of the blue, the bread she'd been holding completely shredded, the circles beneath her eyes the same color as the periwinkle barrettes clipped at her temples. "The guardian angel? Could Bobby be doing this? To try to get to me?"

"Don't think that. Just don't," Becca said, her voice harsh and insistent as she reached over and squeezed Ellie's hand. "No one is going to get to you. I won't let that happen."

Ellie bobbed her head as she inhaled, then wrapped an arm around Becca's neck and pulled her close. Becca patted Ellie's shoulder, used to her demonstrative nature as they all were, until Ellie let her go. She dabbed her napkin beneath her eyes.

"I don't know what I'd do without you. Without any of you," Ellie said, looking around the table, her gaze landing on Thea. "It's safe? You promise?"

Thea crossed every body part she could that she wasn't screwing up these women's lives. "Dakota promised me the money is not coming from anyone any of us have a history with."

"And you believe him?" Frannie asked, dropping a kiss to Robert's head.

"I believe him absolutely. I know what he's capable of, and what he's not. I don't think I've ever known a better man in my life," she said, realizing as she glanced around the table, as she met the concerned and frightened and determined gazes of the women depending on her, that the truth was she hardly knew this Dakota Keller at all.

Cradling a cup of hot tea in both hands, Ellie crossed her legs beneath her in one of the kitchen's cushy, plaid club chairs, brought out of her midnight musings by Thea walking into the room. Ellie had a library copy of *The Hunger Games* open on one thigh, but she hadn't made it very far into the book. She liked it. She could see why Lena liked it. She and Katniss were strong and capable. They could deal with the unexpected.

Ellie could not.

Thea flopped down in the chair beside her, tucking her heels to her hips and pulling her sleeping shirt over her knees until she looked like she was sitting in a tent. A big white tent with tiny little penguins sliding around the background as if on a slope of snow. They were black, and wore red and blue scarves and hats, and had bright yellow beaks. They looked happy.

Ellie did her best to be one of them and smiled.

"Can't sleep?" Thea asked.

Ellie shrugged. She hadn't really tried.

"That was really nice of Lena to bring all that food. I think there may be enough left that we can make another meal out of it. The cheese, at least. We'll have to open a couple cans of our own if we want more soup."

"It *was* nice," Ellie said, bringing her cup to her mouth to sip. The tea was chamomile, which she usually enjoyed, but tonight it tasted like pale boiled water. "*She's* nice. But I think I messed things up."

Thea curled her hands around her bare toes and frowned. "What things?"

It was so stupid, and she knew better, but this happened every time anyway. When was she going to learn *not* to do what came so easy to her? When was she going to learn that not everyone appreciated the fact that she wore her heart on her sleeve? That she cried and laughed and touched, hugging and kissing and holding hands . . .

She shook her head, sighed. "You know how I get all touchy-feely and emotional, and she was *so* amazing talking to little James, and it just made me so happy for him to have that attention. I mean it's not like Frannie ever mistreats him, but he's so curious, and she's so cautious, which is totally understandable—"

"Ellie. What do you think you messed up?"

"James had asked Lena about the rings in her eyebrow so she took them out for him to see. This was all before you got there. Anyway, I showed her to the bathroom so she could use the mirror to put them back in." Ellie closed her eyes and swallowed. "And I kissed her."

"You kissed her." Thea repeated the words, not judging or anything, but as if she wanted to be clear.

"It wasn't a come-on or whatever," Ellie hurried to say. "I only meant it as a thank-you."

Holding her gaze, Thea said, "But you think she took it to mean you're interested in her."

"I don't know how she took it." Ellie dropped her head back against the cushion and closed her eyes. "She didn't move. She didn't say anything. She didn't react at all."

Several long seconds passed before Thea asked softly, "Are you? Interested in her?"

"I am," Ellie said, her hands tightening around her cup. "I really, really am."

"For what it's worth, I don't think you messed up anything. She seemed to have a great time at dinner."

Ellie lifted her head, pushing her glasses up her nose. "She didn't seem uncomfortable? Like she wanted to run as far away from me as she could?"

Thea smiled. "She must've really left you rattled if you didn't even notice how much fun she was having."

"Was she?" Ellie wanted nothing more than to believe that, but oh, it was hard. "I'm so glad. She seems . . . I don't know. Lonely, maybe?"

"What do you know about her?"

"Besides that she works at Bliss?" she asked, and Thea nodded. "She lived with her mother in Kyle until recently. Her mother is a midwife. She's taking some college accounting classes. That's about it. Oh. She likes tomato soup and grilled cheese sandwiches for dinner as much as I do. And she brought all the right cheeses. Did you notice that?"

"That's what good friends do. They pay attention. Kinda like I know how you're pretending to like that chamomile tea."

"You can tell?" she asked, looking down at the weak liquid.

Thea nodded toward Ellie's drink. "You were frowning into your cup when I came in. And you had your mouth all twisted up like you were drinking cat piss. And really. Is there much difference between the two?"

"Ew, Thea." Ellie shuddered at the thought. "But you're right. Not about the cat thing, but that I was pretending. I've never liked chamomile tea."

"Then why do you drink it?"

"Because Bobby did. She swore by the benefits of its calming effects," Ellie said, holding Thea's gaze as the irony bubbled up inside her and they burst into laughter at the same time.

"You sure she wasn't sweetening it with something out of a flask?" Thea asked.

"She probably used it to put out her cigarettes. Then drank the ashes. It would explain a lot," Ellie said, catching herself rubbing at the scars on her arm and sobering. "Are you positive she's not the mysterious benefactor? Those messages she used to leave on my phone, about finding me no matter where I was, about making me pay . . ."

Thea slid her legs out of her shirt, the big paisley-print chair squeaking as she leaned forward, squeezing Ellie's knee. "Dakota knows who it is, and he would have no reason to know Bobby or Todd or Frannie's ex or Becca's Dez. It's no one connected to us. Not like that anyway."

"But why would someone *not* connected to one of us make such an offer? It's not like the house is a blight on Main Street or anything. No one's going to see it unless they come up here, and no one does, which is the whole point." The idea of Bobby finding out where she was . . . Ellie's stomach turned over, and she pressed a hand against it, waiting for it to calm. "There's got to be a huge amount of money involved, and I just can't imagine someone spending that without a good reason. A personal reason. It just doesn't make sense."

"I've been thinking about that," Thea said,

sliding her legs to the side in her chair. "Dakota's sister was one of my closest friends when we were teenagers. She lives here now, and she married into money." Thea shrugged. "We finally caught up with each other the other morning."

"You told her about this place?"

"That I'd bought the house, yes, and that it wasn't in the best shape, but that was all. We were talking about her new house and her old cottage, so it wasn't a big deal. I wouldn't doubt if she's behind this."

That would make sense. "She wouldn't want you to know?"

"We haven't been in touch in years. She might be afraid I'd think her presumptuous."

Ellie thought for a minute. "She knows you. She knows Dakota. She has money. But I still wish we knew. I'd be a lot more comfortable—" She paused on that thought, another taking its place. "I guess we'll all be a lot more comfortable, won't we? Once it's all done."

"That's the plan," Thea said, getting to her feet. "I'm going to turn in. You coming?"

"I'll be up as soon as I rinse this cat piss from my cup."

That made Thea grin. "And you'll stop worrying about things with Lena? At least until you can talk to her again?"

"I'll try."

"Ellie."

"Yes, I'll stop worrying," she said, though she could tell by Thea's face she didn't believe her. Hard to blame her when Ellie didn't believe herself.

❧ *Chapter Fifteen* ❧

Nothing like ripping off the bandage, Thea mused the next morning, standing on the porch of the house on Dragon Fire Hill and watching Dakota's Keller Construction truck make its way up the long narrow drive. It was only wide enough for one car at a time. Thea wasn't sure if that was a good thing or bad.

Frannie almost never went anywhere, so she didn't need transportation. Ellie usually rode her bicycle into town. Becca had an old hatchback that was only a mile or two from giving up the ghost. Thea's Subaru was functional, reliable, and the vehicle that did most of the heavy lifting for everyone. She even had two car seats stored in the front room's coat closet for the rare occasion when Robert or James needed to see their pediatrician, Dr. Barrow.

There was never any shuffling of cars to worry about. She supposed widening the drive should go on her to-do mountain. It might be nice to have room for one vehicle going out, and one vehicle coming in. Except nobody ever did.

She brought her coffee mug to her mouth just as the door opened behind her and Becca walked out.

"And so it begins," the other woman said, bouncing her keys in her palm.

Strangely, Thea was just as nervous when she had no reason to be. "Why don't you wait to go to work? Just in case Dakota has any questions?"

Becca looked over with a frown. "You can answer anything I can."

"I know." Becca was right. Thea's request was completely lame. "But it's going to be hard on Frannie. She'll feel better if we're all here."

"Sure," Becca said, pocketing her keys as Dakota pulled the truck to a stop. "Is he going to be running the crew?"

"I don't know," Thea said, breathing out as relief washed through her.

"That's going to be the toughest part for Frannie. Dakota is one thing . . ."

"It can't be helped. Not if we want to have this done."

As if they'd heard Dakota arrive, both Ellie and Frannie appeared in the doorway, Frannie asking, "Who's that?" while keeping James close to her side. The boy was yawning and rubbing his eyes; in Frannie's arms, Robert sucked on his thumb and dozed.

"His name is Dakota Keller," Thea said, watching him climb from the truck. He wore his usual uniform of work boots, jeans, and a T-shirt. This one was olive drab, and even at this distance, she knew it would give his brown eyes the appearance of gold. The fact that she could imagine it so clearly . . . This was a mistake. It was the only thing she could think as she studied him. He was everywhere she turned now, leaving her heart with a constant, anxious ache.

Shoving his hair from his face with one hand, he approached the house, looking up and catching her gaze. The ache worsened, spreading to encompass her entire chest until she couldn't breathe. He smiled then, as if he liked the idea of her waiting for him, or her welcoming him. Then he nodded at Becca, and raised a hand after Ellie did the same.

Thea finished off her coffee, then set her mug on the porch. She took two steps down before he could climb up. "Frannie Charles, this is Dakota Keller. He works for Keller Construction. I told you about them at dinner last night. They're the firm doing the renovations. Dakota's here to take a look at the house."

Frannie bobbed her head up and down, a quick but nervous understanding.

Then James stepped forward, his feet in a pair of too large purple Crocs. "Did you come here to burn the house down?"

His mother gasped, and snapped out, "James," the sudden sound startling Robert. He let out a cry, and she soothed him with one hand, reaching for James with the other.

Dakota looked from James to Thea as if not knowing what to say, so once Frannie had the boy by the shoulder, Thea dropped down in front of him. "Of course he's not here to burn down the house," she said, wanting to turn back the clock, to call this off. Such a big, big mistake.

But then Dakota moved behind her, squatting at James's level to say, "I'm going to fix it."

"All of it?" James asked, his eyes wide. "Like the holes in the floor and the potty that leaks and the blankets that aren't warm?"

"James, that's enough," Frannie said, squeezing his shoulder and pulling him even harder against her while backing toward the door.

Dakota cleared his throat, and Thea swore she heard him mutter a curse before asking James, "Would you like to see my toolbox?"

"Can I?" James asked him, then looked up to ask his mother. "Can I?"

Thea got to her feet, dreading Frannie's answer and her son's disappointment. She was seconds from telling Dakota she'd changed her mind, but was stopped by his saying to James, "I'll be at my truck. If your mom says it's okay, come on down. But if she'd rather you not, well, it was nice to meet you James." Then he stood. "And you, Ms. Charles. You've got two good-looking boys here." And with that, he brushed by Thea,

233

his chest against her shoulder, and walked back the way he'd come. Thea blew out all the air in her lungs, having felt as if she was going to explode.

"Please, Mommy, can I? I've never in a million years seen a real toolbox."

"I don't know," Frannie said, lifting her gaze to Thea's. "You think he meant it? He really won't mind?"

"He won't," Thea said, the words shaky with emotion she swore she hadn't signed up for, but couldn't hold back if she tried. "I'll walk down with him. He'll be fine."

Of course James beat both Thea and Frannie to the truck and was waiting—not so patiently—when they finally arrived. Thea mouthed, "Thank you," when she caught Dakota's gaze, and got a brief nod in response. From somewhere beneath the bumper he let down a retractable step, then opened the tailgate and showed James how to climb up.

With Frannie's permission—and her help—James did, shuffling with tiny careful steps across the bed to where Dakota waited. He directed the boy to sit on the wheel well while he unlocked and opened the toolbox. Then he lifted out two different screwdrivers and returned to where James sat. He hunkered down in front of him.

"Do you know what these are?" he asked.

James nodded. "They're for turning screws round and round to put broken chairs back together."

Thea looked away from Dakota's searching gaze, glancing briefly at Frannie who had her hand on the back of Robert's head, her lips against his ear, and tears in her eyes. The fact that her son knew such a thing . . .

"It's a screwdriver, right," Dakota said, having cleared his throat. "You use it to drive screws into walls for holding pictures, or for fixing things that have come apart. Now look at the ends. See how this one is straight across, and this one looks like a little star?"

James touched the tip of both while Dakota dug into his pocket and pulled out two screws.

"Okay. Here are two screws." He tapped the top of both. "One of them has a straight line on the top, and one has—"

"A star!"

"Then which screwdriver are you going to use for which screw?"

The boy thought about it a minute, his little fist beneath his little chin, then said, "The star goes with the star, and the straight goes with the straight."

Dakota nodded. "One more thing. This screwdriver is called a flat head. And this one is called—"

"A star head!"

Dakota smiled at that, his expression wreaking havoc with Thea's heart. "That would make sense, wouldn't it? But it's actually called a

Phillips-head. It's named after the man who invented it. His name was Henry Phillips. Like your name is James Charles."

A frown creased James's brow. "And what's your name again?"

"Dakota Keller."

"Dakota is like the United States."

A grin lit up Dakota's face. "You're right. There is a state called North Dakota. And another called South Dakota. Want to hear something funny?"

"Yes!"

"My brother's name is Tennessee. And my sister's name is Indiana."

"Those are United States, *too,*" James said emphatically, gesturing with both hands.

"They are indeed."

Finally, Frannie stepped forward. "Come on, James. Mr. Keller needs to get to work, and you and Robert need to have breakfast."

"But I want to help Mr. Koda screw the house back together!"

"I'm not going to be doing any work today, James. I'm just going to look around and write notes about everything that needs to be fixed."

"I can help with that, too. I know where all the broken parts are. I can show you."

"Well, that's up to your mom," he said, turning his gaze toward Frannie.

She reached for Thea's hand and squeezed. "I wouldn't want him to be in the way."

"I'm going to have a lot to look at. It'll take a couple of walk-throughs. How about he hangs out first time around?"

"That sounds like a good idea," Thea said, hoping Frannie would take the leap of faith. "I'll be with them, too. I'll make sure James is safe."

Her use of the word is what finally convinced Frannie. She nodded, stepping toward the truck bed to help James down. She wrapped an arm around him and gave him a big kiss before swinging him to the ground. Then she looked at Dakota tentatively. "Does he have time for breakfast first?"

"Sure. I need to gather my things."

She nodded, taking hold of James's hand and walking with him back to the house. James chattered about screwdrivers until out of Thea's earshot.

"What things are you gathering?" she asked, rubbing a hand over the back of her neck and trying to still the gyroscope of her emotions. Seeing Dakota's patient engagement with James who needed the attention so desperately . . .

Dakota held up a pencil. "His eating breakfast seemed important to her. Or else she wanted to get him out of my clutches and back to the house."

"There was probably a little bit of that, too," Thea said. "You were amazing with him."

"He's just a little boy. There's not a lot to it."

"For the last few months, he's been around four

adult women. Being in your truck, you showing him your tools . . ." She shook her head. "You should've seen the look on his face."

"He doesn't have a dad?" he asked, frowning.

"Not anymore."

"That's a shame."

"In his case? Not really."

He jumped down from the truck bed, shoved his pencil behind his ear. "Why in the world would he ask if I was going to burn down the house?"

She looked toward the Charles family, wondering if after she told him, he'd be sorry he asked. "Because his father burned down theirs."

Sitting on the stool in front of his brother's drafting table, Dakota stared at the paperwork Tennessee had left him to review. Most of the notes were quotes on materials for the house on Dragon Fire Hill. After Dakota's visit there yesterday, Tennessee hadn't wasted any time. But Dakota hadn't gotten through but one or two of them before his mind drifted to Thea.

The state of her house was appalling. He was trying to think when he'd seen worse. At least worst that wasn't a shack in the woods used by hunters. Or the cardboard boxes homeless men wedged together under overpasses to keep out the rain.

Okay. It wasn't that bad. The house was old. But the problems went a lot deeper than the cosmetic Lena Mining had led him and Tennessee to believe.

He couldn't get a handle on the group of women living there. Becca had told him some of her story, but he knew nothing about Ellie's. Thea had hinted at a bad relationship, one she'd taken too long to leave, but she hadn't said anything about what she'd done with her life since high school. She'd bought the house less than a year ago, but as far as he could tell, she'd done nothing to repair any of the damage she was living with.

And the boy. James. Wow. Just a few little words and the kid had ripped out Dakota's heart. Then to learn the truth from Thea? No wonder Frannie Charles had kept her sons close and looked at Dakota as if he'd come to ruin the new life she was making.

Ruin. Man, if Thea hadn't put a new spin on what he'd always assumed that word to mean. Seemed a man could ruin a woman in more than one way. He wanted to find the bastard who'd ruined Frannie Charles. Find him and do to him what he'd done to Robby Hunt in high school.

Too bad he no longer kept a baseball bat handy.

Thank goodness he'd had errands to run after leaving Thea's house this morning. Double thank goodness she'd already come and gone from Bread and Bean when he finally showed. He wasn't ready to talk to her. He couldn't talk to her until he'd made some sense out of what he'd seen. So far all he'd done was find more questions than answers.

The sound of wheels on the gravel driveway brought his head up. The sedan pulled to a stop behind his truck, and Manny Balleza got out. He ambled into the barn, and asked, "You quit answering your phone for a reason?"

"It's in the truck." Dakota gestured in that direction. "Sorry."

Manny nodded, coming closer. "Figured since you weren't at the coffee shop you might be here."

"Must be important," Dakota said, happy for the interruption. He needed to get his mind off of Thea.

"Not as important as it is bugging me," the other man replied.

"Well?"

He had to wait for Manny to climb onto the extra stool, adjust his jacket, and find the words. "What do you know about the black woman who works at the coffee shop? Becca, I think?"

"Not much," he said, then for no reason he understood added a small white lie. "No more than I know about any of the women working there."

Manny looked off toward the back of the barn as he said, "You do know they don't just work there, right? That they've got something else connecting them?"

Dakota thought for a minute. If anyone else had asked, he probably wouldn't have answered. The women had found each other and what they needed to feel safe. That included privacy.

But this was Manny. And Dakota couldn't think of anything he'd ever held back from the man who'd drawn him as an assignment. Then gone above and beyond to keep him off the grid.

He waited for Manny to look at him again, then offered a vague response. "You figure that out for yourself, or Becca tell you?"

Manny snorted. "Becca's not that forthcoming."

At that, Dakota laughed. "Give it some time. She may surprise you."

But Manny wasn't that patient. "Back to my original question. What do you know about her?"

Dakota thought about the conversation he'd had with Becca York the morning after she'd clotheslined him. He might trust Manny with *his* life, but this was Becca's life. Becca's damage. And so he said, "She's strong as hell."

Manny frowned. "Physically? Or is that some code or metaphor or something?"

Dakota slapped at a piece of paper threatening to blow off the table. "Before we'd even been introduced she tried to choke me to death."

This time it was Manny who laughed. "I would love to have seen that."

"Have you talked to her? Tried to find out what you want to know from the source?"

"Yeah," Manny said, crossing his arms as he nodded. "She's a little bit defensive."

"A little?" Dakota sputtered out the question, glad he didn't have a mouth full of coffee.

Manny shrugged. "Be interesting to see how many customers she runs off the first day."

"I gotta figure Thea knows what she's doing." Or if she didn't, that she was ready for any backlash.

Manny scratched at the side of his hand as he searched for the words. "I'd almost hazard a guess she's playing amateur psychologist."

"How so?" Dakota asked, frowning.

"Putting someone who doesn't like people right in front of them."

Hmm. "Becca's just making the coffee."

"You ever see a Starbucks customer whose order gets bungled? The barista's the one who gets shit on."

Dakota thought again about what Becca had told him, then thought about what Manny had just said. "That connection you were asking about. You know they all live together, too, right?"

Manny's huff said he hadn't. "I do now."

"It's Thea's house, but Becca and Ellie, the baker, and another woman who's got two kids live there."

That had Manny frowning. "Thea footing all the bills?"

"She says she's not, but none of them is

working yet, so . . ." Dakota shrugged. "She said Becca and Ellie are keeping track of the hours they're at the shop, but someone's got to be putting food on the table in the meantime."

Manny nodded, slapped his hands to his thighs. "That's all I needed."

"What's that supposed to mean?" Dakota asked.

But Manny was done talking. "How go the plans to leave?"

He shrugged. "I'll set them in stone once I have the money to do so. I'd borrow it from you but I can tell by the way you dress that you're broke as a joke."

Manny looked down at his white shirt and navy Dockers and brown-suede oxfords. "What's wrong with the way I dress?"

"Nothing. If you're a parole officer."

"Very funny," Manny said, hopping off the stool.

"You going already? You just got here," Dakota said, miming glancing at a watch.

"I got what I came for, and a helping of abuse on top of it. I get that in the day to day. Don't need to take it from friends."

"Manny, Manny, Manny. Since when have we ever been friends?"

"Watch it, Keller," Manny said, pointing a finger. "I know more of your secrets than anyone."

Dakota huffed as Manny walked out of the barn. He'd let the other man think it was true.

He—and Thea—knew otherwise.

❧ Chapter Sixteen ❧

Thea was opening the boxes containing the bread baskets she'd ordered when Dakota came through Bread and Bean's front door. She was lost in thought, caught up in the goings-on at Dragon Fire Hill.

And not just the changes to the structure she'd seen happening over the last few days, but the changes in the women living there. Their attitudes. Their demeanor. The way they moved when they walked. Their laughter, spontaneous and true. Boys running and playing as boys were meant to do.

The house no longer felt like a tomb.

They weren't huge changes, and maybe Dakota, or even Lena Mining, who only knew the others peripherally, wouldn't pick up on the smiles that had been coming easier to Frannie's face, or the length she'd added to her apron strings, allowing James to scamper free outside when she hung sheets to dry.

Thea noticed because she'd been watching Frannie wind James close for months, and do so with pinched lips and a deep vee between her brows. Frannie, more than Becca or Ellie, had arrived at Thea's withdrawn and fearful—with good reason. But she no longer appeared as if she might snap at the sound of a male voice or heavy footstep, which made breathing a lot easier for all.

But even Ellie had been singing more when in the kitchen kneading bread, her fingers like vise grips, her hands like hammers. And Becca. Well, Thea had caught her several times talking to one or another member of the crew from Keller Construction, answering questions, running small errands between rooms of the house. None of what was going on was flirting; it was simple adult conversation.

Thea had even walked in on one of the workers trying to save a pot of soup Becca had inadvertently oversalted. He'd even accepted when Becca had offered him a cup to go with the chips and sandwiches he'd packed for his own dinner. And the fact that Becca had made the gesture was nothing short of a miracle. Thea hadn't minded a bit. Beans were a perfect comfort food and went a long way.

Dakota's shadow fell across her then, and she reached for another of the boxes instead of looking up, ignoring the tremor in her fingers, her shortness of breath. Damn him for making her itch, and want things that were impossible, and wish her whole life had been different, and that they weren't both so . . . ruined.

"Shouldn't you hold off on getting that put together?" he asked. "You don't want your bread baskets to have a half inch of construction dust in the bottom."

She pulled another basket from the box, then from its protective plastic sleeve. "I'll cover it all back up. I want to make sure everything arrived in good shape in case I need to make a return before we open."

He took in the jumble of baskets surrounding her. "You have all of those custom-made?"

"Not made-to-order, but I did buy them through a place that makes everything by hand. They're set up a lot like Bread and Bean. Sort of a . . . co-op," she added, realizing she'd already said more than she'd meant to. "Everyone pitches in and the profits support all the members and their art."

She looked up and met his gaze. He stood with his feet spread wide, his hands stuffed in his jeans pockets, his gray T-shirt pulled tight over his shoulders and tighter around his upper arms. His hair appeared to have grown several inches since he'd come into the shop that first day. It couldn't have, really. Not enough time had passed. But with his head tilted down, his hair fell forward, adding shadows to his already shadowed jaw. The scruff there had her itching to kiss him, to feel his cheek scratch hers.

And that's what she was having trouble with. Accepting that this very imposing man was the boy she'd loved so desperately. She wasn't desperate any longer, and she didn't want to think about then when now was so very different. He wasn't going to hurt her. She knew that, but too often she found herself conflating Todd's insecurity-driven damage with Dakota's that was authentic and earned in unspeakable ways.

"Co-op, huh? I guess that works."

"What do you mean 'that works'?" she asked, bristling.

He crossed his arms, the motion increasing the sense of his towering over her. "It works because it tells enough of the truth without revealing the parts that need to stay secret."

Need to stay secret. Not she needed to *keep* secret. He'd taken the onus off her as if he understood the sticky wicket surrounding Bread and Bean and the house on Dragon Fire Hill. But if he was digging for information, he wasn't going to be getting any. "I was thinking it might be a good idea to go over the timing on the construction projects. I don't want to fall behind on the shop because you're tied up at the house."

"I'm not assigned to the house, in case you haven't noticed. Tennessee's got that under control."

She'd noticed. Every night when she'd gone home. Six or eight men, two trucks, neither one of them his. "About that," she said, setting the basket in her lap. "Why were you the one to do the initial walk-through?"

"I thought it would go easier for your . . . room-mates if the first person they saw was someone they knew." He shrugged as if his thoughtfulness was nothing when it was everything. "The two who'd already met me anyway. I'm not sure any of this is going to go easy for Frannie."

"You might be surprised," Thea told him. "She's still cautious, of course, but she's actually coming out of her shell a bit. And she's given up some of the helicopter parenting, too."

The smile that came then nearly melted her. "I'll bet James likes that."

"He's having the best time watching everyone work. One of the men, Frank, I think, brought him a little box with plastic tools. He carries his *flat* screwdriver everywhere," she said with a laugh. "Frannie said he's even sleeping with it. Of course, Robert thinks anything that's James's is his, too, so there have been a lot of lessons lately in sharing and respecting the property of others."

"You ever sorry you didn't have kids?" he asked after a moment and out of the blue.

Gee, thanks. "I do have a few good years left in me, you know."

"Sorry. That didn't come out right." He dragged over her folding chair from her makeshift desk and spun it around to straddle it. "It's just that I've been thinking a lot lately about how badly parents can fuck up their kids and not even know it."

Okay. This was new. And interesting. And obviously coming from a very personal place. "You were thinking about it because . . . of your own parents?"

"Tennessee and I were talking about them the other day," he said, his arms crossed on the chair back, his gaze cast down. "Did you know they haven't come home to see Georgia May since she was born? Their only grandchild, and they can't even be bothered to send more than a congratulatory postcard, which, by the way, was all about the children they're caring for in some storm-ravaged Laotian village."

That sucked. "I guess Tennessee can't be too happy about that."

He snorted, then slammed a hand against the chair back. "What is wrong with them? They shit on the three of us growing up, so I guess I shouldn't be surprised, but . . . a baby. The first Keller grandchild. It's like they don't have a clue what it means to be a family."

"They aren't the only ones, you know," she said, slipping the basket back into its sleeve. "I'm pretty sure you met my mother."

He nodded. "You two still in touch?"

Because he knew not to ask if they were still close. They never had been. "I haven't heard from her in probably ten years. I don't even know where she is. The minute I left home, so did she. As if she'd been waiting for me to find someone else to live with so she could get on with her life."

He shook his head. "I always hated that for you. Sometimes I wondered if she even liked you."

"She didn't. I reminded her too much of him. My father."

"And what about him? Still no contact?"

She shook her head, old bitterness leaving a bad taste in her mouth. "I'm surprised she didn't just drop me off at some fire station and be done with it. She never wanted me. She made that very clear. Though I guess she needed a whipping boy. Or girl. Someone, me, to blame for the big fat mistake she made, me, that cost her a pretty hefty inheritance from her parents."

"Runs in the family then, does it?"

"Cutting off your kid? Yeah. But not the part about getting pregnant." She thought about all the condoms they'd used, how they'd joked about a subscription service, or buying by the case. "I heard for years how I'd ruined her life. No way was I going to let a baby ruin mine."

Time ticked by, the word *ruin* hanging in the air, Dakota finally saying, "So you let me do it instead. At least for other men, wasn't that what you said? Which I guess could be one and the same. I mean, if you had your heart set on a relationship and it was true."

"I didn't let you," she said, sighing heavily. "It just happened."

"I'm good with being a whipping boy," he said, and Thea finally looked up.

She held his gaze, searching for . . . something, anything, she didn't know. A truth, maybe. "You and I wouldn't have had that last night together if she'd given a shit about me."

"I'm not sure that makes what you went through living with her worth it," he said, his tone gruff and regretful.

She didn't want him to have any regrets. "If that night helped you get through, then yeah. Growing up with her for a mother was worth it completely."

His eyes softened. "We're getting kinda deep here, Clark."

"Seems to happen every time we talk about the past."

"Probably why we agreed early on that we wouldn't. Should've stuck to that I guess."

"Stupid, really, to think it wouldn't keep coming up since it's a known quantity and neither one of us has a handle on the present," she said, then wanted to bite back the words when he cocked his head inquisitively.

"I thought you had everything figured out, your house, your business . . ."

She allowed herself the briefest of smiles. "I do all my flailing in private."

"I think I'm disappointed," he said, and she laughed.

"Be glad you weren't around a couple of years ago."

"Okay, now I'm really curious," he said, standing to turn the chair around and settling back down as if for a show. "I mean, we're already talking about the past . . ."

"Trust me." She tossed the basket back into the box. "You don't want to hear *this* part."

"The part with your ex?"

She hated him doing that. Hated it. "Stop digging. And stop reading my mind."

"What was his name?"

She closed her eyes. "Todd."

"Did he hurt you?" he asked.

She'd never realized a tone of voice could be both soft and mean. "Not physically," she said, looking at him. "Well, once or twice. But nothing like what Ellie or Becca suffered." She thought about Ellie's burn scars, about the whip tracks across Becca's back.

"Their abuse being worse doesn't make yours okay."

"I didn't say it did." Ugh. This more than anything she did not want to explain, but since it was Dakota asking . . . She stretched out her legs, pointing her toes before drawing herself into a ball and hugging her knees close. "Todd was well-off. Very well-off. He thought having money meant he was right about everything. That he was entitled to get his way no matter what anyone else wanted. He wasn't so . . . insistent when we first got together. It escalated over time."

"How long were you together?"

"Six years."

"What did he do to you?"

"I'm not going to talk about that." There were some things she would rather Dakota not know.

"Where is he now?"

"Honestly? I have no idea." This was the part she was least comfortable sharing. The part she'd never told another soul. "He was on a trip with some friends. His idea of friends. More like sycophantic hangers-on. It was some adventure thing. Hiking. Rafting. There was an accident. Two of them made it out. Two did not. When search and rescue went back, they couldn't find them. I only learned about this later from the news. He'd barely been out the door before I emptied his safe and the bank account I had access to. Then with the help of some contacts I'd made, I went underground to make sure he never found me."

He leaned forward, his elbows on his knees, rubbing at his wrist with his thumb. "The authorities didn't connect you to the money?"

She shook her head, still amazed she hadn't been found out. "No one would've known about the cash he kept in the safe, or the jewelry he'd bought me. And since the money from the account was withdrawn before he'd had time to get on the plane, it could easily be assumed he took it with him."

"How long ago was that?"

"About three years."

He let that sink in, then said, "And when you came up for air, you thought you'd go into the underground business."

"It's more complicated than that"—*so* much more complicated—"but that's the gist."

Frowning, he thought for a minute, then asked, "Is it safe for you to be using your own name?"

"He didn't know me as Clark. No one did," she said, her chin propped on her knees. "Not the bank. Not the people I was working with when I met him and before he insisted I quit my job. Our friends were his, not mine. He basically locked me away."

"Shit, Thea," he said, collapsing back in the chair, lacing his hand on top of his head, shaking it. His expression broadcast as much disbelief as it did anything.

He didn't ask for more, but she wanted him to understand that she hadn't just given up. "He was . . . persuasive. And it took a while before I realized what he was doing. By then I had no way to fight back. No job. No money of my own. No car. I lived in luxury, but I was still a prisoner."

"Why weren't you going by Clark?"

"I dropped my mother's name after high school.

Todd only ever knew me as Thea Bateman. Which is just as well."

"Why's that?"

She swallowed hard. It was silly, but . . . "I like you being the one to call me Clark."

Sitting on the front porch, her legs dangling over the edge while she ate the very boring bologna sandwich she'd fixed herself for dinner, Becca watched yet another car make its way up the drive to the house. It wasn't one she recognized, but there had been too many lately to keep track of. Keller Construction was a lot bigger deal than she'd thought, being able to bring on so many men at such short notice.

For not the first time, she wondered about Thea's guardian angel. No one was supposed to know about the shelter. It was a safe house, and in Becca's particular case, it was doing a very good job keeping her out of her ex's reach. She hadn't dated for years after her discharge from the service. She would've been smarter to remember why than to take the chance she had. But she'd been lonely, and Dez had been so sweet.

She'd met him at a honky-tonk in Fort Worth, a working cowboy, a man who lived close to the land, who talked about his horse as if the animal was his best friend, who knew what it was like to scrabble for a living, who expected to be handed nothing he hadn't worked his ass off to earn. He smiled easily. He laughed readily. He loved as if no woman before her had existed. As if no woman would exist in his world once she was gone.

He also had a thing for his whip, and a temper that was as robust as his sex drive. If she'd known that in the beginning, she could've saved herself a lot of grief. And bruises. And trips to the clinic for stitches. Teach her to let down her guard. To let a man close enough to make her want to. She knew better. It was why as much as she blamed Dez for the disaster that had sent her into the night alone and bleeding, she blamed herself.

You'd think she had learned something in the navy, she mused, stuffing the rest of the white bread, mayo, and lunch meat into her mouth to chew, but apparently not. She dusted her hands together, then wiped her palms on her jeans and her mouth on the inside of her T-shirt. That's when the slam of the car door brought her head up.

Of course. Her mouth was full and she was still covered with the grime she'd picked up crawling around beneath the kitchen floor, looking for a piece of copper tubing in a recess the plumbing dude couldn't squeeze into. It made perfect sense that the man she most wanted *not* to see was the one walking toward her.

"You again." The one who kept trying to get under her skin by doing no more than being observant.

"Manny Balleza," he said, nodding with the introduction.

Sigh. She really didn't want to know who he was, or his name, and so far had successfully avoided learning it. Knowing was the first step to caring. To interest. To thinking he'd be different than the others. She wasn't going to make that mistake again. "Dakota's not here."

He shoved his hands to his hips and grinned as if he was looking through her. Reading her mind. Letting her think what she wanted to. For now. "I'm here to see Frank Stumbo."

Huh. "Why?"

"That's between me and Frank."

"I'm not just going to let you inside the house," she said, but then it didn't matter. Frank had come out through the back door and circled the house to his truck. He saw her, saw Manny, raised an index finger in greeting and continued on, his work boots kicking up dust on the way, his overalls sagging on his thin frame. "And now I guess I don't have to."

"No, I guess you don't—"

"Are you a cop?" she interrupted him to ask.

"Excuse me?"

"A cop. You have that look," she said, waving one hand.

He frowned as he glanced down at the sport coat and dress shirt and Dockers and shoes she knew a cop could afford. "Not sure what that look is, or why suddenly everyone's so interested in my clothes, but no. I'm not a cop."

"Fine." She got to her feet, having no idea what he was talking about, and dusted porch dirt from her hands to the seat of her jeans. Then she jumped down beside him. "I'll be right here keeping an eye out."

He tried really hard not to grin. "I need to speak to him privately."

"I didn't say I was going to listen."

"You're not exactly the trusting sort, are you?"

If it wouldn't have made her seem flighty, she would've laughed. "I don't trust anyone without a very good reason."

"Frank can vouch for me, and obviously you trust Frank."

She and Frank had spent some quality time over a pot of navy-bean soup. She'd messed up the seasonings. He'd looked through everything in the fridge and the pantry and tossed in what would fix it. He hadn't told her she was stupid for not paying attention or for reading the recipe wrong and using garlic salt instead of garlic powder. She'd been distracted. It happened.

Frank had just heard her yelling at the beans and come in to see if he could help, and she'd been frustrated enough at possibly having wasted the food to let him. She'd had a soft spot for Frank ever since.

"Go on then," she said, crossing her arms. "Have your little talk with Frank."

Manny backed up a step, then turned, but didn't make it any farther before coming back to her. "Do you have something against my clothes?"

"I didn't say anything about your clothes."

"Then what did you mean about me having *that look?*"

She shrugged one shoulder. "You look . . . tired, I guess. Worn out. And you do dress like a cop. The jacket and everything, but none of it really tied together."

"Oh, so you were referring to the fashion police."

She looked at him, blinked, then laughed, quickly covering her mouth as if she could hold back the sound. It was just one bark, but it sounded so strange, and felt even weirder in her chest. Damn him for making it happen, she mused, then laughed once more, this time at herself.

She was a piece of work, wasn't she? "No. I was not referring to the fashion police."

"Well, that's good, because pot and kettle and all that."

This time instead of laughing she gasped. "You're mocking the way I look? When I've been on my hands and knees crawling around under the house?"

"You've got a little of the house in your hair there," he said, waving one finger. "Some insulation or something."

She reached up and swatted at her hair, finding nothing, then shaking her head when he said, "Other side."

She swatted again, more aggravated that she regretted not looking in a mirror than that she hadn't done so.

"Here. I'll get it," he said, plucking the fibers before she could stop him from getting that close.

"Stop it," she said, swatting at his hand this time.

"Want me to put it back?" he said, holding it out like an offering.

"No, I don't want you to put it back. What is wrong with you?"

"Nothing," he said, dropping the fluff of pink and watching it blow away. "Just trying to lighten things up. Get you to laugh again. You've got a great laugh. A great smile."

Oh, no. Oh, no. "Do not even tell me you're coming on to me."

"You know," he said, frowning as with hands at his hips, he looked off into the distance. "I haven't had to come on to a woman since my twenties when I thought that's how things were done. Now if I'm interested, I just let them know."

"Yeah?" Cocky ass. "And how's that working out for you?"

"I've been single about ten years," he said, and looked back, his expression completely serious save for the humor flashing through his eyes.

She tried not to laugh again. She really, really tried. But the way he so easily made fun of himself . . . No. *Enough.* She was not going to start thinking he could be one of the good guys. She'd thought Dez was a good guy, and look how that had turned out.

Still, she couldn't keep herself from asking, "Well? Are you?" though she was surprised she'd been able to get out the words with her throat all twisted up with wondering what he would say. Wondering what she wanted him to say. Wondering why she was wondering anything at all.

"Interested?" he asked, and she gave him a single sharp nod.

"I'll have to get back to you on that. Frank's waiting," he said, canting his head toward the other man's truck. She rolled her eyes as he turned to go.

What a loser she was. *Loser.* Letting him get to her. Letting herself almost, just almost care. She had just reached the porch steps when he called out, "Becca!"

She looked over—not caring, not letting him get to her, not a loser—to see him walking backward and nodding.

"Yeah. I am," he yelled, giving her a wave as he turned and slapped Frank on the back.

All she could do was stand where she was and do her best to remember to breathe.

✌ Chapter Seventeen ✌

Sitting in the passenger seat of Becca's car where she'd parked it behind Bread and Bean, Ellie flipped through the notebook that was her constant companion these days. She wanted to do her absolute best by Thea and the shop, and she'd been trying out a variety of breads, buying most of the ingredients on her own dime, though Thea had said she'd reimburse her.

It just didn't seem right, having the boss pay for her mistakes, her trial and error, though she supposed Thea could write off the expenses on her taxes. Ellie just wanted to have the recipes perfected by the time the shop opened. She wanted customers to know which day they could get fresh ciabatta, which day French baguettes would be available, which day focaccia.

Every day would bring white and wheat or at least a multigrain. She'd never known many folks to really be fans of pumpernickel or rye, so she'd offer one of those every other week until she got a feel for the demand. And she'd schedule in fresh cinnamon-raisin swirl for weekend French toast. Sourdough was another thing entirely. Who didn't love sourdough?

She was having the most trouble coming up with a gluten-free loaf she would actually want to use for a sandwich. Tapioca starch and brown-rice flour seemed to work well as basics, but when she added potato starch she got a better crumb. Unfortunately, she hadn't yet figured out the proportions; every time she put slices through a griddle or panini press, they burned.

She knew she was close to getting it right. The bread wasn't heavy like the one she'd made with sugarcane fiber and plum puree. That loaf had been stuffed with flax and sunflower seeds, too, and the flavor had been sweet and nutty, but it wasn't what she wanted to use for peanut butter and jelly. Or even grilled cheese.

Setting her pen in her notebook, she reached up to rub both hands over her face. Why did she have to think about grilled cheese? Why? She'd been doing *so* good since talking to Thea the other night, though obviously she was only fooling herself or she wouldn't fall apart thinking about sandwiches. Sandwiches and soup and Lena Mining.

She thought the three might just be linked forever in her mind.

A knock on her window brought her head around. She pressed her hand to her chest where her heart was thudding, then started to roll down the window. In the end, she opened the door. She needed to get out of the car anyway. Why not kill two birds with one stone?

"Lena, hello. How have you been? It seems like

ages since I've seen you"—*way to be casual, El*—"though I guess it's only been about a week."

"An insane week. Truly insane." Lena shook her head and shuddered as if shedding layers of stress. "I forget that summer class sessions are shorter so they're way more intense, and I'm so bad at knowing when to call a debit a credit, and vice versa."

"Isn't it like the source is credited and the destination is debited?" When Lena offered her a curiously pleased smile, Ellie shrugged, and added, "I read that somewhere once."

"It sounds so simple like that, but I still can't keep it straight. Which is why I'll continue to work in a confectionery, and my mother can hire a CPA."

Ellie reached back into the car for her tote bag and notebook, then locked and slammed the door. "Are you quitting school?"

"For now," Lena said and nodded. "It's early enough in the semester that I can drop the class without a penalty. I'll register here soon for something in the fall."

Ellie tucked her notebook down in her tote as she asked, "You have an idea of what you want to study?"

Lena shook her head. "I don't know if I'm cut out for a career, you know? I like too many different things, and I want to do them all, and experiment to find out where I fit."

"It can take a while." And sometimes it never worked out. Ellie's dream was still to teach art, but she couldn't imagine ever having another chance. Not without changing her name, cutting her hair and dying it, wearing contacts . . . Bobby would be looking for her until the day one of them died. The thought was just too much to deal with today. She was so very tired of being afraid.

"Honestly?" As if shy, Lena glanced down at the Doc Martens she wore with dark-green combat pants that were as baggy as her long-sleeved T-shirt was form-fitting. The pants hung low on her hips, and Ellie wondered if the boots were comfortable for being on her feet all day. It was safer than wondering if her bra, visible through the shirt's fabric, was really a camouflage print. "What I want to do more than anything is open an animal shelter."

That snagged Ellie's attention and had her smiling. "Like for rescue dogs?"

Lena nodded. "It's just that there's so much involved. The land, and licenses, and zoning, and regulations, and veterinary care. I'll get it figured out."

"Sounds like it would cost a fortune." Also like a good use of a business degree. Why in the world had she ever majored in art?

"It probably will," Lena said with a laugh. "But my grandparents left me a very nice inheritance. I think they'd like the idea of me spending it like this."

So maybe her dream *would* come true. That made Ellie happy. Truly. "It's nice you have that luxury."

"I have a cushion. Not sure I'd call it a luxury. Besides what I have from my grandparents, I have an insurance payout from my father. He died when I was a senior in high school, and left me and my mom the money. Ten years of interest on that and investing makes it a lot easier not to worry about where my next meal is coming from." And then she suddenly stopped talking, staring at Ellie like she wanted to take everything back. "That was really crass. I'm sorry. I know better than to talk about money."

But Ellie was still back on what Lena had said first, and she reached out to hold Lena's wrist. "I'm so sorry. About you losing your father. It was wonderful that he provided for you."

Lena shrugged, her expression tender as she covered Ellie's hand with her free one. "I guess. I mean, I still have to work. I have bills," she said with a laugh. "But I don't have debt. I pay cash for everything. I spend more than I should on my hair, changing it up all the time, but I don't have a thing for designer bags, so I figure it's a fair trade-off."

"And here I was just thinking that I spend too much on specialty flours."

"Flowers? Like hybrid roses or something?"

That had Ellie smiling. "No. Baking flours. Like spelt and teff."

"I didn't even know those were things. But if the breads turn out half as good as your sourdough, then it's worth the splurge, don't you think?"

Reluctantly, Ellie pulled her hand away. "So you liked the sourdough?"

"I *loved* the sourdough. The loaf you gave me? I made toast out of it every morning for breakfast. Sometimes with garlic butter. Sometimes the butter was plain, which I'm sure made Callum a lot happier since I didn't smell like some vampire repellent all day," she said, her cheeks coloring. "I made croutons for my salad one night, and used it to mop up the juice from a rotisserie chicken. You do good bread. Bread and Bean is going to be a huge success thanks to you."

Ellie didn't even know what to say. "You should come to the house this weekend and bake with me."

"Seriously?" Lena's eyes widened. "I would love that."

"Fair warning. The place is a mess now with all the construction. But this should be the last weekend before the kitchen is finished."

Lena looked down again. "How's that coming along?"

"The place is going to be a showpiece when

Keller Construction is done. Or at least once they're done and Thea can implement all her decorating plans."

"That's awesome."

"It really is. We were so lucky to have—" Ellie stopped, cutting herself off. "Anyway, do you have plans on Saturday? You could come watch me inaugurate the new kitchen. Or get your hands dirty if you wanted to. Unless you're busy."

"Since I won't be going to class, I won't be busy with anything that won't keep."

"What time would be good for you?"

"What time do you want me there?"

"Is ten too early?"

"Ten is perfect. I'll see you then," she said, her smile wide and excited. "But now I gotta run before Callum docks me for being late."

"Oh, tell him it's my fault. I shouldn't have kept you."

"I'm just kidding, El. He's too smart to mess with the best thing that's ever happened to him. Well, not counting his girl and his fiancée."

Ellie didn't know about Callum, but one thing was true: Lena Mining was the best thing that had happened to her in her entire life.

Pencil in hand, Dakota sat at the Keller Construction drafting table that served as his brother's office going over the progress report from Tennessee's foreman on the project at

Dragon Fire Hill. It really wasn't any of Dakota's business; the company belonged to Tennessee. He'd put together the crew and handed out the jobs, but Dakota was curious.

He was the one with the most personal investment because of his connection to Thea. Also because of the things he knew to be fact about the women living with her, as well as the things he suspected were true.

He'd told Thea the crew would be in and out as fast as they could, but he was surprised to see the list of smaller tasks that had already been completed. At this rate, the house would be done before the coffee shop. Then again, the house had a half dozen men putting in twelve-hour days.

Dakota's was a one-man show.

He was supposed to be outlining his headway at Bread and Bean for Tennessee to look over, but the notes he'd jotted so far were all about Thea. The particulars she'd shared about her life. The things she'd left out. The questions he had about both. And yeah. He had reams worth of questions.

The notes he was having the most trouble with, scribbles, really, because no one would ever be able to make out the words, were the ones about why he cared as much as he apparently did. If he didn't, he'd be able to forget everything she'd told him about her life since he'd seen her last and move on. But he couldn't. And he hadn't.

So . . .

He looked down at what he'd written.

Thea had been involved with a wealthy man who'd stripped her of everything that made her who she was. Who'd kept her locked away like an animal. Who'd used her when in the mood like he would any of his playthings. Cars. Bikes. Boats. Planes. A football team. A private island. Whatever the rich spent money on. Very little of it on Dakota's radar. None in his budget.

He'd arrived in Hope Springs with a backpack, a bedroll, a cell phone, and a couple changes of clothes. He had a tent, but he never traveled with more cash than he could afford to lose.

He'd done a lot of his moving around by hitching rides with friends of friends, but had pedaled his way through the Pacific Northwest, and hoofed it almost as many miles as he'd traveled by bus or train on his way across the country. On his way home.

Vagabond was a good word.

Home he was having more trouble with.

A gust of wind through the barn helped blow away both and return him to Thea. The smells of fresh-cut pine and cedar fencing and the tall grass outside filled his head as he thought about the girl he'd known in school, the girl he'd *loved* in school—because he had to face it; nothing else described the emotions of those years—who would never have allowed herself to be bundled away and brought out on a whim.

It was a wonder she'd been thinking clearly enough to escape when she had, that the traumatic bonding she'd described hadn't won out. Stockholm syndrome. It was the only thing that made sense. The absolute rage he felt for what she'd gone through did not. Anger was something he no longer had truck with. Anger was the emotion that had changed his entire life. Changed his brother's life. His sister's life.

He would not let his feelings about Thea's past mess up what either of them had now.

The sound of a vehicle's wheels on the gravel drive brought his head around. Dolly Pepper's Prius made no other noise. He swiveled on his stool, then watched her exit the front door, only to open the back door and reach for something there. Usually she came to work with a bag of needles and yarn. Today she held a pan of food. She smiled as she approached and offered it to him.

The dish was still warm when he took it and reminded him that he'd skipped lunch. "A woman bearing gifts. My favorite kind."

"You're favorite kind of gift?" she asked with a laugh, her eyes twinkling behind her glasses, her short gray hair catching shimmers of sun. "Or your favorite kind of woman?"

She really had the sweetest laugh. Dakota didn't know if he'd ever met a woman as warm and genuine as Dolly Pepper. Funny how his mother would be about the same age, yet he couldn't picture how she might look. He hadn't seen her in over a decade. "I'm going to have to say both."

Dolly set her purse on a stack of boxes. "I might hold that against you if bringing food to a man who doesn't take the time to eat wasn't one of my favorite things to do."

He frowned down at the covered dish that smelled so good. "Tennessee's not here."

"I'm not talking about Tennessee," she said, reaching out to pat him on the arm. "I'm not sure that brother of yours has ever missed a meal. At least not since he's been married to Kaylie."

Oh good. Then it *was* for him. "You don't usually work this time of day."

"It's been slow at Two Owls today for some reason," she said, digging into her purse for the fork and napkin she'd brought and handing him both. "Mitch and Kaylie have everything under control, and I really do have a small mountain of paperwork to catch up on. You Keller men have been keeping me busy. So much work with these new jobs."

About that. "Has Tennessee talked to you about how to code the Dragon Fire Hill costs? Not that it's my business—"

Dolly cleared her throat softly. "You mean has he told me not to share what I know with anyone who might ask? And to give him all the relevant invoices to handle?"

"I'll take that as a yes." His stomach rumbling, Dakota unfolded the napkin to find the fork.

"I do find it curious that he's not billing out the labor costs on this project. With as large of a crew as is working, that's a hefty amount to absorb, though of course it's not my concern."

Even though Tennessee was her stepson-in-law, and his finances affected her stepdaughter, too. Dakota dug into the huge serving of sour cream chicken enchiladas. "It was Tennessee's idea. A way to help out with the philanthropy. The . . . person covering the materials is getting hit hard, so Tennessee's paying the men out of his own pocket. And mine."

"Well, that's extremely generous of you both," she said, removing her glasses and frowning at the lenses before finding a cloth in her purse to clean them. "Especially since everything I've heard about the women living there leads me to believe they could use all the help they can get."

His mouth full of cheese and chicken and fresh, warm corn tortillas, Dakota just nodded. Not for a moment did he believe Dolly was digging for information, but he wasn't sure what all Tennessee might've told her, and he didn't want to say something he shouldn't. It was bad enough he'd admitted to his and his brother's altruism. If Tennessee *hadn't* told Kaylie . . .

"Tennessee is worried about you, you know,"

273

Dolly said, the complete change of subject bringing Dakota's head up.

"Because I told him I'd be leaving after this job?" he asked, his mouth still half full.

"He's not worried about that," she said, crossing one leg over the other and smoothing the fabric of her pants over her knee. "Though he's not happy about it."

"I don't get it."

Dolly pressed her lips together, as if it helped her form the right words, then said, "He doesn't think you're going to find whatever it is you're looking for by leaving."

Right. Since he was having so much luck finding it here.

Here . . . where Thea was? Here . . . where for the last few weeks, getting out of bed hadn't had him calculating how long he needed to stay to feel like he'd given his siblings what they needed?

Here . . . where arriving at work meant seeing the woman who'd been the girl who'd been the reason he'd survived prison in one piece?

"He may be right. I might never find it." Or could be he already had, and was only just now coming to realize that particular truth.

❧ Chapter Eighteen ❧

With all the construction going on at Dragon Fire Hill, and that at Bread and Bean, Thea had almost forgotten about Butters Bakery until she and Peggy arrived at their respective businesses at the same time, parking in their designated spaces in the through street behind the building they shared with Callum Drake and Bliss. Thea slammed the door of her Subaru and waved.

"Hi, Peggy. Do you have a minute?"

Peggy, her black hair sporting but a smattering of gray, was dressed in her usual uniform of black slacks and white athletic shoes, with a camp-style blouse that skimmed her heavy thighs. Today's blouse was a tangerine and lime plaid. "Certainly. Come have a slice of coffee cake. And a cup of coffee. Though I imagine what you're brewing is a lot better than what I have."

Thea hit the locks on her doors and laughed, recalling Dakota's griping about the bitterness in a recent pot. "At the moment, I wouldn't doubt we're brewing the same thing. You know how it is. Save the best for guests."

"Especially when they're paying," Peggy said, extracting her keys from the door and tugging it open, tote bags slung over both shoulders. She set them on a table just inside the door.

Thea stepped in after her and closed her eyes, breathing deeply of the smells that were already pervasive at this hour. Sugar and cinnamon and sweet vanilla and even sweeter maple syrup, and beneath it all, chocolate. Like a big bowl of cake batter waiting for her to scoop a spoon through and lick clean.

Then again, Pat had probably had the ovens going for hours. "Morning, Thea," he said with a nod as he hefted a bag of flour and measured out what she was certain was ten cups.

He was at least a foot taller than Peggy, his hair fully gray, his beard and mustache, too. Along with his hair net, he wore white pants, a white T-shirt, and a big white apron that Thea wouldn't doubt had been the same apron he'd had on the day the bakery opened. It looked as thin as a well-worn sheet.

"How's it going, Pat?"

"I'm still here. I'm still kicking. I'd say it's a damn fine day."

Peggy flipped on the lights in the small office she kept just inside the back door. "Pat, hon, please tell me you've got a coffee cake that Hyacinth hasn't put out in the case yet."

"I believe there's one still in the pan on the cooling rack."

"Good. If I go into the shop, someone will

waylay me, and Thea will never see me again." Peggy had crossed the room while talking, and now picked up the whole pan rather than the slice Thea had expected. "Let's talk in my office. I've got utensils and dishes in there, and a coffee pot."

Thea caught a whiff of the cake's coffee and butter aromas, as well as that of toasted pecans, as Peggy passed her, and her stomach rumbled. Oh, she definitely needed to stop by more often, if just to get the sugar high. "Nice to see you again, Pat."

"Don't be a stranger," Pat called back, flipping the switch on a giant mixer, the motor whirring to life.

"Go ahead and shut the door," Peggy said, pulling out plates and forks from a file cabinet drawer as Thea walked in. "Too hard to talk over Pat's noise."

"Does he do all the baking?" Thea asked as she closed the door.

"Not all, but a lot, yes. Here, you cut while I start the coffee. Hyacinth holds down the fort out front until I get here, then I spend most of my days out there while she works with Pat."

And here she'd assumed Peggy was the one baking, Thea mused, slicing off a square of cake and then another, trying not to be too greedy. As hungry as she was, having skipped breakfast, it wasn't easy. "Has Hyacinth worked for you a long time?"

"She's been here almost as long as we've been open," Peggy said, popping a K-Cup into the Keurig machine. Thea smiled at Peggy's having called it a coffee pot. "Her daughter, Iris, has been here ages, too. She started in high school, working afternoons until close. Now she takes care of her father while Hyacinth is here, then comes in around noon when her mother goes home. I don't know what we'd do without them."

Loyal employees. Loyal employer. "Becca York, my soon-to-be barista, mentioned you telling her you were retiring and selling the bakery."

"We are." Peggy nodded, handing Thea the first cup of coffee along with half and half from her office fridge and an old baking powder can stuffed with sugar and sweetener packets. "And I can't believe it, but I haven't had a single second thought since we made the decision."

"Had enough?" Thea asked, stirring her coffee.

"Enough of Pat getting up at four a.m. and groaning through his aches and pains all morning." Peggy finally settled into her desk chair and picked up her fork. "It's tough on a body, all this baking. But then look who I'm talking to. You know exactly what I mean."

"I've done my fair share of kitchen duty, but Ellie's the baker in the bunch. The bread anyway." Thea reached for her coffee, the aroma rich as she brought the cup closer. "Becca's in charge of desserts at the house when we can manage them."

"We've talked several times," Peggy said, surprising Thea as she sipped. "She said she did a lot of baking in the service, but I guess you knew that."

"I did, yes. It was her dad who instilled the love in her."

"She told me he'd worked in a commercial kitchen."

Thea nodded. "He started as a dishwasher. When Becca was in high school, he decorated sheet cakes for a grocery store's bakery. One of the chains," Thea said, her hands cold around the hot coffee cup. "He died while she was overseas. A heart attack."

"Such a shame. She told me both of her parents were gone. I'm not sure she really meant to." Peggy cut into her cake as she talked. "We were out back one morning early. She seemed to need someone to talk to. I guess she has an ex who gives her trouble?"

Thea nodded again. If Becca had already spilled, no need to hedge.

"I thought rather than talk about a bad part of her past, she might feel better talking about something good," Peggy said with a shrug, slicing into her cake. "I'm not much of a therapist, but I've got more than my share of common sense," she added, forking the bite into her mouth.

"Thank you. For being kind to her." Thea wanted to laugh as much as she wanted to cry. The words were such a weak representation of the gratitude she wanted to shower on this woman. "There hasn't been a lot of kindness in Becca's life since she left home."

"You've shown her more than anyone. She told me so," Peggy said, adding an emphatic nod. "It explains why she's so protective of you."

The picture of Becca's forearm at Dakota's throat played in Thea's mind. "I hadn't realized she was until recently." A moment of silence passed before Thea spoke again. "You know Becca wouldn't be able to buy the bakery herself."

"Oh, I didn't think she would be." Peggy sounded apologetic as she reached for her cup. "I almost didn't mention it, but I thought with her history, it would be something she would enjoy thinking about anyway."

"She was thrilled that you asked her about it."

"Is that why you're here?" Peggy arched a brow and asked. "To talk about the bakery?"

Thea took a deep breath. "Do you have a buyer yet?"

Peggy looked at her over the rim of her cup as she sipped and shook her head.

"Then can I ask you a few questions?"

This time Peggy gave her a nod, her eyes above her cup sparkling.

"How much of what makes this *Butters* Bakery

are you selling? The name? The recipes? Or only the ovens and the display cases and the lease on the space?" If one could even sell such a thing, which would require Thea to hire an attorney to discuss. She took another deep breath. "I'm not even sure it's within my reach to buy it. But I need to know more to know that."

Peggy considered her for a long moment, then set down her cup and asked, "Do you want it because of Becca?"

Thea nodded. Swallowed. Until this very moment, she hadn't realized how important this was.

"Will she be involved as an owner, or an employee?"

"We'll set up a partnership. There are four of us. But, yes. It's for Becca. As an owner."

Peggy reached for her phone. "Our attorney, Ian Payne, can tell you everything you need to know," she said as she dialed. She waited for the call to be picked up.

"Cindy? It's Peggy Butters. Does Ian have any spare time this morning?" She held Thea's gaze while on hold. "Ten-thirty? I think that works," she said after Thea nodded. "I'm sending a young woman named Thea Clark to see him. She'll be there right on time."

Becca wasn't sure why she'd thought Bread and Bean would offer more peace and quiet than the house on Dragon Fire Hill. Both places were hosting crews from Keller Construction. Both places were nothing but hellholes of constant noise. Hammers and drills and power saws and men laughing. Men cursing. Men stomping around with their big feet in big boots and hefting stacks of plywood as if they weighed nothing.

Her bed in her room in the still of the night was the only place these days she could think. As if she had anything to think about that couldn't be done in the midst of distracting interruptions. It wasn't like she was the deep thinking type. No philosophy or theology or pondering of the state of the universe. All she had on her mind was staying safe, and figuring out if she could afford to leave Thea's and live on her own.

Stupid, really. Where was she going to go? She wasn't one for trust; she'd pretty much had that whipped out of her. Her fault for thinking a man cruel enough to use a whip on an animal would hesitate to use it on her. Last time she went for a cowboy, though her experience in the military hadn't been a lot better. Too bad she didn't have it in her to love women. Then again, look at what Ellie had gone through with hers.

No, she was done with relationships. Frannie had thought she'd had things good. And she probably had. Until she hadn't. And though Becca didn't know all the details of what Thea had gone through in her past, it was pretty clear the other woman was done with men, too. What other reason could there be for her not to be all over Dakota Keller?

The man could not keep his eyes off of Thea, though Becca had to give him credit. He hadn't once stepped out of line; if he had, he wouldn't still be around. And he'd been so amazing with James, and even with Frannie. Too bad the good ones never stuck around. Or if they did, something always happened to fuck things up—

"I thought I'd stop by for a coffee."

At the sound of the deep male voice, Becca froze behind the half-finished barista station where she'd been making notes on the drink menu she and Thea were working to finalize. She took a deep breath and turned, then stretched out her fingers that had been balled into fists.

"We're not open yet," she said to the man with the cheap not-a-cop clothes. The man who'd liked her cake.

The man who had told her he was interested in her.

"Does that mean I can't get a cup?" Manny Balleza asked. "Nothing fancy. Just coffee. Maybe some sugar. Some cream."

Nothing fancy, but still with the extras. Though that was just her being bitchy. "You need a specific temperature? A certain grind? A mug with a smiley face on it? Or are your only demands sugar and cream?"

Holding her gaze, he rubbed at his jaw, then set both hands at his hips. "They weren't demands, Becca. I can drink it black."

Manny. She rolled his name around in her head. She didn't want to say it. Hearing him use hers was making her itch in a way she liked but didn't want to. It was easier to give him a hard time. Doing so made for a great first line of defense. Most guys tucked tail and retreated.

"Black it is," she said, heading for the table with the espresso machine and the stainless steel carafe. Which, of course, was empty. Damn construction hammerheads, drinking her dry *and* giving her a headache with all their power tools and pounding. "I'll need to make a new pot. Or I can pull you a shot."

His mouth grew tight, his frown menacing, or maybe just concerned. "A shot."

He said it as if he was expecting her to offer him José Cuervo or something. "Espresso. It's coffee. But only if you've got an iron gut."

He came closer, but not too close, as if he were actually one of the smart ones who could read the signs. Then he punched a hand against his stomach the way some guys did to show off the steel of their abs. "I guzzle industrial-grade garbage at the office all day, and half the cups I get on the road taste like they've been sitting for a week. Plus, I've never met a jalapeño I didn't like. Bring it on."

Thing of it was, he wasn't showing off anything. He was just making a point. She could make one, too. Show him what real coffee tasted like. She reached for the filter basket and packed it full. "What do you do on the road?" she heard herself asking, thinking she really needed to get a grip. He might be interested, but she, most definitely, was not.

He shrugged. "See clients. Visit friends. Check in on folks I work with. And those I'm interested in."

And there it was. The subject she'd been trying so hard to keep buried. Except she'd known she wouldn't be able to. Dakota wasn't here and she was. That didn't leave much in the way of a reason for Manny to have stopped by, and she wasn't ready to deal with his interest.

She shoved the filter handle to secure it and hit the button to start the machine, thoughts of their encounter at the house refusing to go away. But at least it gave them something to talk about, she mused, watching the espresso cup as it filled. "So Frank's a friend? A client? Are you in construc-tion?"

"You could say that," he said as the machine finished and she shut it off.

Lord save her from men. "If you're going to be all cryptic," she said, handing him the clear glass, the espresso topped by a beautiful crema layer, "you can get your coffee in a can at the

285

Dollar General. And if you tell me you've drank that swill—"

"A time or two," he said with a nod, his eyes blacker than coffee and twinkling. "If I'm with folks who offer. If that's all they have."

She didn't know what to say to that. Did he drink it because he wanted it, or was he actually that nice? She wasn't even sure Thea would be, and she was the nicest person Becca knew. Hell, she wasn't sure she'd had that much niceness in her before it had been beaten out.

"So, Manny," she said, crossing her arms. "Is that short for something? Manuel?"

"It is," he said, and held her gaze as he sipped.

The small cup's double wall of glass served as insulation, so he didn't have to use the handle at all, but he did, sort of mashing it between his thumb and the rest of his fist. And that was when she saw his knuckles and the scars running across them like a railroad track.

She wanted to ask him what they were, but her head was full of the sound of Dez's whip, and the tracks he'd left on her shoulders and down her spine like hash marks used for counting. He'd called it a brand, said she should be proud to be marked as his.

She supposed it was better than having had her skin burned with a branding iron. Or a lit cigarette.

"Would you like to go to dinner?"

"With you?" She blurted it out without thinking

and wanted to kick herself in the ass. "Sorry. That didn't come out right."

His mouth pulled to the side, and she really hoped it was because he was enjoying the coffee, and not because he was laughing at her. "Yes. With me."

"Why?"

"Because it's what people who are interested in each other do."

"I never said—" Then she stopped because one of his eyebrows went up. He was right and she was a liar. "Look. I can't be interested in you, and you really shouldn't be interested in me. I'm flattered—"

"No you're not."

What was wrong with him? "Excuse me?"

"You're scared. You think I'm a jerk, which I can be," he said with a shrug, downing the rest of his espresso then frowning into the cup. "Most of the time I'm not, but it happens. And you don't want to make a mistake, or get hurt again, or risk the progress you've made getting over your past. You don't even want to think about your past, and if you decide to date again there's really no way around it because—"

"Okay. Okay." Sheesh. She'd heard all of this in therapy. "I'll go to dinner with you."

"Because you want to?" His head was still tilted downward, one hand in his pocket, the other holding the cup. But he did lift his gaze to meet hers. "Or did you say that to shut me up?"

"Can it be a little bit of both?" she asked. It was easier than admitting the truth.

A smile started up at the corner of his eyes. "It can be anything you want it to be."

"Does that mean it doesn't have to be a date?"

"No. It's definitely a date."

She blew out a long audible breath.

"You make it sound like the end of the world."

"Some dates have turned out to be just that. For the women."

"You watch a lot of crime TV?"

"And there you go. Being a jerk."

"I'll be more careful." He stepped closer to give her the empty glass, holding on to it just long enough that their hands couldn't help but touch. "Thanks for the coffee."

"Next time I'll make you a latte," she said once he'd let go. "And draw you a big fat middle finger in the foam."

"Now see? That's what I like to hear," he said, as he headed for the door. "Next time. Has a nice ring to it." Then he pushed it open and walked out, leaving Becca standing there, and staring, and so very hungry for things other than dinner.

Having arrived at Bread and Bean earlier than usual, Dakota found Ellie in the shop's kitchen baking bread. He'd known she was there before poking his head in. The smells coming out of the other room had made him regret skipping breakfast, as did the third cup of coffee he'd finished five minutes ago. He needed to eat, and had just decided to break for an early lunch, when Thea walked in through the front door.

She headed straight for her table and her laptop, a frown on her face as she booted it up. Then she dug in her messenger bag for a legal pad, and jotted some notes, checking the calculator on her phone as she did. She looked more tired than usual, as well as more frazzled, and obviously she had something on her mind as she still hadn't noticed him. Or maybe she had but was too caught up in whatever was going on in her head to have time for hello.

He started to go back to work on the shelving unit, not sure why lunch seemed less pressing now, but that meant the electric sander, and he was just about to ask if it would bother her when she heaved a huge sigh and collapsed, laying her head against her arms on the table.

He left the sander where it was and headed for the coffee pot and cup number four, asking the lame, "You okay?"

It took her a minute to respond, as if she didn't have the energy to lift her head, but finally she did, shaking it as she used both hands to hold her bangs away from her face. "I had a meeting with an attorney earlier. To go over some numbers. Finances, taxes, stuff like that."

"For the business?" he asked and she gave him a pretty vague shrug. "Didn't it go well?"

"Why do you ask?" she asked, her mouth twisted sardonically.

"Because you look like you're in over your head," he said, then turned back to the coffee pump.

"I have a ton of stuff to do today is all," she said, then added, "Is it that obvious?"

Probably best not to mention how shredded she appeared, the circles under her eyes, her topknot that had fallen down the back of her head. The streak of dirt on the front of her top. "You want a cup?"

"Sure. Not that it will help."

This time she leaned her head back and closed her eyes. He glanced over once while her cup filled, thinking what she needed was a nap. "You getting any sleep?"

"Apparently not enough if you're asking," she said, adding, "Thanks," when he handed her the drink.

"You just look a little rough around the edges is all." He blew across the top of his cup then sipped, sucking back a sharp breath at the burn. "Like you've got a lot on your mind."

She sipped more slowly, then set the cup down and gestured toward her makeshift desk. "It's not on my mind as much as it's in a spreadsheet and financial statement I'm not sure I've got it in me to decipher."

"Want some help?" he asked, pulling up a milk crate and flipping it over to sit before she answered.

"Because this is high school, you mean? And you whizzed through Mrs. Agee's accounting class? Or was that Mr. Meyer's algebra? Neither one of which I would've ever gotten through without you."

"Left brains. Right brains. We all have different strengths."

"Says you with the engineering degree you're not using."

"Are we going to talk about me now?"

"I think we should. I mean look at me. What the hell do I know about running a business? I'm Muriel Clark's unwanted kid. I barely graduated high school. I worked in fast-food joints until I was twenty-one and able to work clubs. Then I met Todd, who looked *so* much like you that I put on blinders—"

"Whoa, whoa, whoa." Seriously? "Hold on just a minute now. Are we back to that ruining thing again?"

Her hands weren't quite steady when she brought her coffee to her mouth, sipping then shaking her head. "It's not that. It's just . . ."

"What? It's just what?"

"I missed you," she said, slamming her cup against the table and sloshing coffee onto her legal pad and one of his arms. "Shit. I'm sorry." She scrambled to move the paper, using the edge to scrape some of the spill onto the floor, while Dakota pulled up the hem of his shirt to dry his arm.

"It's okay," he said, then caught her staring at the skin he'd revealed, and the scar that had been a part of him for so long, he'd forgotten it was there. He finished with his arm then covered the damage, not sure if he wanted to answer the questions he knew she had, or get back to her missing him. Six or a half dozen . . . "Spit it out."

"What happened?"

"I ran into another guy's sharpened toothbrush in the shower."

He left it at that. He didn't want to explain the circumstances or the aftermath or how much the stitches had hurt or the wound breaking open and bleeding in the yard and his ignoring it while doing pull-ups adding to his crazy-man rep. And when Thea finally did react, it wasn't what he'd expected at all, which made him wish he'd asked her about missing him instead.

She reached over, not to lift his T-shirt and look closer, but to brush his hair away from his face. Her fingernails scraped along his temple and his scalp above his ear, and his hair went right back to covering his forehead so she did it again. Shivers traveled down his spine as if riding on razor blades, the emotion in her eyes too stark for him to avoid.

He felt her desperate ache to make things better

as if the words had come out of her mouth, and so he said those that were trying so hard to get out of his. "I missed you, too."

She leaned her elbow on the table then, propping her head in her hand, her eyes damp, her fingers now toying with the ends of his hair. He sat where he was, wanting to touch her, too, but more afraid of what would happen if he did than if he remained unmoving.

But almost as soon as he had the thought, she straightened and pulled away. "I have to go. I have an appointment for lunch. And my whining about all these numbers is keeping you from work."

"Actually, it's keeping me from grabbing some grub. I'd been on my way out when you came in."

"You should've gone," she said, getting to her feet and waving him toward the door.

He shrugged. "You looked like you needed a friend. Or at least an ear."

"I needed both. Thank you. And," she said, her tone strangely shy, "please don't cut your hair."

"You like it, huh?"

"I do."

"I've worn it long since getting out," he said, standing and flipping the milk crate back into place. "I figure if it worked for Samson . . ."

Gathering up her legal pad and laptop, she laughed. "Just don't get sucked in by a Delilah."

"Not going to happen." Besides, he was pretty sure his temptress had a different name.

❧ Chapter Nineteen ❧

Her meeting with Ian Payne on her mind, Thea left Bread and Bean and drove across town to Two Owls Café on the corner of Second and Chances. Facts and figures and the idea of taking on another business had her drowning, and flailing while she did. Why in the world did she think she could manage a second shop when her first wasn't even off the ground and the reputation of the second was more than she'd ever be able to live up to?

Todd talking again. And here she'd been so successful lately at blocking his disparaging remarks like they were browser pop-ups. She wasn't sure why doing so seemed easier these days. Possibly because after many months of uncertainty, things were finally looking up. She wasn't sure if that was because the women in her life were showing obvious signs of healing, or because of how much better she was feeling with the best friend she'd ever had back in her life.

It had taken her a while to come to terms with the truth, but as wonderful as it had been to see Indiana again, nothing came close to the comfort of Dakota being part of her days. And it made perfect sense when she viewed the past from the now and admitted that hanging with Indiana had been a means to an end. At least at first, until she'd gotten to know her. And, yeah. She'd tried to gloss over it since, not wanting to accept what a jerk she'd been as a teen.

Selfish, self-centered, self-involved. Those had been her three most noticeable—and obviously intertwined—traits. She'd been the only one interested in how she turned out, so it made a perverse sort of sense. Then she'd met Dakota, and for many months they'd been selfish together. She'd given him what he wanted, and she'd gotten the same in return. Then they'd started spending time together outside of bed, and time in bed talking.

That was when everything had changed. He'd been a senior. She'd been a freshman. Indiana, in eighth grade, had still been a middle-schooler, so they didn't see each other as often as they had the previous year. It had been harder to use Indiana as an excuse for showing up at the Keller home. Fortunately, the Keller parents paid little attention to their kids' comings and goings, and if they were there, sent Thea upstairs, ostensibly to see their daughter.

Making the turn onto Second Street, Thea reached over to aim the A/C vent at her face. Her palms were damp, her nape, too. Perspiration bloomed between her breasts. Damn Dakota Keller for making her sweat, and from no more than the memory of those long intimate nights.

The dreams and desires. None of which they'd ever believed would come true.

It would be good to see Indiana today, though she wasn't as thrilled to be having lunch with Kaylie and Luna. It wasn't like her to be social. She was, in fact, one of the least social people she knew. At least that's the way it was now. Before Todd, she'd been the life of the party. He'd liked that about her. Her outgoing nature was a big part of why they'd hooked up.

It was part of why she'd hooked up with Dakota, too. She hadn't been the least bit shy about going after what she wanted, even when it had meant using Indiana to get to him. Still, it had been worth it. For all of Dakota's claims that their last night together had kept him sane in prison, their entire relationship had kept her from being completely stupid and quitting school.

She didn't think she'd ever told him that.

After parking and exiting her car, she headed toward the café's porch, only to be intercepted by a waving Indiana. "Thea! Back here!" Detouring away from the sidewalk and onto the well-worn footpath through the yard, Thea met Indiana halfway, where they stopped to share a big hug, Indiana's cloud of dark hair smelling of sunshine.

"I'm so glad you could get away," Indiana said, linking their arms. "Between the shop and now the house, I wasn't sure you'd be able to."

Thea laughed, aching so badly to ask her friend

if she was her guardian angel, but not wanting to put Indiana on the spot. Who else could it be, really? "You realize I'm not the one doing the work, don't you? I'm not even supervising. I've got one of your brothers seeing to things on the hill and the other taking care of everything in town."

"And you have my complete sympathy," Indiana said as they walked. "Being at the mercy of one of those two would be enough to drive me to drink. But both? At the same time?"

"Guess it's a good thing I gave up alcohol. Then again . . ."

This time it was Indiana laughing, her joy infectious, the diamond in her wedding ring set flashing in the sun. "Come on. I'm dying for you to meet everyone, though I guess Luna is the only one you don't know."

Obviously Kaylie had told Tennessee they'd run into each other at the park, and Tennessee had shared the news with his sister. That was the way it worked with the Keller siblings. At least with those two, which had Thea wondering how tight their bond had grown during Dakota's absence, and if he sensed some of that now and felt left out, or as if he didn't belong, or wasn't needed, because of it.

Once Thea and Luna had been introduced, and their six degrees of separation narrowed down to their having Angelo in common, Kaylie pulled foil from the casserole dish in the center of the table, while Indiana uncovered the salad bowls, and Luna poured the iced tea. The three chattered and jostled comfortably, their movements showing off the simpatico of their friendships.

Not for a moment did Thea feel like a fifth wheel. The three's interaction wasn't quite that of Thea and the women she lived with, but then their situations were hardly the same. Thea's lunch partners were happily married. They didn't spend their days looking over their shoulders, their nights in the dark waiting for their locked doors to shake.

They didn't look at fresh deli soup and a variety of real cheese as a splurge. They didn't live hand-to-mouth, day-to-day, and yet they, too, were survivors. Suddenly Thea wished Ellie and Becca and Frannie were here to see their future. They would have this, all of them, one day. Thea would see to every bit of it.

"Here you go," Kaylie said from across the table, handing her a basket of bread. "Take one and pass it on. There's butter, honey, and Dolly's fresh strawberry jam."

Thea pulled aside the napkin, her eyes going wide as she reached for a roll and bounced it in her palm. "I have never in my life seen a hot roll this size. This one could serve as a softball."

"It's my foster mother's recipe," Kaylie said, pouring a drizzle of dressing onto her salad.

"They were one of the best parts of growing up in this house."

Thea stopped in the act of splitting open her roll. "I didn't know that about you. That you'd grown up here."

"I did. I came back and bought the place a little over three years ago. And thanks to Luna," she said, passing the dressing to the other woman, "I was able to reconnect with my birth father. Then when I wanted to put in the garden at the back of the lot," she added, waving in that direction, "Tennessee got in touch with Indiana."

"It was the first time we'd seen each other in years," Indiana said, stirring sweetener into her iced tea, and surprising Thea with the admission. She'd assumed the siblings had been the rock each needed. And she wondered if Dakota knew of the rift. "After everything that went on with Dakota, we drifted apart. Both of us feeling guilty, I guess." She shrugged, then she smiled and nodded towards Luna. "This one here managed to find Angelo again on her own."

"It was completely unexpected," Luna said, with a laugh, the sun catching on chunks of her sharply cut and very black hair. "But I really like how it worked out."

"I can imagine." Thea had met Angelo. He was definitely a catch. She set aside Indiana's confession to ask, "How did you know him?"

Luna gestured with her salad fork while she

chewed, then said, "His younger sister and I were best friends in school. She was killed in a car accident at the beginning of our senior year. It was the same accident that eventually took Oscar, Indiana's husband's brother."

Thea's stomach dropped. "I'm so sorry. I shouldn't have asked."

"No, please. Don't worry about it," Luna said sweetly. "Anyway, I bought the house that had belonged to the Caffey family, and Angelo found out. I went by after closing, and looked up, and there he was on the porch."

"And they lived happily ever after," Kaylie said, the three women laughing again. This time Thea joined them, though she wondered how much of what any of them felt was less joy than relief at having recovered from their emotional ordeals.

Luna's next words gave credence to her thoughts. "We've laughed about it a lot, and still do, as you've no doubt noticed. We've got sort of a survivor's club thing going on here."

Thea stabbed her fork into her vegetable lasagna, coming up with a zucchini slice, then asking, "Can I throw my hat in the ring for membership?"

"Is this about your seeing Dakota again?"

Thea shook her head in response to Indiana's question. She wiped her napkin over her mouth, then sat back, looking from one woman to the next. She had never told anyone the full story of her years spent with Todd. But these three women had made it. They had gotten beyond their tragedies, or at least learned to live with them. And that was exactly what Thea wanted for herself and the others she lived with.

"My ex kept me locked in our condo for nearly two years. The last two we were together. He chose what I would wear, what I would eat. Who I would see. What I would say when I saw them. He made me into someone that wasn't me. He hurt me during sex, then soothed it all better. I thought I could save him, you know. Being there for him. Listening. It had to be me, no one else. Turns out he couldn't be saved. Big surprise."

Then she took a deep breath and reached for her tea, feeling bizarrely relieved—though considering her earlier thoughts about the others, was her relief really that strange?

Seemed she did fit in.

"Oh, Thea," Indiana said, tears filling her eyes. "I'm so, so sorry. I had no idea."

"But you got out?" Luna asked, completely somber. "And you're okay?"

"I'm out, but I'm not sure about the okay part," she said with a strained laugh. "Though I am working on it. Every freaking day."

"You'll get there," Kaylie said, reaching across the table to take hold of her hand. "I promise. Just look at us."

"How did you do it?" Thea asked, blindsided by

the rush of charged emotion she felt at learning the bits and pieces the women had shared. "Get past the, well, past?"

"We didn't. Not really," Indiana said. "We are all our past."

"She's right," Luna added. "You don't need to move beyond it, as long as you don't look back. There's no need. You're not going that way."

Dakota was sitting on the top of the cottage's front steps, a longneck in his hand, when Thea's Subaru turned off Three Wishes Road into his driveway, and came to a stop behind his truck. She'd been scarce today around the shop. He'd talked to her this morning, then she'd disappeared for a long time around lunch. He'd heard her again this afternoon, but just briefly. More girl chatter before she'd come to fetch some paper-work from her desk. He'd had his table saw going, so no chance to say hello.

He'd missed that. Saying hello. Saying any-thing that came to mind and having her listen. Having her say what she was thinking without walking on eggshells, afraid the wrong words would break him. It had taken him weeks after arriving in Texas to convince his siblings they didn't need to couch things *just so* to keep from hurting his feelings, or risk him spiraling into some deep dark place. But Thea hadn't bothered.

Probably one of the reasons it was so easy to love her—

Aw, hell.

He brought his beer to his mouth and tried not to pay attention to the way she looked walking toward him. It wasn't easy. Instead of her usual knee shorts and baggy tanks, she had on those pants that stopped midcalf—in black—with sandals and a black-and-white striped shirt that was a little bit classier than a T. She also had on big pink sunglasses. The same color as the polish on her toes. Huh. First time he'd noticed that.

What he was noticing and in a very big way was her hair. Since the day he'd walked into Bread and Bean and seen her there on the floor, she'd worn her hair in a loose topknot thing that usually fell one way or the other, and always had pieces sticking this way and that like a rooster's tail. It was cute. He imagined it was cool. And it was completely Clark. She'd shoved it out of the way similarly in school, and hadn't taken it down in bed.

It was down now. And it was a lot longer than he'd realized. Almost to her elbows. With the wispy bangs that hung in careless points to her brow in some places and nearly into her eyes in others. It was laid-back hair. Messy hair. But cut to be so, and he liked it. Seeing it catch the breeze and blow around her shoulders, watching her reach up to clear it from her face, looking at the way the sun glinted off the lightest of the strands . . .

Yeah. He shouldn't have had a fourth beer. Then again, he'd had no idea she was going to stop by. She hadn't stopped by once since he'd lived here, and had only come to breakfast at his invitation. Besides, he was only on his way to being lit, not yet all the way there. He'd be okay, having her here, the unexpected temptation showing up when his guard was down and he was more vulnerable than he liked to admit.

Aw, hell.

"Long time no see," he said as she reached the steps.

"I had lunch with your sister today," she said in way of greeting.

He didn't know why that came as a surprise. "And lunch took all afternoon?"

"Kaylie was there," she said. "And Luna."

"That would explain it," he said, adding as casually as he could, "Nice hair, by the way."

"Thanks." She crossed her arms on the porch steps handrail. "I decided a lunch date deserved a little effort."

He lifted his bottle and drank, then backhanded his wrist over his mouth. "I see where I rate."

"You are not a lunch date. You're the hired help."

"Right."

She sighed, then propped her chin on top of

her arms. "Do you ever feel as if the universe is trying to tell you something?"

"How so?"

"Every time I turn around it seems like someone is telling me to stop worrying about the past and pay attention to the present, yet the past is so much a part of my present, I don't think I can."

"Want a beer?" he asked because he didn't want to comment on her observation. It cut a little too close to home.

She shook her head, pushed off the handrail, and came closer. "No thanks."

"I've got tequila inside," he said, jerking his chin that way.

"I don't drink anymore."

Well. This was interesting. "Because of the ex?"

"Because I like having a clear head."

"To think about the past?"

She shot him a look, then climbed the steps and sat beside him. "How was your day?"

"This is what we're doing now? Sharing the events of our days?"

"Why not? We're friends."

Friends. "I thought that was a couple's thing. Man comes home after a hard day at the office, listens to the little woman tell him her woes."

"That has to be the most sexist thing I've ever heard," she said, smacking him on the shoulder before leaning back on her elbows and lifting her face to what was left of the sun.

Dakota chuckled, staring at the steps between his feet instead of at the length of her neck. But it was her neck that he saw. Her neck that he couldn't get out of his mind. Her neck, and the way her hair fell to drag against the porch, and the smooth skin of her chest above her shirt's neckline, and her breasts beneath the fabric . . .

Aw, hell.

He leaned away from her to set his bottle on the porch, and then he leaned toward her because he couldn't help himself any longer. He'd been thinking about kissing her for weeks now. He probably thought about it a dozen times every day. It was hard not to when she was within reach again and he'd known her so well way back when.

Before she could open her eyes, he slid his forearm beneath her neck, bracing himself as he hovered over her. Her lips parted as if to speak, and then she looked at him, there above her. She blinked, her lashes fluttering, as if trying to clear him from her sight. He waited. He didn't want to scare her, or make her uncomfortable.

Finally she rested her head on his arm and reached up with one hand, raking her fingers into his hair and along his skull. Her wrist scraped over his cheek, and he rubbed against her, then turned enough for his lips to find the heel of her palm. He kissed her there, nipping lightly at the muscle as he lowered his gaze from hers to her mouth.

Still he waited, wanting to get this right. Her nostrils flared briefly, and her chest rose with her quick, rapid breaths, and then the tiniest sound escaped her mouth. A moan, a sad one, as if she were giving up instead of giving in, and he hesitated, lifting his head just enough to signal his intent to put a stop to what had never really started.

He was not going to screw this up. He was not going to give her a single regret.

"Stay." She whispered the word, and it wasn't the least bit sad.

"Only if you're sure."

"I am," she said, nodding as she did. "It's been so long. Years. Forever. My whole life."

It seemed that way to him, too. But the second his lips touched hers he forgot all the time he'd waited and fell into the moment, all of it so familiar and yet completely new. Her lips were soft, and she took no time parting them; her tongue had found his within moments.

He didn't press, keeping things on an even keel, one he could deal with without losing his mind, though he feared he was looking at a lost cause. This was Thea, not one of the other women he'd had the pleasure to know during the years he'd been unable to face home.

She slid her tongue along his, then pulled away

to tug at his lower lip and breathe. His heart had swelled until his chest hurt with it, and the pounding had reached the base of his skull. He wanted to blame the beer. Damn, he wanted to blame the beer. But he couldn't.

It had been this way with them every time. And the fact that nothing had changed left him feeling punched. He hurt with what she made him feel as her lips played over his, her teeth catching him lightly, her tongue hot and wet and wistful as she swept it through his mouth.

He pushed harder against her because it was what he had to do. He'd never thought he'd have her again. Not this way. Not outside of the past he remembered as if it were yesterday, not when they hadn't been teenagers and life hadn't gone to hell. They weren't teenagers now.

Thea loved him with her mouth as if he mattered, as if nothing else did, and he loved her back the same, telling her with his hand sliding down to her hip what it was like to know her again, with his fingers at her cheek and her jaw how much he'd missed her, how he'd wanted for so long to open the door and find her there. With his mouth, how he hadn't realized any of this until just this very moment. He sighed then, and lifted his head. Trouble. They were in so very much.

"What was that?" she finally asked him, having spent the seconds since their parting blowing out long, slow breaths.

"It's been a while since I've done it, but I'm pretty sure it was a kiss," he said.

"That wasn't any kiss I've ever known."

"I hope that's a good thing."

She didn't respond to that, saying instead, "It's only good if we're not heading into a relationship. I don't think either one of us is ready for that."

Yeah. He'd pretty much known that when he'd started. "You're getting a little deep on me, Clark. I was just having fun."

"And you're forgetting how well I know you. You don't do anything for fun. Not anymore."

The thing of it was, she was right. About both. The fun part wasn't a big deal; he could live with it. Having Thea Clark knowing him as well as she did . . .

Aw, hell.

Chapter Twenty

Baking bread with Ellie Brass turned out to be a great way to spend a Saturday. Lena learned things about the science of food she'd never even imagined. Ellie knew everything. How different ingredients reacted when barely whisked together. How they reacted when heartily stirred. How baking soda and baking powder were not the same thing. How salt that wasn't even noticeable made things taste so much better.

Frannie and her boys were in and out as she did laundry and other chores. James helped as much as he could, and when Ellie had downtime waiting for loaves to rise, she scoured the kitchen. Lena helped, though it bothered Ellie for some reason that she did. Ellie said Lena was a guest and guests didn't need to clean. Lena insisted she was a friend and friends pitched in whenever and where ever they could.

It seemed a foreign concept to Ellie, which had Lena wondering yet again what the other woman had been through that had left her so insecure, and so fearful that she wasn't doing enough. As if her own needs weren't important, but she was responsible for meeting those of everyone around her. Something had gone very wrong in her life. Something Lena wondered if she'd ever be able to work her way past.

"When did you start baking? How did you figure out how to do all of this?" she asked with a wave of her arm, encompassing the cooling loaves and those that were rising and the table loaded down with oats and seeds and honey and a half dozen types of flour. "Because I am so totally impressed."

"I worked in a bakery after losing my teaching job," Ellie said with a shrug. "It's not a big deal. Lots of people bake. But I don't know anyone who can make candy."

"I don't make the candy," Lena reminded her. "That's all Callum."

"Still, you know how it's done." Ellie tossed the long braid of her hair over her shoulder before bending to tap a wooden spoon on the top of a loaf ready to come out of the oven. "You could probably wing it if you had to."

Leaning against the counter in front of the sink, Lena laughed. "Not a chance. What Callum does is art. Just like what you do is art. And I'm dying for a slice of that art, all buttery and warm."

Ellie closed the oven door and gestured toward the table with the spoon she still held. "The honey wheat is cool enough to slice. Is that okay?"

"I'll be happy with anything. Trust me. And it's even better knowing you made it."

Avoiding Lena's gaze, Ellie set down the spoon and dug for a serrated bread knife in a drawer. Her smile was weak and nervous. "You don't have to say that."

"I know I don't have to," Lena said, hating how hard it was for Ellie to accept a compliment, and wondering again how such an accomplished woman had been stripped of her confidence. It was bullshit, whatever had been done to her. "I want to because I mean it."

"You're just being sweet—"

"No, Ellie," Lena said, frustrated, and reaching for the other woman's wrist. "I'm serious. I think it's incredible—"

And then she stopped because Ellie had dropped the knife and was doing her best to pull down her sleeve and cover her forearm where Lena still held her. Lena looked down, her gaze drawn to Ellie's burn scars she'd noticed the day they'd met.

She took Ellie's other hand in hers to stop her. "I'm sorry that happened to you. I'm sorry you were hurt."

"I didn't want you to see." The words came out on a whisper, Ellie's eyes red and watery and sad. "It's a souvenir of a relationship I'm never going to get rid of. The souvenir, I mean, though sometimes I wonder if the relationship won't haunt me for the rest of my life."

"It won't if you don't let it," Lena said, then added because she needed to be one hundred percent certain: "Shitty boyfriends suck."

Ellie took a long moment to respond, holding Lena's gaze, her own searching and nervous as she said, "So do shitty girlfriends."

And now she was. Certain. Lena swallowed. "Yeah. A lot of people don't get that."

"Right?" Ellie said, shaking now, her breathing ragged. "Like one woman can't beat the crap out of another. One she swears she loves while she's still holding the flashlight responsible for the blood dripping from the other's forehead."

"Ellie. Crap. Let me see," Lena said, reaching

up to brush aside Ellie's bangs. "Oh, man. Oh, baby." Swallowing so much hurt she thought she would choke from it, Lena outlined the V-shaped gouge of a scar with her finger, a touch so light she could barely feel Ellie's skin.

Ellie shivered, and the tears in her eyes fell silently, streaking her cheeks. "I'm sorry you didn't know me before all of this. I was so much more fun then."

Lena thought she might explode with the rage burning through her like a lit rocket. "What're you talking about? There's nothing wrong with this you. Nothing at all."

"Besides the fact that I can't walk without bumping into people because I'm looking over my shoulder? Or that I can't live on my own because I can't afford windows with bulletproof glass? I can't get a job that pays enough for cheese to go with my bread because I need the protection of Thea's network in case I need to run?"

"Why would you need to run?" Lena asked, frowning as she absorbed all that Ellie had just told her, truths Lena couldn't imagine anyone outside of this house knowing.

Ellie shook her head, her braid falling forward. "You don't want to know."

"Yeah. I do." That was one thing she needed Ellie to understand. "But you don't have to tell me. I can respect needing to keep some things to yourself."

"Do you have them? Things you don't want anyone else finding out?"

Lena looked down at her hands still holding Ellie's, at the scar at the base of her thumb. Most of her scars ran deeper, but this one was easier to talk about. "My mother did this to me," she said, pulling one hand free to point. "It's my reminder of how someone you've known all your life can turn out to be someone you didn't know at all."

"I guess I misunderstood," Ellie said, frowning. "I thought you and your mother were close."

"We are close."

"But if she did this—"

"It was an accident. She was trying to save me from my father. Save us both, really."

"Your father was abusive?"

Abusive wasn't a strong enough word. "My father was a monster. My mother didn't know it when she married him. She didn't know it when they had me. I didn't know it the years she worked and he stayed home and cooked me breakfast and got me to school. Not for the first few anyway."

"Maybe he wasn't a monster then. Did something happen?"

Lena shrugged, remembering things she didn't want to remember. "He lost his job. His industry was in the toilet and he couldn't get another one.

He started drinking with dinner. Then drinking with lunch. Then drinking his first shot of the day with his morning coffee."

"Oh, Lena," Ellie said, her voice breaking.

"It's okay, El. I survived. My mother survived. He left us in a pretty comfortable way, the insurance and all, which a part of me thinks he would've hated."

"Why would he have hated it? He was the one who took out the policy right?"

Nodding, Lena said, "He liked to threaten my mother with it. He would tell her if she didn't do this or that when he ordered her to, he would cancel it. So when he told her to jump she did. If it wasn't high enough she did it again. I guess he finally forgot about it. Or was never sober long enough to follow through."

"What a horrible way for you to grow up."

"It was a lot worse on my mom than it was on me, but yeah. I hated that she had to put up with that bullshit.

"I can imagine. I was really lucky. I had an all-American childhood. It was later when things went to crap."

"You can say shit you know. It's okay with me."

Ellie laughed at that. Then she grew somber, rubbing at the mark on Lena's thumb. "Strange that of all things we should have scars in common."

"I'm sure we have more than that," Lena said,

hope like bread dough rising. "It will just take time to find out."

We are all our past.

The thought had stuck with Thea since leaving Two Owls Café and had been the reason she'd gone to Dakota's last evening instead of home to the house on Dragon Fire Hill. And what a big mistake that had been, though Dakota had started it, and Dakota had been the one behind a few beers, not her.

That didn't absolve her of participating, or wanting to erase everything Todd from her life and everything prison from Dakota's, or wishing they could start over as two brand new people sans baggage.

We are all our past.

She hated to say it but she was almost glad Dakota had decided to leave. Their not living in the same small town would make her life so much easier. She wouldn't find herself drawn into his drama. She had enough of her own to last a lifetime; how could she take on his, too?

Yet how could she not? How could she separate wanting him as the man he was from having wanted him, having had him, when what they'd known about life had been contained in their own small spheres?

We are all our past.

Life was so unfair, *so* unfair, taking him away

from her when she'd needed him the most, bringing him back when she couldn't have him. *She could not have him.* She was up to her eyeballs with paying back what she owed, and doing what she could to pay forward. He would consume her, and she was helpless.

Funny how she'd gone all these years unaware of how much she'd missed him until he'd been a daily fixture in her life once again. And speaking of the very devil walking in when she least expected him.

"I didn't think I'd find you here on a Saturday."

"I hadn't planned to be, but the house isn't conducive to anything requiring concentration these days." She didn't ask him what he was doing here. She didn't want to hear him say he'd come looking for her just as much as she didn't want to hear him say he hadn't. Right. That kiss hadn't screwed her up or anything.

He came closer and glanced down at her paperwork. "What're you up to?"

"Looking at some numbers I got from Peggy Butters and her attorney. Trying to decide if I, if the *co-op,* can afford to buy her bakery."

"Huh. I didn't know she was selling," he said, and moved to the coffee pot. "Is that what all the cake eating and watching the traffic flow was about?"

The coffee was fresh. She hadn't even had her first cup. "I don't think it's common knowledge.

And, yes. It was."

He looked over while his mug filled. "So the *co-op* has enough money to do that?"

"Not that it's any of your business," she said, more irritated than she'd realized and for no reason that made sense, "but no. I would provide the initial investment."

"Just like you did here?"

She shook her head, ignoring the fit of his T-shirt and the hair at his nape caught in the neckband. She squeezed her pencil tighter. "Bread and Bean is mine. Ellie and Becca and Frannie are my employees."

"The bakery would be different?"

She nodded. "We would set up a partnership. But there's a lot more involved than money."

"Like whether or not they're going to stick around," he said, lifting his cup, blowing across the surface, his mouth drawing her gaze and taking her back to their kiss.

Why was he here? *Why?* "I wouldn't put it that way, but yeah. I mean, I'm staying. I bought the house. I'm opening the business. But the others . . ."

He took a sip of the coffee, his gaze still holding hers. "They're only living with you while they get back on their feet."

Now he was just being nosy. "Something like that."

"And they may not want to call Hope Springs

home once they do."

She tossed her pen to the table and sat back in her chair. She was done with him prying into this part of her life. "I guess that would depend on how happy they are living here."

Dakota grinned, his gaze on his coffee now, dimples pulling deep into the scruff covering his cheeks. "Point to Clark," he said, then changed the subject. "You told me about the beans. But why coffee? And bread?"

Fine. Memory Lane was better than an ongoing Q&A. She got up and found her mug, pumping it full from the carafe and breathing in the heady steam. "I went to Spain one summer with my ex. While he was off doing his extreme-sports things, I explored the cities we were in. One of my favorite spots was a tiny coffee shop. It was open-air, with tables outside under an awning. The owners also sold bread and pastries. We stayed there nearly a month.

"I didn't know there were that many extreme things to do in Spain, but between the surfing, the rafting, the hiking, my ex stayed busy, and I studied that little shop like I'd be given a test and my life depended on it. I paid attention to what the regulars ordered, what the tourists ordered. Which breads sold the best. Which were offered on which days. Which had customers lining up before the shop opened." She looked down into her cup, smiled at the memory. "You can't begin to imagine the smells. I could've lived there. I got to know the owners well enough to get a look at the kitchen. I don't think I've ever been as happy anywhere as I was that month. It felt like home."

She stopped then, her hands shaking, the surface of her coffee rippling as she raised the drink to her mouth. She sipped, wishing for the first time in years that she hadn't given up alcohol. She couldn't remember the last time she'd felt such a strong urge for a crutch. And she couldn't figure out why.

The trip to Spain had been the best time she'd had during her years with Todd. She'd been able to deal with the nights in his bed, the mornings after, the long dresses to hide the bruises that shorts would've revealed on her thighs. And maybe that was it. Everything she had now, everything she was, had been born during that month.

It was when she'd decided to leave him the next time he left her alone.

"You never have said if you're happy living here."

Dakota's comment brought her back, and she returned to her chair, glad to be faced with the simplicity of construction and business woes. "I'm too busy to be anything but tired. But I'm not unhappy."

"Why Hope Springs? I mean, I know things

weren't great for you in Round Rock, but why not go back there where things were familiar?"

She drank half of her coffee while deciding what to tell him. She ended up telling him the truth. "I never left Round Rock."

That had him stopping with his cup halfway to his mouth. "I thought you said you'd been all over."

"Been. Not lived. Todd's company was headquartered in Austin. He commuted. I stayed home." Not that their condo had ever been a home as much as it had been a cell. A cushy cell. With all the amenities. But still a cell.

"How did you meet him?"

Good grief. "Why are you asking me about my past again?"

"Because I want to know."

She closed her eyes, stretched her arms overhead then side to side. "I was working as a waitress at a club in Austin. He was a regular. That's all. And don't look at me like that's *not* all because you're not getting anything else."

He moved to lean against the barista station. "But why come to Hope Springs?"

"Do we have to do this now?" She was exhausted, and she didn't want to get into something deep, and she certainly didn't want to bring up the kiss, but it was right there in the front of her mind and . . . and . . . and . . .

She got up from her paperwork and headed for

the espresso machine. She needed more caffeine like she needed another hole in her head, but it was either fool with the coffee and the filter basket and the dials or thread her fingers into Dakota's hair and pull him close.

"Do what?"

"You nearly walked out on me the first day you were here because I brought up the subject of prison. My past with my ex feels like that to me. I did things I'm not proud of when I left that relationship. Things that might not exactly be legal. But I didn't stop to ask. I needed to get out."

"Thea—"

"Your kissing me doesn't change anything."

"My kissing you?" His eyes widened, then almost immediately narrowed. "What about your kissing me?"

She didn't want to talk about that. She didn't want to think about that. It had been a moment of weakness she couldn't admit to him. It was bad enough she had to admit it to herself. She had to be resolute. There was no room in her life for anything short of absolute strength. She would not kiss him again.

"We can't do this, Dakota," she said, spinning on him. "We can't be anything anymore besides friends. I came here to start over, not to go back."

"You think I'm asking you to go back? What in the hell makes you think I would ever want to go back?"

The truth was going to hurt. But that's what truth did. "Maybe because nothing I've seen has me believing you've done anything about going forward. And I can't be with you when we're moving in two different directions."

Walking into the Back Alley Pub beside Manny Balleza felt as wrong to Becca as it did right. No. It felt more wrong. Completely wrong. In fact, nothing about it felt right at all. Nothing. Zero. Zip.

For one thing, she hated going out in public. She hated being in public. She shouldn't. There was very little chance of Dez finding her. There was very little chance he was still looking. Knowing him as well as she unfortunately did, there wasn't a doubt in her mind he'd found someone new to receive his particular brand of love after doing his time for loving her so thoroughly.

But Dez had a lot of friends, and those friends weren't particularly happy about their good buddy getting jail time for the stripes he'd put on her back. It had been two years ago, sure. Everyone should've moved on by now. But Becca had received enough threats after Dez's sentencing to put the *moving on* in her court.

The domestic abuse counselor she'd been assigned while hospitalized had facilitated her transfer to the women's shelter when released. That was where she'd met Thea and Ellie. And when Thea had struck out on her own, Becca had come soon after. Ellie had followed a few weeks later, once the windows and doors had been installed in the house on Dragon Fire Hill. Unlike Becca's ex, Ellie's had never been prosecuted for the abuse the bitch had inflicted. Becca couldn't imagine Ellie and Lena going out to dinner at the Back Alley Pub, or anywhere.

Then again, she'd never imagined herself doing so, yet here she was, rights and wrongs and Manny Balleza's hand hovering in the small of her back as they followed the hostess to their booth.

"Will this table be okay?" the girl asked, her skin the same color as Becca's, her hair worn natural, too, but cropped close.

"It's fine," Becca said without checking with her date. She should have, she supposed, but she was more interested in sliding into the high-backed booth than she was his opinion. Which was why she didn't make for a very good . . . date. She'd almost said girlfriend, but stopped herself in time.

"Your server tonight will be Carey," the hostess said, her smile plastic, her gaze moving from Becca to Manny and back. She arched a brow, still fake smiling. "He'll be right with you."

"Thanks," Becca said, again more concerned

with sitting than being served, though a part of her wanted to get in the hostess's face and ask her if she had something she wanted to spit out. Manny hadn't said a word since they'd walked inside, letting Becca run the show. But now she turned to him and asked, "Which side do you want?"

He rubbed at the fuzz on his chin, which had a whole lot of white hairs mixed in with the black, and looked from her to the booth and back. "I get a choice?"

She came very close to flouncing out. It was his smile hiding behind his hand that stopped her.

But not her sarcasm. "Yes, you get a choice."

"About what I eat, too?"

The man was asking for it. "Left or right? Choose one, or I'm going to."

"What if I want to sit next to you?"

She swallowed, her stomach tumbling. "Why would you want to do that?"

But instead of answering he shook his head and scooted into the seat on the right, leaving her the left or the extra room beside him. She chose the left, then opened the menu the hostess had set on the table.

"I don't bite, you know," Manny leaned forward to say.

"Actually, I don't know," she said. And then, to see how he would react, and for no other reason, she said, "Though biting's not such a bad thing.

When done right."

"I'll remember that," he said, opening his menu without looking at it at all, his gaze having room for only her.

Laid back. Unflappable. Did nothing ever bother the man? Not that she wanted to bring sex into the equation, but his even keel bugged her more than it should have, and she didn't know why.

Carey came then to take their order. She decided on a nutty brunette brown ale and a bacon-and-blue-cheese burger. Manny listened to her choices then told their server to bring him the same. Once the kid collected their menus and left, Becca said, "They have a whole lot of other things to eat, you know. If you'd looked at your menu, you would've seen that."

"I know what they have. I've been here before." He leaned into the corner, stretched out one arm along the back of the booth. "What you're having sounded good."

"If you say so," she said, reaching for a sugar packet and tapping it against the table.

"You don't believe me?"

"I don't know you. I don't know what I believe. You could be serious. You could be mocking me. You could be scamming me because you want something, the least of which is sex."

He waited for a long moment, Carey arriving with their beers as if he'd been hovering and

326

waiting for Becca to take a breath before delivering them. Once he'd set the two foaming glasses on their napkins, he left, giving Manny the floor.

"I have no secrets, Becca," he said and reached for his beer. "And I don't expect you to tell me yours. Ask me anything. And tell me whatever you want me to know. It's really not that hard."

"Fine." She started where she had no business going, but they couldn't do this on a regular basis if he didn't know where she'd come from. "Do you know why we all live on Dragon Fire Hill? Together?"

"I don't know the particulars," he said, returning his glass to the table and leaning forward, one arm on the table. "But I've seen the doors and the windows, and I can take a guess. And I'm sorry you have to live like that. No woman ever should, no child, no man."

She nodded. The words sounded nice anyway. "You work with criminal types, don't you? Like Frank?" she asked, having heard some of Frank's history from the man's own mouth. "And Dakota?"

"I'm Frank's parole officer, yes. And I was Dakota's years ago. The men I work with, that I send to Keller Construction, are men who've done things they shouldn't have, but for reasons that, quite frankly, are often hard to argue with."

"Like Dakota protecting his sister."

"You know Dakota's story?" Manny asked, and

when she nodded, he went on. "Then you probably know that his choice wasn't the best one he could've made."

"Because it was more about avenging than protecting," she said, and Manny remained silent as their food was placed in front of them, giving Becca a chance to continue once they were alone. "Sometimes avenging is the only thing you can do."

He shook his head as he spread his napkin over his lap. "It may feel that way. And it may feel better that way. But answering one act of violence with another is never the only thing you can do."

Uh-huh. "You work for the system. Of course you'd say that."

"You've got that backward."

"How so?"

"I work for the system because it's what I believe." He lifted his burger. "That there's no need for violence to beget violence. Encouraging that mind-set only makes things worse," he said, biting in.

"And I guess you hug trees, too," she said around a bite of her own.

He shrugged. "I've been known to sing to my plants. Or at least sing along while playing them some Boz Scaggs."

"Who's Boz Scaggs?"

He set down his burger, reached for his

napkin, and pointed as he said, "And that right there is why I'm way too old for you."

She ignored him to say, "You probably wouldn't believe that if you'd had a family member victimized, or been a victim yourself. The violence thing. Not the Boz . . . whatever."

He was slow to respond, taking a long swallow of beer, returning his cup to its napkin coaster, finally letting it go. "I have been a victim. My wife was murdered less than a year after we were married."

His words sucked the air from her lungs. She didn't know what to say. She couldn't even look at him. But neither could she stay where she was and let him think he was alone, think she didn't care. She might come across as a bitch, and she admitted to cultivating the skin, but that's all it was, and it was suddenly important for Manny to know the real Becca York.

She scooted off her bench and scooted onto his, moving as close to him as she could without touching him. Then moving another inch as she pulled her plate in front of her. "Manny—"

"I'm okay," he said before she could get out more than that. "I survived. It was more than a decade ago, and there's not a day that goes by that I don't think about her, about Alisha. But I don't base every move I make on what happened to her."

Then it hit her, and she had to turn on the booth to face him. "But you do. Because you chose to work with ex-cons because of her. Didn't you?"

He arched a brow as he looked at her. "You're not supposed to be that smart."

"Oh, yeah?" God, but he was really gorgeous this close. "What am I supposed to be?"

"You tell me," he said as Carey returned with their check. Manny tossed cash on the table to cover it. She waited for him to nod, then she left, heading out the front door to his car.

What was happening to her? This was why she didn't need to be in a relationship. It was so much smarter, so much safer, so much easier on her nerves to keep things simple and stick to being friends. But she knew even as the words tumbled through her head that being friends was not what was happening here, and it frightened her even more than her past.

"What do you want from me Manny?" she asked, hearing him walk up behind her.

His laugh was a throaty threat. "I'm not sure you want to know."

She wanted to. She desperately wanted to. She clenched her jaw so tight she thought her skin might pop. Arms crossed, she looked out into the night, seeing the twinkle of lights in Hope Springs.

Hope was such a stupid emotion. Hope never came true.

Manny moved in closer. She heard his steps on the pavement, felt the heat of his body when he came near, smelled the aftershave she hated that on him she'd grown used to.

"I want you, Becca York. I'm crazy for you. But I'm not going to sleep with you until I know without a doubt it's what you want, too. Not the sex. Me," he said, and set his hands on her shoulders. "I'm not about to screw up what we might have here by rushing it."

Her voice shook when she said, "I'm so scared."

"Don't be." And then he lowered his head, and parted his lips against her neck, right where it met her shoulder.

It felt so good to be wanted. To be more than wanted. To be treasured, because that's what he made her feel.

His hands slid down her arms, squeezing her biceps, cupping her elbows, finding her wrists, then lacing their fingers, keeping the whole length of his arms against the whole length of hers. He nuzzled the skin beneath her ear, tugged on her earlobe with his lips, rubbed his nose against her jaw.

She was shivering everywhere, shaking where she stood, and still he held her, pulling her into his hips where she felt cradled and sheltered. Where she felt safe. And as securely as he held her, she knew she could step free at any time. He wouldn't keep her against her will. He wouldn't force her.

Moving away was the last thing she wanted, but

she did so she could turn and lean into him, and wrap her arms around him. She found his jaw with her lips, setting them there, then kissing his stubbled skin. He was warm, and she was growing warmer, and parts of her body that had been asleep for so long were waking up, and oh were they suddenly demanding.

"Becca—"

"Shh," she said, laying her index finger against his lips. "Please don't talk. Just be here with me. Please."

"Becca—"

"Manuel. Manny." She stopped, swallowing her fear and misgivings and every doubt she'd had. "I'm so tired of looking behind me. I want to look ahead."

"Then you've come to the right man," he said, slinging an arm around her and covering her mouth with his.

Chapter Twenty-one

Dakota had just turned off the kitchen light, having rinsed out the sink after cleaning the ketchup from the plate he'd used for dinner, when he heard the car outside. He hadn't cooked. He'd picked up a bacon cheeseburger basket at Back Alley Pub after work. Unfortunately, the pickles and tomatoes had soaked the bun and the wrapper both, and when the paper had torn under duress, he'd slid everything onto a plate.

He walked to the front door. It stood open in the early summer night, the breeze cutting through the house to exit through the screen in the kitchen. If he'd been home during the day, he would've run the A/C, but since he was only here to sleep, he gave himself the luxury of fresh air and a tiny little power bill. Looking outside, he saw the blue Subaru. Then saw Thea talking to herself as she walked toward the cottage.

Thea, climbing the steps to the porch.

Thea, holding his gaze while his heart cracked behind his ribs.

Thea, planting a hand in the center of his chest right where he was breaking, and pushing him into the room, kicking the door shut behind her. She took one of his hands in hers and turned toward the bedroom.

"What—"

She spun to press her finger to his lips, whispering, "Shh. Don't say a word or I'll change my mind. Unless you want me to change my mind," she added, letting her finger slide down his chin, his neck, over his Adam's apple and into the hollow of his throat. Then she hooked it over the band of his T-shirt and pulled.

He went willingly, silently, desperately, and anxious, wanting to ask her what had brought her here, but he feared the answers even more than he wanted to know. And so he kept his mouth shut and walked through the darkness to the only bed in the house. The window was open in here, too, the curtains fluttering, light from the moon shining in on the sheets he'd left crumpled this morning.

They weren't exactly dirty, though they certainly weren't clean, but Thea was toeing off her shoes and slipping off her tank top, taking away that particular pleasure he would've loved for him-self. He reached for the hem of his T-shirt and pulled it off. Then he moved his hands to the waist of his jeans. Thea stopped him.

She released the top button with shaking fingers, then freed the rest until his fly parted, dragging the backs of her nails from his boxers through the hair on his abdomen and up his chest. Once there, she spread out her fingers, flexing them against his pecs, then slid her hands to his neck and pulled him down.

He groaned, wrapped his arms around her waist and lifted her against him. She hooked one leg behind his hips and leaned back. They fell to the bed together, and lost the rest of their clothes in a flurry of hips wiggling and hands tugging, and Dakota didn't even bother with his socks.He was naked enough, and she was beside him, and nothing else mattered.

He rolled to his side, facing her as he brought up his hand to cup her face. He remembered this, touching her softly, being gentler than he'd ever known he could be.

She smiled, a tentative movement of her lips, then she turned her head and kissed the center of his palm, holding his hand in place with her own, hers so small, her fingers so slender when she threaded them through his. He'd forgotten so many things about his past, but he still knew every bit of Thea, even though what he knew belonged in the long ago when they hadn't known shit about making love.

Leaning close, he brought his mouth to hers. Her lips were soft, and they parted without reservation, and she squeezed his hand until it felt as if she would cut off every bit of blood flow to his fingers. He wiggled them and pulled free, running his palm from her shoulder to her elbow, then sliding over the curve of her arm to her waist, to her hip, to the back of her thigh which he lifted and draped over his.

She ran her foot up and down his calf. "I don't remember these muscles."

"And I don't remember these," he said, his hand once again at her shoulder and squeezing.

"I still can't do but one or two pull-ups, but I can kill a punching bag."

"I'll bet," he said, pushing her down and crawling over her, then pinning her arms above her head. "Something tells me this would be a really good time for a pair of handcuffs," he said, then wished he hadn't, and waited to see if he'd ruined everything.

But all she did was laugh, sliding her feet along his legs and tucking them next to his. "A real punching bag, silly. I'm the last person you'll ever see using another person instead."

Because she'd been used as one. Maybe not literally, but emotionally, mentally. Though for all he knew some of her damage could be found on her body in scars. He wanted to run his hands over her, to find them, to feel how deep they ran, to learn how she'd been marked.

But he didn't. Instead, he held her wrists with one hand, and slid his other between their bodies, finding her wet and ready, and guiding his sheathed cock between her legs.

She gasped when he pushed into her, rising up against him, then taking him with her as she settled back onto the bed. She hooked her heels beneath his rump and held tight with her legs as he stroked, shoving deep, pulling free, sticking with a rhythm he knew well. A rhythm that had always worked for Thea. A rhythm she'd taught him she liked.

That had been so many years ago, yet looking into her eyes now he saw the girl she'd been as well as the woman she was. It left him confused, left him aching. He closed his eyes and dropped his forehead to hers, breathing in the air she breathed out as they moved. Their hearts pounded as one, their body heat rising, their skin growing slick in the warmth of the room.

It was hard not to give in and let go. They had all night. They didn't have to make this more than it was or needed to be. Not this first time after so many years and so much history. Not after living for a third of his life with the memory of their last time and how it had saved him, kept him sane, left him wrecked for every other woman he'd known. Not—

"Dakota?"

"I'm here."

"Hurry."

He chuckled, and lifted his head from hers, and looked into her eyes. "I can do that."

"Then do it now," she said, squirming beneath it. "Make me mindless. Make me disappear. Make me forget everything. Make me come."

Her hands roamed his back, one reaching his head and her fingers threading into his hair to urge him down. She opened her mouth beneath his and kissed him, catching his bottom lip between hers, and tugging playfully until he was gasping for breath and had to pull free.

And that was it. They moved as one until neither of them had any reason left to hold on, and they both let go, coming together, coming apart. Coming to know nothing after this would ever be the same between them. Coming. Coming.

Coming.

• • •

"Tell me something," Thea said, snuggling up to Dakota's side. All these years later, and here they were, warm and comfortable, like a coat taken out for the winter, or a favorite childhood blanket that smelled of home. It was as if there had never been prison or Todd or the need to buy the house on Dragon Fire Hill for a shelter. As if nothing had come between them. As if they'd been here together all along. It was a wonderful feeling, and she never wanted to let it go.

Strange how she knew his body so well, yet didn't know it at all. This wasn't the body she'd curled up against all those years ago, the body she'd allowed into hers, the body she'd taken with hers. His differences made her wonder about her own, or at least the ones she couldn't see.

She was narrower in her waist, heavier in her hips. That much she knew by the fit of her clothes. Her bustline hadn't changed much, though gravity was doing its best to drag things down. Fortunately, weight lifting had given her some pretty buff shoulders, and her triceps weren't anything to laugh about. Funny the toll life took on joints and muscles.

"What?" he finally asked after a long minute of thinking and breathing and little else.

"Pick something. Anything." She wanted to listen to him talk. To hear what he had on his mind. Doing so had been one of her favorite parts of their past: sex first, every other thing in the world that mattered next. It was almost as if they'd needed to make that visceral, physical connection to allow the rest of what they shared to find a way out.

Oh, but they'd shared a lot.

"The earth is round."

So it was going to be like that, was it? Not that his reticence to be revealing surprised her.

This Dakota, older and wiser and broken in ways that went far beyond her ability to deal with, wasn't much for talking. Even with her understanding of damage, she hadn't been very successful in finding a chink in his armor. Crazy how much she wanted to.

She prompted him. "Tell me something about your life. Where you've been. What you've done. More than the barista, cattle wrangling, and construction stuff."

"I thought we agreed not to revisit the past."

"That was before."

"Before what?"

"This," she said, spreading out her fingers over his belly, threading them into the coarse hair growing low there.

"The way you showed up out of the blue, I thought this might be no-strings-attached sex."

"It is," she said, trying not to think about the promises she'd made to herself, that sex, when she was brave enough to explore such intimacy again, would be wrapped up in glittery ribbons and bows. That it would tie her tightly to the man she found deserving. That strings would be everywhere. Hundreds of them. Thousands. She wanted to know the emotional ties were tight, and that she was safe before indulging.

Yet sleeping with Dakota . . . She didn't feel like a sellout at all—a thought she tucked away to look at later. For now she chalked up the urge that had sent her here to finding comfort in the favorite and the familiar. Dakota Keller was both. He'd always been a part of her. She thought he always would.

He grunted in answer. "Not sure I believe that, but it's your party."

"Then that means I should get my way," she said, pushing a tangle of sheet from between her feet so she could find his. "Talk to me like you used to. I loved that, you know. Listening to you after sex. It was the only time you really talked. About things that mattered anyway."

"Except that last time."

The one place she hadn't expected him to go. The one place she wasn't sure she wanted him to. "I fell asleep. When I woke up you were gone. If you talked to me, I didn't know."

He raised one arm, tucking it beneath his head. The other he wrapped around her shoulders, securing her against him. "When I got back home, that last night before prison, my lawyer was waiting there with my parents. My dad was pacing the kitchen. Tennessee and Indiana were sitting on the stairs, like they'd been in bed and heard me come in so had gotten back up. I guess my folks were afraid I had split. That I was regretting what I'd done and didn't want to have to pay for what was a big fat mistake."

"Did you?" she asked softly, spreading her fingers over his chest. "Regret it?"

"No. And it was never a mistake. Tennessee knew that. When I picked up the bat that night, we looked at each other. I didn't say anything, and all he did was nod, but he knew I was asking him if going after Robby for what he'd done to Indiana was the right thing to do."

"And it was?"

He didn't answer her question, continuing on as if she hadn't said a thing. "My lawyer took me outside, away from my folks. They were absolutely useless. Nothing new there, but that was the first time I realized the extent of that particular truth." He went silent for several seconds, as if reliving the moment of awareness. "He told me I had to be strong, and I thought *what a worthless piece of advice,* but then he grabbed me by the arm and wouldn't let go.

"I jerked, trying to get away, but I didn't really fight him, and he held tight. He wasn't a big guy, not much taller than me, but obviously a whole lot stronger. Yeah, I knew how to swing a bat, but

341

that was nothing. And that was his point. I was going into a place where men waited for fresh meat. Especially young meat. And pretty meat." He snorted. "First time I'd ever hated my looks."

Thea shivered. "Oh, Dakota."

"He didn't just tell me I had to be strong. He showed me why, just by holding me there, then he explained in very crude detail what I was going to be up against. Once I'd finished hyperventilating, he went into the how of making it happen. A very specific how. Crunches and push-ups and squats and running in place. Jumping with an imaginary rope. I started the first day, as soon as I rolled out of bed. I earned a rep as a crazy man not to be messed with. I went in with one body, came out with another. Indiana said the day I got out that she didn't recognize me until I'd walked past them and gotten into a cab."

She raised up on her elbow, wanting to see his face. "You didn't know they were coming? You didn't look for them?"

"I knew," he said, staring at the ceiling. "But I didn't want to see anyone just then. It wasn't just the shape of my muscles that had changed."

"You weren't the same man mentally or emotionally either."

He shook his head on the pillow and tightened the arm holding her. "I needed to find out for myself who I was on the outside before I could be of any use to either of them."

"You didn't want to tell them that? To see them first?"

"Of course I wanted to see them," he said, rolling onto his side to face her. "But I knew if I did I'd be going home with them and I couldn't do that. It was probably the hardest thing I've ever done in my life, walking to that cab and getting in, knowing they were there waiting."

"I'm so sorry," she said, reaching up to brush his hair from his face, the palm of her hand skating over the scruff on his cheeks. She shivered and did it again. "For all of it. For everything."

He took hold of her wrist, turned his head and pressed his lips to her skin. "Your turn. Tell me about the women's shelter you're running. Bread and Bean. The house on the hill. The co-op. The ballistic-resistant windows. Becca and Ellie and Frannie and the boys."

She closed her eyes. She'd been so afraid of screwing up. And obviously somewhere she had. She didn't mind him knowing, but the house being a shelter and its location common knowledge . . . Surely it wasn't. She hadn't said a word to anyone. The others wouldn't have done so. Speculation she understood, and with the construction going on, the men in and out having to work around those windows and the nearly impenetrable doors . . .

Yeah. She could see where the guesswork was coming from. "How long have you known?"

"Officially? About three seconds. Unofficially? I've suspected for a while," he said, frowning when she shook her head, as if her incredulity unsettled him. "But not everyone you run into is going to know you as well as I do."

That didn't exactly make her feel better. "No one else knows?"

"Manny's got a pretty suspicious head on his shoulders. It's what makes him a good parole officer. And Tennessee and I talked about the possibility when the guardian angel offer came in."

"Which means Kaylie knows, too," Thea said with a groan. "And that probably means Indiana. And Oliver. And then there's Luna. Angelo did my shutters, so if they start comparing notes . . . I might as well put out a sign."

"I don't know that Tennessee's said anything to Kaylie."

"They're married," she said, then she thought back to her conversation with Kaylie at the park.

"And married couples don't keep secrets?" he asked.

Some did, she supposed. "What do you want to know?"

"How did you meet Becca York?" he asked, hooking his thigh over hers and pulling her close.

She tucked her hands between their chests and cuddled up against him. "It's hard to explain that without telling you how the whole thing came

344

together. And I really can't talk about that without breaking a lot of rules."

"Sworn to secrecy?"

"Yeah," she said, and nodded.

"Then tell me what you can. Tell me about you."

"It may be more than you want to hear."

"You think I can't take it?" he asked, his brow arched as he reached to sweep her hair over her shoulder.

"It's not great."

He huffed at that. "I spent three years in prison, Clark. I nearly beat a kid to death. I'm pretty familiar with not great."

"Some of this you already know, but okay," she said, rolling onto her back. "Todd traveled a lot. Sometimes business. Sometimes pleasure. Toward the end, he'd made it where it was next to impossible for me to leave the condo. The door-man would tell him if I'd gone out. The garage attendant kept tabs on the car I used. I finally learned to sneak out through the maintenance elevator, taking it to the basement then climbing the stairs to street level. Disguised, of course. I used the Internet at the library to research shelters.

"I started with ones for homeless women. I explained my situation and that I needed out and eventually was put in touch with a group who could help. I went underground for a while, changed my name back to Clark, then decided to put Todd's money to use in the way he would most hate. Giving women their lives back. And opening my own damn coffee shop and bakery and filling myself up on carbs and caffeine, fuck him very much."

Once she finished, he climbed over her, staring into her eyes as he stretched his body the length of hers. It felt so good to have told him. It felt even better to have him know. Living off the grid, wearing disguises so as not to be recognized, sneaking around so as not to be seen . . . It had taken its toll. She was tired. Exhausted. Weary from the weight of the secrecy, watching every step she took, every word she spoke, every move she made.

She'd done her best. She wouldn't beat herself up over what others thought or assumed. She brushed his hair from his forehead to better see his eyes, and felt him hardening against her. That made her smile, and then he said, "You're a hell of a woman, Clark. So either have your way with me again, or let's go to sleep."

Chapter Twenty-two

Though Tennessee's was the name behind the Dragon Fire Hill project, Dakota had a vested interest that took him to the house every day. Some mornings he made the trip before heading in to Bread and Bean. A few times he took an actual lunch hour and drove up to check on the progress, pitching in when Frank or one of the other Keller crew members needed help.

Most of the time, however, he waited until he was finished at the coffee shop then headed that way after work. He'd walk the grounds, get an up close look at the exterior changes, but he never went inside unless invited. Sometimes it was James who saw him first and asked him in. Other times it was Thea. But he only stayed long enough to say hello.

He had to admit Tennessee knew what he was doing. Dakota had been working with his brother a year now, and was aware of that instinctively, but watching him pull together the monstrous job of Thea's house had Dakota looking at Tennessee with new eyes, and a lot of respect, and more than a little bit of envy. That emotion was less about what Dakota had missed out on and more about what Tennessee had built for himself: his ability to take care of his family and to give a leg up to a lot of ex-cons.

Manny had come through in a big way, finding enough men to outfit a crew willing to work the long hours the project would take, because Keller Construction was determined to live up to their promise to get in and out pronto. After the morning he'd walked through the house the first time, when he'd seen Frannie's fear and Ellie's withdrawal and Becca's fists ready to punch through walls, he'd gone back to Tennessee and told him they'd need to do the job fast or not do it at all.

Heading from the Keller Construction barn back out to his truck in search of a drill bit he was going to need tomorrow, Dakota shook off the memory of his initial trip to the house, and focused on how many things were going right. The house had obviously been in sound structural shape or Thea wouldn't have bought it. And Dakota had seen people living in a lot worse. But it was good to know Thea and the others could put their money toward things like food instead of pouring it into a pit.

It was a hell of a house. Plenty of space inside and more than enough out. Rooms for working in and playing in, room for storage, room for life. He could see Thea and the others living there as long as they needed the safe haven. Funny thing, though, he mused, pulling the trays from his toolbox and setting them in the bed of his truck. He could see himself living here, too. With Thea. If that's what she wanted. Because he was pretty sure he did. No. He knew that he did. Problem was getting there from here.

He wasn't sure if their sleeping together had helped or hurt the cause, but damn if it hadn't been exactly what he wanted. What he'd needed. Thea's body beneath his again. Thea all over him, pleasing and pleasuring. No woman had ever been able to take him apart so completely. He'd looked. He'd waited. But no one compared.

The idea of fate made him itch. Thea made him better.

He'd been set on leaving for weeks now. He hadn't made plans. He had no place in mind to go. He wasn't sure if that had changed when they'd fallen into that first kiss, or when she'd barged into his house and taken him to bed. What a welcome surprise that had been. And what a night. She was a hell of a woman. A hell of a lover. But an even better friend.

And wasn't that what had been missing for the last decade plus of his life? A friend who was more than someone to shoot the shit with over burgers and beer. More than someone to catch a ride to work with when buckets of rain were coming down. More than someone to ask for help unloading a panel van full of crates and bags of dog food donated to a rescue group. He'd had all of those friends.

It was Thea who he'd been missing.

Look what she'd done with her life. Look what she'd survived. Dakota had no truck with her taking her ex's money and using it for good. Thinking about it like that, her crime fell into the same category as what he'd done: using a baseball bat to beat the kid who'd tried to rape his sister. It was the same with the men Keller Construction hired. The men Manny Balleza recommended. The men who'd done the work on the house on Dragon Fire Hill. All of them were ex-cons. All had done a bad thing for a good reason.

He couldn't hold Thea's crimes against her when they were the same as his. He'd served time to get out from under his debt to society. She'd turned around the lives of three women and made them productive members of the community. Or that's what she was in the process of doing anyway.

He would never have imagined the Thea he'd known in school turning into the woman she had. And he hated thinking it was due to some asshole who'd treated her no better than an animal, caging her and stripping away the self-sufficiency she was only just now finding again. The independence he'd loved seeing in her.

The strength he still did.

Thea hadn't visited the Keller Construction barn since either of her projects had been underway. After losing her first contractor to health issues, she'd called Tennessee's firm and talked to the woman in his office, who she'd later learned was his stepmother-in-law. It had been Dakota, however, and not Tennessee, who'd arrived to do a more thorough assessment of the job.

But Dakota hadn't been to Bread and Bean today. And he hadn't called. And all she could think was that he'd stayed home to pack. That after she'd left his bed, he'd made his decision. That her arrival at the cottage had been the catalyst. That her plans to show him how much she loved him, and needed him, how much she wanted him had backfired in an absolutely sensational way.

She supposed she shouldn't be surprised. She knew Dakota, and had since they'd been too young for the relationship neither one of them had been able to say no to. They'd needed each other. The bond they'd shared had been forged in sex, but it had been so much greater than any physical affair. Yet it had taken her seeing him again as an adult to realize that, and to understand it, and to accept that she'd never put away that bit of her childhood and moved on.

She arrived to find him hunkered down in the bed of his truck, tools spread out around him. The day was bright, and he squinted as he looked up and saw her. Those sexy crow's-feet around his eyes made a lot of sense now, as did his looking a lot older than thirty-five, though he was getting pretty close to thirty-six, if she was remembering her dates correctly.

The sun had done a number on his hair, too, during the decade-plus years he'd been gone, turning the caramel color into fifty shades of brown and gold. She loved that he wore it long, tying it back with a band when working, leaving it free the rest of the time to blow in the wind. Like now. He scraped it away from his face as she walked toward him.

He'd changed so much in the short time since she'd first seen him again. She had no idea if the year he'd been in Hope Springs prior to walking into her shop had been good to him, but she thought the last few weeks had. And she was just confident enough to take some credit for that. It was a confidence that came with knowing how much she'd changed because of him.

She was so much more comfortable now with who she was.

"What are you doing here?"

How many times had they asked each other that question lately? She reached up a hand to shade her eyes. "I came by to see you and Tennessee. Is he here?"

He shook his head. "He just left. Dolly's car's in the shop so he gave her a ride home. You need me to pass along a message?"

No. I just need you.

The words came out of nowhere and hit her so hard she had to stop walking for a moment to catch her breath. "I came by to tell him thank you. For taking on the job at the house. I know he's getting paid but I have a feeling he's not getting paid enough."

"What's enough?" he asked, his attention on his tools again. "He's getting paid what he wanted."

"Yeah, but is *he* getting paid?" she asked, crossing her arms along the truck bed's frame and resting her chin on her stacked hands.

"That's Tennessee's business," he said with a shrug, wiping a red shop rag over a pair of greasy pliers. He tossed them into a tray she thought must fit the toolbox that sat behind the cab, then he picked up the same two screwdrivers he'd showed to James.

His mouth a grim line, he said, "I still want to go all *Walking Dead* on the man who destroyed those boys and their mother."

Thea supposed he was talking about screwdrivers as deadly weapons shoved deep into skulls. "They're not destroyed. They're doing really well actually. They've all come out of their shells a lot these last few weeks. It's amazing to see. It truly is."

"Not knowing them before, I'll have to take your word for that."

Time for some of what she'd come for. "People do recover, you know. Get over tragedies. Move on. We actually talked about this the other day at lunch. Kaylie, Luna. Your sister."

"There's a lot of damage there for sure," he said, tossing the screwdrivers on top of the pliers, then standing and walking to the open tailgate.

Thea followed, moving away and giving him room to hop down. "There's also a whole lot of happiness. A lot of peace. A lot of forgiveness."

"Just not any forgetting," he said with a snort.

She took a deep breath and forged ahead. What did she have to lose? "I don't think forgetting is the goal. Take Kaylie and her father. Don't you think her knowing about the years they lost makes what they have now that much more valuable? And if Luna had forgotten about her friendship with Angelo's sister, would they be together now? And Indiana—"

"Uh-uh." His gaze was sharp and cutting, his words equally so. "You really think my sister wouldn't want to forget what she went through? What our whole family went through?"

She took a step back before she realized what she'd done. He wasn't a threat. Even in anger. She knew that. "I think she's accepted that the assault happening is why she's where she is today. And if she hadn't bought the Hope Springs property to be close to Tennessee because of it, she might never have met Oliver."

Dakota leaned against the tailgate, head shaking as he crossed his arms. His ankles, too. "I don't see it."

"Why do you think forgetting is going to make anything better?"

"Don't you want to forget what happened to you?"

"I never will, so I've never thought about it," she said, coming to stand in front of him, taking him in from his worn boots, to his worn jeans, to

354

his T-shirt that had seen better days. The clothes clung to his body, as comfortable a fit as his skin. As the weight of the past he refused to shed.

"Seriously?" The word brought her gaze up to his. "You've never wished that you could put it all behind you and make it vanish for good? Hell, make it not exist?" he added with a wave of one arm.

She reached up and rubbed at her forehead. "What good does it do to wish for something that will never happen? I lost my favorite cat to a speeding car. He was a roamer, a hunter. He loved his outdoor life. But he also loved crawling into my lap. For weeks after, I pictured him walking through the door. I'd look over when I woke up in the mornings, thinking magic would have happened and he'd be lying there as he always was, waiting to be fed. All I was doing was making myself miserable. Of course, I wish he was still here, but that sort of wishing is so emotionally destructive. It's a waste of energy and time."

He pushed off the truck to stand straight. "So now I'm destructive and wasting my time? Just because I like to imagine what life would've been like if I'd never picked up that bat?"

She was losing him. He was going to leave her, and she loved him, but she would not keep him caged. She would never wish that life on anyone. "I can tell you how it would've been. You would've gone to school and played ball, and maybe made it to the minor league with a degree in something useless. You would've married a cheerleader. You would've bought a house in a gated community. You'd have an eight- and six-year-old who'd both be sports nuts. You'd see Tennessee and his wife, probably someone other than Kaylie, for holidays. Indiana would be growing vegetables in third world countries. You might never see her.

"You wouldn't know what it was like to wrangle cattle in Montana, to breathe in the sort of air that feels like it's going to freeze your lungs. You wouldn't have the thighs you do from pedaling across the Pacific Northwest. You wouldn't appreciate fresh-caught salmon, or the sound of a tree's branches crashing through those still standing as it falls to the ground. You wouldn't know how to build a barista station or a front counter for a coffee shop. And you would be shit at latte art. Absolute shit."

"That's what you think would've happened?" he asked with a dry snort of a laugh after letting her words swirl around them and settle.

"Don't you realize you wouldn't be who you are today, the man I most urgently, most desperately love, if you hadn't gone through everything you have?" She didn't want to cry. She didn't want to appear weak. But dammit . . . "I understand you don't like thinking about the past. I get it. I really, really do. So don't. Don't think about it. But don't wish it away either. It's ugly and painful, and I would do anything to make that part vanish, but without the bad, there wouldn't be the good, and—"

"Did you just say you loved me?" he asked, his voice gruff and raw and torn from his throat.

"Oh, Dakota." She sobbed out his name, and then she just sobbed because she was beyond being able to deny the truth any longer. "I've loved you since I was fourteen years old. I've spent my whole life loving you. I've looked for you in every man I ever shared as much as a cup of coffee with. And the man I finally settled for, thinking close enough would be good enough—"

He cut her off, hooking an arm around her neck and grabbing her to him, not to kiss, but to hold against his body while the truth ravaged him. He shook as he cried, and he did so silently, purging himself of years of pent-up emotion. Emotion he'd had no one to share with, no one to under-stand. It broke her heart, seeing him this way, yet *this* had been inevitable from the beginning.

How in the world had he survived so long on his own? Because she knew, without a doubt, if he left again, this time he wouldn't.

Though Lena had invited Ellie to her place more than once before she'd finally agreed to come, Ellie still wasn't comfortable being here. Her discomfort had nothing to do with Lena and every-thing to do with being somewhere unfamiliar and out of her comfort zone.

For months now, nearly a year, she'd lived in one shelter or another, until coming to stay with Thea. She hoped it would be the last change of address she made until she was out on her own, though more and more she wondered if that would ever happen. If she could get past the fear of Bobby hunting her down and inflicting more than just the lit end of her cigarette to leave scars . . .

Since she'd ridden to Bread and Bean with Becca this morning, she'd come here with Lena in her car, the cutest little Mini Cooper ever, and she'd spent half the trip looking in the passenger side mirror. She had no reason to think they were being followed—that *she* was being followed—but the possibility was never far from her mind when she was away from the shop or the house.

Even on the days she rode her bike to town, she was a wreck by the time she arrived. She tried so hard to be brave, but all she could think about was Bobby chasing her down, catching her, holding her, burning her, telling her she didn't deserve anything good.

Shuddering at the memory, she followed Lena out of the elevator and down the hall to the door, her hands shoved in the pockets of her skirt while she waited for Lena to open it so she could get inside. There wasn't anyone else in the hallway, but someone could have seen her—

"Here we are," Lena said, walking in. Ellie took a deep breath and followed, giving Lena enough room to close the door before stopping. She looked to one side, then to the other.

The loft was huge. The second floor of the warehouse had been divided into two living spaces, and Lena had one whole side of the building to herself. It was extravagant. The idea of so much space for one person. Then again, it was smaller than the house she'd lived in with Bobby.

"This is your place?" she asked, still standing just inside the door and twisting her hands at her waist. Why was she so nervous? Why was she always thinking the worst? Nothing was going to go wrong. This was Lena. She was safe.

"Only for the last couple of months," Lena said, dropping her cross-body bag onto the seat of the closest chair. A chair that wasn't broken in, or stained. A chair with fabric that wasn't torn. "I'm subletting from Callum. He bought a house for him and his kid, but his lease wasn't up here, so I took it on."

Ellie crossed the room to the wall with the long row of casement windows. "Are you going to stay? When it is up?"

"I haven't decided," Lena said, but her shrug

wasn't exactly convincing. "I hate the idea of moving again, though eventually I'll have to."

"But this is so close to Bliss," Ellie said, peering across the tops of what buildings she could see.

"I'm not planning to work at Bliss forever."

Of course she wasn't, Ellie mused, smiling as she turned. "Right. The animal shelter."

Lena took a deep breath, and nodded with a weak smile. A strangely nervous smile. "If you ever want to stay here, you can. Like you said"—Lena shrugged—"it's close to work. No one has to know where you've gone."

"I'd have to tell Thea," Ellie said. She was certain Lena had been referring to Bobby.

But Lena was shaking her head. "I don't see why. As long as you show up for work, what does it matter?"

Confused, Ellie frowned. "I owe her so much."

"More than you owe yourself?"

"That's not fair," Ellie said, feeling defensive as she crossed her arms. "If not for Thea, I wouldn't even be here."

"You don't know that. You're resilient, El. I can see it."

"I'm glad one of us can." Ellie dropped her gaze to the hardwood floor. "All I can see are the years I spent being weak."

"How were you weak?" Lena asked, and Ellie sensed her frustration. "You didn't have family.

You didn't have friends. Doing what you had to do to survive does not make you weak."

Oh, but Ellie wanted to believe that. "I could've tried another shelter. I could've lived on the street. I could've—"

"Stop. Just stop. Now. Please."

"I'm sorry." She had to get it out. "I shouldn't have kissed you. I mean, I'm not sorry that I wanted to do it. Or that I gave in to that want. I'm just too impulsive sometimes and I don't stop and think about what I'm doing—"

"Ellie—"

"Not thinking has gotten me into so much trouble." She pressed trembling fingers to her forehead. "You'd think I'd learn, but no. Stupid, stupid—"

"Ellie—"

"I'm going to go," she said, holding out both hands like stop signs, which made her want to laugh. She could've used them back when she'd opened her mouth and said yes to coming here. "You don't need me here fucking up your life—"

This time she wasn't stopped by the words coming out of Lena's mouth. There were no words. Just her lips pressing to Ellie's, her hands on either side of Ellie's face holding her head still. The kiss was soft and sweet, and would have been chaste if not for the flutter rising from Ellie's stomach to her chest and into her throat.

Once there, it beat with tiny, persistent, and

oh-so-hungry wings. "I didn't know—" she tried to say, but Lena cut her off with a gentle, "Shh," and an even gentler pressure as she tilted her head, her breath warm on Ellie's skin, and comforting. Ellie reached up and held on to Lena's wrists.

It was welcome in ways Ellie had wondered for so long if she would ever know again. Except she'd never known this at all, not even once, not ever. Lena cared, and Ellie had been too wrapped up in her past to see it. But she could feel it, and she wanted to weep with the wonder of losing herself, with forgetting, even though she knew she never would.

"Your hair is beautiful," Lena whispered against the corner of her mouth. "I love the color."

"That's because you've never been a red-headed stepchild," Ellie said, her laugh tickling as Lena found her mouth again, kissed her solidly, holding her head as if to make sure she got it.

But not so securely that Ellie couldn't cut and run if she wanted. Lena wanted to make sure she knew where they stood. That it was her choice to be here. To have something this good if it was what she wanted.

She totally did.

"C'mon," Lena said, suddenly letting her go. "My turn to make you *my* favorite comfort food."

Ellie pushed her glasses back into place. "You don't have to cook for me."

"Sure I do. It makes for a great first date, lot of prep time for conversation, then a totally fab meal."

"Is that what this is?" Another flutter. "A date?"

Lena nodded, her eyes sparkling, her earlier nervousness crushed by their kiss. At least that's what Ellie hoped. "It can be. If you want it to. Or it can be two friends hanging out and having fun."

"What do you want it to be?"

"I'm pretty sure I heard the word *date* come out of my mouth. Also, I just kissed you."

"Are you sure? Because I haven't been on a date in years, and even then it didn't feel as right as this, and I would love more than anything in the world for this to be one. A date."

"Then it is. Though a working date because I've got to start the chicken and could use some help with chopping the mushrooms, onions, carrots, and celery for the pot pie."

"Goodness." Ellie clasped her hands against her chest where her heart was singing at the top of her lungs. "Homemade chicken pot pie. This may just be the best date ever."

❧ *Chapter Twenty-three* ❧

"I'm trying to imagine the last time a full meal, a *real* meal, was cooked in this room," Indiana said. Dakota glanced over to where she hovered between the cottage's small table and the kitchen. He'd banned her from the room where he was using every available surface to cook.

Tennessee was doing his hovering from the table itself with a beer. He was close to being too big for the bistro chairs, even if they were a welded wrought iron. He sat with his legs spread for balance, the cushion crushed beneath him, his forearms on the table's glass top.

It was almost as if one small move would cause his precarious perch to collapse and he'd go tumbling. He wouldn't, of course. He'd sat in the same chair while they'd scarfed down pizza or wings nights after working late, and he'd eaten with Indiana when she'd lived here.

Still, Dakota wasn't going to miss that table at all. Assuming he wouldn't be living here much longer and using it. Not that he really ever used it. Most of the time he ate on the couch in front of the TV, leaning over the coffee table. Unless he was using the table as an ottoman and his T-shirt to catch his crumbs. He probably wouldn't be able to get away with that in his new place.

"I hardly ever cooked," Indiana was saying in lieu of blowing off nervous steam. "I used the microwave a lot. I had a panini press." She came closer. "What exactly are you making anyway? Because it smells amazing. And I have absolutely no patience and want to know *now*."

Dakota smiled to himself but kept his gaze on the pot in front of him while he whisked the remaining ketchup and brown sugar glaze. Satisfied, he opened the oven and drizzled it over the meatloaf that was as perfectly brown as it was ever going to get. As were the potatoes. "It smells amazing because it is amazing. Or it always was when Granny Keller made it."

Indiana brought up both hands to cover her mouth and lowered herself slowly into the chair across from Tennessee's. "You made Granny Keller's meatloaf and Aunt Ruthie's potatoes. My favorite comfort foods in the world. Do you know how long it's been since I've had either?"

"If Kaylie saw all the cream and cheese in those potatoes, she'd kill me," Tennessee said, his stomach rumbling.

Indiana turned to him and huffed. "Please. There's just as much in most of Two Owls' casseroles. Not to mention the sugar and butter in all those brownies."

"She doesn't feed *me* the casseroles *or* the brownies," Tennessee said as he finished his beer.

"Which is why I'm going to do my best to eat myself into an early grave tonight."

"Better to ask forgiveness than permission?" Indiana asked with a laugh.

"You betcha."

And there was the opening Dakota had been looking for. He reached for three plates, put three forks and two serving spoons on top, and held them out to his anxious sister. "Take these. And grab those hand towels for hot mats. Food's done."

The smells of beef and onions, garlic and tomatoes, wafted through the small house as Dakota pulled the pans from the oven. The table creaked under the weight of the casserole dishes, and the juggling of plates, bottles, and glasses, and knees bumping its legs.

Though the reason for the meal had him wondering how much of an appetite he would manage, Dakota's plate was soon full. Tennessee mounded his with at least two helpings each of the meat and potatoes. Indiana had enough of both that Dakota figured she'd need a to-go box.

But that was good. That was fine.

He wanted his siblings comfortable because what he had to say to them wasn't going to be. He frowned as he lifted his fork and licked the glaze from the tines, then he set it down and spread his hands over his thighs. He flexed his fingers, stared at the remains of the ink on both of his middle fingers.

"I need to talk to you both about something," he said, looking up to see Indiana's face pale as she lowered her fork to her plate. Tennessee just dropped his, then sat back and shook his head.

Arms crossed, he said, "You're leaving. That's what this is about. Get the whole family together one final time. Big good-bye. The last supper before you hit the road. *Adios, amigo.*"

Dakota didn't react. He'd expected his brother to be angry and bitter, his sister to be confused and hurt. Those emotions and others had simmered beneath the surface for a year now because the three of them hadn't really talked. They'd exchanged words while walking on eggshells. That was no way to live. No way to stay close.

"But it's not the whole family, is it?" He sliced the side of his fork into his meatloaf, looking from his sister to his brother while he chewed. "I think that's pretty much why we're all in this pickle now."

"What pickle?" Indiana asked, wiping her napkin over her mouth, then twisting it in her lap, her fingers tight, her legs crossed. "Is Tennessee right? Are we here so you can tell us good-bye?"

He'd get to that in a minute. "Do y'all ever wonder how things would've turned out for us if our parents had been around? Or think about how often they weren't there? How they're still not? I know Tennessee does." He gave his brother a nod. "We talked about it the other day. They've got a year old granddaughter they haven't bothered to come back to the states to meet."

Indiana frowned, and instead of answering his question, asked her own. "So you're not leaving?"

"You with the one-track mind," Dakota said, stabbing his fork into his potatoes and taking a bite.

She growled beneath her breath. "Answer me, dammit, before my fork accidentally flies across the table and stabs you in the eye."

Dakota glanced at Tennessee. "Your influence, no doubt."

"I don't recall ever stabbing anyone with a fork. Now a knife is a whole other . . . ball . . . game. Crap." He cut himself off, shook his head. "Sorry, man. I didn't mean anything by that."

"It's okay. I did what I did and I've never been sorry about it. But I *am* sorry that I didn't know any other way to deal with what Robby had done. Or later, after everything, how to deal with what I'd done to both of you." He frowned down at his plate while he cleared his throat of the regrets rising there. "I walked away after prison because it's the one thing I learned from our folks."

"What are you talking about?" Indiana asked.

"At the prison that day. When I got out"—

whoo, boy—"I knew you were both there but I couldn't come home. I couldn't face either of you until I was in a better place mentally."

"But we could have helped with that," she said insistently.

He shook his head, aware her sincerity was one hundred proof. "I appreciate you wanting to, but I had to figure things out on my own."

"Things like what?" she asked, almost in tears.

He pushed a string of onion around on his plate. "What I wanted to do with my life—"

"Besides working construction—" Tennessee interrupted to say.

But Dakota wasn't finished. "And how to make up for all that I put you through."

"You didn't put us through anything—"

"I did," he said, meeting his sister's gaze. "I couldn't live with what Robby had tried to do, or the fact that we'd treated him like one of the family. I should have seen what he was—"

"Why?" Indiana asked, her napkin so snug around her fingers the tips had grown bloodless.

"None of us saw it," Tennessee said, heading for the fridge and another beer, his voice gruff and sorrowful. "Why should you be the one to take on that burden? Robby deserves the blame for where we are now. It's his fault."

"And mine," Indiana said softly.

That had Dakota frowning. "How is it yours?"

"I led him on—"

Uh-uh, he mused, tossing his fork to his plate. He wasn't having any of that. "Did you say yes? Did you once say the word *yes?*"

Indiana shook her head. Her tears ran down her cheeks to her chin. She used her napkin to wipe them away, but finally gave up. They weren't going to stop.

It took all the self-control Dakota had not to break something. "I brought him into our house—"

"No," Tennessee said. "I did that. We both knew him. We all hung out. But I brought him home. And I convinced Dad to let him stay with us during that spring-break week."

"None of this matters." Taking a deep breath, Indiana waved a hand, then reached for her iced tea. After a long swallow, she put on a brave smile. A survivor's smile. "Who did what to whom and when is in the past. I'm sure we've all suffered remorse. I know I have. But we're here. We're happy and healthy. We're all in good relationships, and don't tell me you and Thea haven't hooked up again," she said, when Dakota started to interrupt.

"That so," Tennessee said, lifting his longneck to drink and trying to hide a grin.

Dakota made a zipping motion across his lips. He wasn't talking *about* Thea until he talked *to* Thea.

"There's only one thing left to settle tonight.

The rest can be worked out in years of group therapy," Indiana said teasingly, though her words had Dakota and Tennessee exchanging a terrified glance. "Are you staying?"

Dakota looked at Tennessee, who raised an eyebrow, then looked at Indiana, whose hands were clasped beneath her chin as if in prayer. Then he got up and carried his dishes to the sink, realizing what an amazingly lucky man he was to be here, past and all.

He was looking out the window into the dark night when he said, "I'm staying," and he'd braced himself against the counter preemptively, so when Indiana launched herself at him with a joyful screech, they both—miraculously—stayed upright instead of crashing in a heap of limbs, laughter, and sibling love to the floor.

"Do you want to do this by yourself?" Dakota asked, his voice drifting softly down to Thea where she stood at his side. The pebbled walk beneath her feet was new, and led from the newly set concrete driveway to the new front steps. Those rose to the new porch wrapping all the way around the house on Dragon Fire Hill. Sturdy steps. A sturdy porch. A sidewalk without cracks. A driveway that wouldn't turn into mud and wash farther away with the next storm.

Thea had done cartwheels across the porch last night and laughed until she'd nearly made herself sick. Oh, but it had been glorious. No loose boards to unbalance her. No jagged nail heads catching the soles of her shoes. No splinters gouging her palms as she'd tumbled. No fear of crashing through rot to the ground beneath.

The driveway continued on to the back of the house and the new carport. On the other side of the carport was a new sandbox Frank Stumbo had used his own money and his own time to build. He'd given Robert a set of pails and shovels to match the colorful plastic toolbox he'd given James. Then he'd given them both matching trucks.

Frannie hadn't known what to do with the attention, until Frank brought his wife to visit—with Thea's permission. Turned out the visit was less about showing a kindness to Frannie and her boys and more about giving Letha Stumbo a reason to bake cookies again.

She hadn't touched her Mixmaster or baking sheets or food coloring or cookie cutters, he'd told Thea, since their five-year-old grandson had been killed three years earlier by a drunk driver. Frank had made certain the driver wouldn't ever get behind another wheel.

"Well?" Dakota asked. "Would you rather do this alone? Do you want me to wait out here?"

"Absolutely not," Thea said, rubbing her hands up and down her bare arms even though it was already in the mid-eighties and she wasn't the least bit chilled. There was just something about this house and the way the magic had touched others who'd moved unexpectedly into its sphere.

Frank. Manny Balleza. Lena Mining. Thea wondered who she'd missed. If Dakota might have been caught up in its spell, too. *Please, please let him stay.* She couldn't imagine life without him. "I want you here every step of the way. This wouldn't have happened without you."

"Without Keller Construction, I'll give you," he said, his arms crossed as he canted his head to the side to take her in. "But I didn't have much of anything to do with it."

"I refuse to believe you being at Bread and Bean wasn't directly responsible somehow." But she wasn't going to push him more than that. Not about her benefactor. Not about the rest. *Please, please let him stay.* She'd done all she could; if he was leaving, then she'd move on without him, as devastated as doing so would leave her. As lonely. Though not alone.

A shudder ran through her at the thought. She shook it off and changed the subject, pressing both hands to her cheeks. The new coat of dove-gray paint, the black shutters, the white porch columns, the matching rockers scattered along it. Those had not been part of the renovations but a gift from Kaylie, Indiana, and Luna. "Oh, Dakota. It's absolutely gorgeous."

"Gorgeous owner deserves a gorgeous house."

She rolled her eyes because he tickled her so with his purposefully provocative remarks. "There you go, being all sexist again."

"Hey, gorgeous dudes deserve gorgeous houses, too.

"Uh-huh."

It was all she said before grabbing his hand and pulling him down the sidewalk and up the stairs to the porch. The flower beds could use some work, she realized, casting a glance along the front of the house. The yard, too, eventually, but Keller Construction didn't have a landscaping arm.

She wondered if they'd thought about adding one, what with the bedroom communities on the outskirts of Hope Springs expanding. She wondered if that was something Dakota might have an interest in. *Please, please let him stay.* He was so good at bringing what laid dormant to life.

When she reached for the door, Dakota stopped her, doing the honors himself with a gentlemanly bow that had her giggling as she scampered by. Once inside, she spun circles through the living room, inhaling the scents of fresh paint and wood and varnish, all of it new, all of it clean. Every bit of it hers. It didn't even matter that the furniture was secondhand. Or that even now the room was dim, the lamps dark where they sat on their tables as always.

Her greatest wish was that one day soon, once Bread and Bean was open, and with the possible added Butters Bakery income, they wouldn't have to keep the lights off. That they could afford the bump in the power bill that came with running the A/C more than a few hours a day.

For now, all she wanted was to celebrate. The porch, and the living room, and oh, the kitchen. The hardwood floor gleamed nearly as brightly as the glass-fronted cabinets. The countertops went on forever. Ellie was going to have so much room for baking. And the oven . . .

Thea had never seen anything like it outside of a commercial kitchen. She ran her fingertips along the edge of the stainless steel and turned|to look at Dakota. "This cost a fortune, you know. This oven. Did Keller pick this out or was this our guardian angel's doing?"

Dakota pressed his lips together and mimed zipping them, the corners of his eyes crinkling, his dimples like sideways smiles in the scruff covering his cheeks.

Beautiful, beautiful man, she mused, her heart in her throat making it hard to speak. *Please, please let him stay.* "You're really not going to tell me."

"I don't make promises I can't keep, Clark," he said, and she hoped he wasn't giving her a warning. "I figured that would be a mark in my favor."

"Are we keeping a tally now?" she asked, strangely excited that he would care what she thought, though still wary. This was a new Dakota. As if a weight had been lifted. A decision made. She found herself holding her breath.

"You want to look at the rest? Or just stand here and ogle your oven?"

She nodded toward the back door and the new laundry room. "Let's go."

The appliances were a glossy onyx and top of the line, and there were almost as many cabinets in here as there were in the kitchen. "You know you went overboard with some of this."

Dakota held up both hands, a gesture of surrender. "Don't look at me. I had nothing to do with what went on around here. This was Tennessee's baby. Tennessee's crew. Which was why he could do in a month what I haven't yet finished in almost two."

"Right," she said, because she didn't believe him, but she couldn't prove otherwise.

He tapped the top of the dryer with one hand. "You think Frannie's going to want to keep hanging the sheets? Or will she actually use this?"

"She hangs them because she likes the smell. Though our old dryer did have to run through two cycles to do even a small load."

From the laundry room they climbed the back staircase. It spilled out onto the second floor hallway in the corner near Thea's room. She pushed open the door and stopped, looking from the interior to Dakota and back.

She'd expected to see her unmade bed in the center of the room, her bedside lamp and the art from her walls still in boxes, drop cloths covering everything while the paint dried. But that wasn't what she found at all.

The room looked exactly as it had the last time it had been put together. The navy curtains and sheets were in place, along with the frolicking dolphin comforter that fell to pieces a bit more with each wash. The white-cane ceiling fan whirred overhead, and the side table she'd painted herself held her lamp and the book she'd last been reading.

The only thing different about the decor was a circular throw rug of braided rags in shades of complementary blue. "This wasn't here before," she said, kicking off her sandals and flexing her toes into the fabric. "It matches perfectly. I love it. Do you know where it came from?"

"Dolly helped me pick it out," he said, dropping the bomb as if she should've known he'd been the one to buy her such a perfect house-warming gift.

She swallowed to clear away the swelling in

her throat. *Please, please let him stay.* "You bought this?"

Hands stuffed in his pockets, he nodded, still standing in the doorway, still watching her.

"Why?" she asked, the rest of the house suddenly unimportant. She needed answers. She loved him. She had to know where they were going from here.

He shrugged. "I thought you might like it."

"I love it." *Take it slow, Clark. Take it slow.* "But why are you buying me gifts?"

Rather than answer, he asked, "Are you going to keep using this room?"

She adored this room. She'd done so much work on it before moving in, and it looked almost the same, only better. "Why wouldn't I?"

"You don't like the one in the attic?" he asked with a glance skyward.

Good grief. Could the man not respond to her questions? "Well, sure. But I was thinking it would be a lot more practical for someone like Frannie. For as long as she's here. And should anyone else with little ones need to stay a while."

"I get that," he said, frowning as he looked down at the floor. "But it is your house. And since you're staying, and since I'm staying, I thought maybe the attic could be our room."

"Our room?" The words tumbled out but she was clueless as to how. Her mouth was dry, her ears ringing with what he'd said, her mind whirring. And then the rest of it hit her.

He was staying. *He was staying.*

She pressed the fingers of one hand to her heart, trying to keep it in her chest.

"If you want me to move in, that is." He lifted his gaze, his expression searching, frightened. Vulnerable.

Oh, but she loved this man. Tears threatened, and she blinked them away, pushing her next words past a ball of choking emotion. "You did say *our* room, didn't you? As in you and me, sharing a room, living in the same house, together?"

He nodded. "I did."

"Aren't there a couple of steps missing here?" she asked, the question creaking out because her heart was slamming all the air from her lungs.

"Such as?"

She curled her toes into the rug again. "You love me?"

"C'mon, Clark. You know I do." He shrugged, a sheepish grin on his face. "I always have."

"I don't know anything of the sort," she said, her palms sweating, her nape sweating, the skin between her breasts growing damp. Her voice felt shaky, which she supposed was as close as it could get to perspiring. "Not once in my life, present or past, have you said anything to me—"

He crossed the room and grabbed her to him, staring down into her eyes and brushing her bangs to the side with one hand as if to get a better view. "I love you, Thea Clark. This me. Here. This you. Now. I love you. I *live* you. I breathe you. I will for all time. Until I'm gone."

"But not gone like leaving," she said once she found her voice.

He laughed at that. God it felt good to hear him laugh. "Not gone like leaving."

"You're going to be here. In Hope Springs. Forever." She had to be sure.

"Forever. Or as long as you're here anyway. You make me happy, Clark," he said, his voice breaking. "You're my favorite person in the entire world. Why would I want to be anywhere but where you are?"

"I can't think of a single reason," she said, grabbing handfuls of his T-shirt and pulling him down onto her bed, kissing him, loving him, wrapping herself up in him.

It was the most comfortable place she'd ever known.

It was exactly where she wanted to spend the rest of her life.

In love with her very best friend.

❧ Acknowledgments ❧

A book is made so much better with the \perfect editorial eye. A big thank you to Charlotte Herscher for seeing things so clearly, and another to JoVon Sotak for the hook-up.

❧ About the Author ❧

Alison Kent is the author of more than fifty published works, including her debut novel, *Call Me*, which she sold live on CBS's *48 Hours*, in an episode called "Isn't It Romantic?" The first book in her Hope Springs series, *The Second Chance Café*, was a 2014 RITA finalist. Her novels *A Long, Hard Ride* and *Striptease* were both finalists for the *Romantic Times* Reviewers Choice Award, while *The Beach Alibi* was honored by the national Quill Awards and *No Limits* was selected by *Cosmopolitan* as a Red Hot Read. The author of *The Complete Idiot's Guide to Writing Erotic Romance*, Alison decided long ago that if there's a better career than writing, she doesn't want to know about it. She lives in her native Texas with her geologist husband and a passel of pets.

Center Point Large Print
600 Brooks Road / PO Box 1
Thorndike, ME 04986-0001 USA

(207) 568-3717

US & Canada:
1 800 929-9108
www.centerpointlargeprint.com